Tales of the Aerocorp

THE
RAY OF DOOM

JEFF THOMSON

Tales of the Areocorp:
The Ray of Doom

ISBN: 978-0-6456581-6-3
First published 2018
Second Edition 2023

Cover Design: Jeff Thomson
Typesetting by Rack and Rune Publishing
https://rackandrune.com

Dedicated to the spirit of
Natalie Etherton

Contents

I

The Lucifer Appears

It was the Year 233 in the Radium Age. The Britannic Empire was the most powerful empire on earth. Five years after the Third War, in which she and the Coalition of Nations; which included Espania, France, and Italio, had defeated the Germanian/Russland Alliance, Queen Aurelia and her consort, Prince Henry, Duke of Buckingham, were participating in the annual parade to honour that victory and to respect the fallen. I, along with other journalists, had been assigned to cover the event. My editor at *The Chronicle* wished me to write an article for the following morning's newsvid, and so I stood with my comrades watching the parade. Standing with me were Flint, from *The Imperial Tempo*, Ross, from *The Londinium*, and Barrett, from *The Courier.* We all took holos with our pads, or typed notes to be expanded upon later. The masses of Londinium were turned out to cheer on their soldiers and their Queen. The soldiers marched along, the sound of their feet in time with the band that was playing in front of the palace. Resplendent in their uniforms, each unit represented the different forces that were under Her Britannic Majesty's command. Flags of the different units added their bright colours to the display, and each officer who led their detachment held their electroswords at guard, electric arcs playing up and down the blades. Those blades had conquered in Her Britannic Majesty's name; from Indi to China, Europa to Russland.

In the forefront of the parade marched the men of Her Britannic Majesty's Dirigible Service, their dress grays and long black boots immaculate. Britannia's Senior Service, they were the most respected armed force in the Empire. Their airships had brought justice and peace to every corner of the world. Upon their right breasts was emblazoned their symbol; a dirigible rising into the clouds, with the Britannic lion standing beneath, roaring defiance.

"I've never seen so many medals," Ross said. "Look at that chap there. He can hardly walk for all the stuff pinned on his chest." He laughed.

A woman standing with a group of young ladies in front of us turned and regarded Ross with a frosty stare. She looked him up and down with undisguised distaste. Her companions looked us over, and their attitude was plainly in accord with hers. She was much older than them, and was obviously their chaperone. By her side, a pretty young blonde girl looked at us as though we were something odious that she had just had the misfortune to step in.

"You should show more respect, sir," the older woman remarked haughtily. "*That* is Captain Nathaniel Smith, Commander of the *Victorius*, the flagship of Her Britannic Majesty's Dirigible Service. He has fought in many battles for the Britannic Empire, whilst you are but a scribbler. Pray hold your peace."

Embarrassed, Ross fell silent, and blushed furiously while the smile ran away from his face. He was a young man, recently come to Londinium from the country, and the dictates of society were unknown to him. He stared down at his feet, stung at the rebuke.

I stepped forward, and taking off my hat, I bowed to her. "Please forgive the lad, madam. He is unfamiliar with such ceremony. He is from the countryside, and has only recently came into the city, and is therefore unfortunately ignorant of its ways."

She regarded me. "Then I suggest you inform him of how a gentleman behaves in polite society." She sniffed disdainfully.

I nodded. "I shall, madam. Rest assured."

She turned her gimlet stare upon the boy again, and shook her head.

The band struck up a different marching tune, and the girls squealed and tried to surge forward, but were stopped by a mounted trooper. They moved restlessly, excitement emanating from them.

"Auntie!" The blonde girl cried breathlessly, "here they come!"

The witch spun about, her bombazine dress whirling, and gave her attention to the approaching marchers.

I put my hand on Ross's shoulder. "Don't worry about it, lad." I leaned in close, and whispered: *"She's just an old shrew."*

That brought the smile back to his face. We turned our attention back to the parade.

Coming along now was a detachment of the Royal Air Service, dressed in pale blue uniforms the colour of a cloudless sky. They stepped out smartly, led by an officer who was decorated with as many medals as Captain Smith had had pinned upon his chest. His electrosword was drawn and displayed also. The witch turned and fixed Ross with an icy gaze. Ross doffed his cap, and smiled. She frowned, and turned back around.

"Ian! Ian!" The pretty young blonde cried, waving furiously.

The officer leading the detachment looked straight ahead, and made no sign that he had heard the girl. They continued on, and passed us, as she continued to call out. Then they were gone.

The blonde turned to the witch, and cried: "Oh, auntie, he didn't even *wave* to me!" She wailed, and lay her head on the old woman's shoulder. "There, there, my dear," she soothed, patting her young charge's back.

"I believe that was Commander Ian Symes, a Squadron Leader in Her Britannic Majesty's Royal Air Service, who leads a squadron of autogyros," I said. " He is an excellent pilot, who has many kills to his guns, most of which were scored in the Third War. Whenever the Britannic Empire is involved in any conflict, he and his fliers are in the thick of it."

The harpy turned to me. "You are well informed, sir." The girl was still sobbing on her shoulder.

"I had the good fortune of interviewing the commander during the war, madam. I found him to be a gentleman of the highest quality." I came over to them. "Don't be upset, miss. The officer's aren't allowed to let anything distract them while they are on parade. Commander Symes is just doing his duty."

The witch smiled. "You see, my dear? Ian didn't ignore you."

As the girl straightened up, and wiped her reddened eyes with a handkerchief, the old woman said: "Thank you, sir."

I bowed to her and rejoined my companions.

"I think she fancies you," Flint said suggestively.

"Shut up," I said, even though I knew he was only teasing.

The band struck up another tune; this time it was the music associated with Her Britannic Majesty's Ground Forces. Here they came, the finest soldiers to ever take to the field of conflict. Their red dress uniforms were as immaculate as the other unit's had been. Gold braid flashed in the sun, and at their head marched another officer, his chest festooned with medals. He held his electrosword proudly, and marched with a swagger.

The band changed their tune again. This time it was a rousing march, filled with the sound of drums.

Then the mounted cavalry rode along, they and their mounts accorded a lusty cheer by the watching populace. The bravery of these men was well known. They had never failed to achieve any objective that was set them. However, in the modern age in which we found ourselves, replete with hovertanks, there were those who said that their time had come and gone. But for the present, they were hailed as heroes.

When they had passed by, the band fell silent. A group of a dozen trumpeters stepped forwards, and raised their shining instruments. A fanfare rang out, echoing in the clear air. Then the band struck up again, playing the National Anthem.

In a glittering golden steamcoach, Queen Aurelia and her Consort, Prince Henry, proceeded towards the palace. Surrounded by mounted officers, and followed by a marching detachment of the Honour Guard, they drove along the Mall. The populace cheered, because they were most beloved. As a ruler, Her Britannic Majesty was well respected, for she treated her subjects most fairly, and her dealings with the governments of other countries were beyond reproach. She had led the Empire into its days of glory, and during the Third War, had shown that she had a will of iron. She and the Prince waved to all and sundry, basking in the love that their subjects displayed.

The steamcoach had proceeded down the Mall and had stopped outside of Buckingham Palace, when all of a sudden, a huge red airship appeared, and hovered above the multitude. One moment there was empty sky, and then the immense craft had swiftly hove into view. No markings were displayed on her hull, and no sound of engine could be heard. She hung there soundlessly. A silence fell over the crowd as they gaped at this marvel. My companions and I quickly took holo's of this new arrival. The Queen's Honour Guard formed up to protect the steamcoach in which the Queen and the Prince were riding. Rifles were loaded, and aimed. The silence dragged on, with the crowd looking on expectantly. Mounted escorts tried to soothe their horses. The band ceased playing as the stillness became uncomfortable.

Suddenly, a large hatch opened in the belly of the airship, and a shining mirror like object descended. It was shaped like a large bowl, and in its centre, there was a long tube that extended outwards. The bowl moved, angling downward until it was aimed at the steamcoach. At the same time, other hatches opened up on either side of the airship, and dark figures in black battle armour appeared, flying through the air with the aid of rocket packs that they were wearing. They were carrying strange looking weapons, which they flourished menacingly.

There came a deep humming sound, and a purplish vortex began to form at the tip of the projector's central tube, spinning and crackling. Suddenly a violet ray shot forth from the mirror, sweeping over the Queen, the Prince, and many of the Honour Guard. All fell senseless as they were struck down by the ray.

The flying figures descended, firing at the masses below them. Their strange weapons gave off a blue flash as they fired, and an unusual sound, like that of a whip cracking, came from them. The populace panicked, and scattered in all directions, screaming. Horses reared and capered in terror. Shots rang out from those members of the Honour Guard who had been lucky enough to escape the violet ray. Several of the dark invaders fell, shot from the sky, but their comrades dove towards the ground, firing indiscriminately at soldier and citizen alike. Pandemonium ensued.

The ray swept over the crowd again, this time cutting a swathe through the crowd of citizens. Many of them fell, and the others screamed in terror and desperately scrambled for safety. Men trampled their comrades, and women and children were thrown down and trodden upon by the frantic mob. The group of journalists and the ladies scattered like startled pigeons, but I ducked behind a tree, taking cover as the unbelievable spectacle unfolded before my shocked gaze. Two soldiers who were running by me were hit by a burst of fire, and their blood sprayed over me in a hot shower of gore. I threw myself to the ground as a hail of bullets ripped into the tree. I glanced up to see more of the invaders issuing from the airship.

Several of the black clad soldiers landed, and advanced towards the Queen's steamcoach, firing as they came. Men of the Honour Guard were shot down, but others took their place, firing at the invaders. One of the mounted officers cried out an order, and he and his comrades spurred their horses forward, drawing their electroswords. The dark figures fired at the oncoming assault. Half of the mounted escort went down, but the others rushed the invaders, and struck them down with their flashing blades. I believe I cheered at the sight.

Another wave of the flying soldiers descended, firing their weapons. The brave cavalrymen were slain in a hail of fire. They and their horses went down in a spray of blood. The black figures landed and advanced upon the steamcoach, where Queen Aurelia and Prince Henry lay senseless. Only a dozen of the Honour Guard remained, but they were determined to protect the Queen, or die. The sound of their weapons echoed across the palace grounds.

A huge explosion drowned out the rifle fire. I looked up, and saw the ray projector disintegrating, and falling in shining shards towards the ground. A voice cried out: *"Look there!"* and the attention of all turned to another airship that was approaching fast. She had a large gun turret mounted on her forecastle, and it was evident to all that it was she who fired the shot. As the wreckage of the mirror was dashed to pieces on the road, she fired again, and a massive hole was torn in the bow of the invading airship.

At that moment, all of the black soldiers stopped their attack. Then, as one, they leaped into the air, and began to retreat back to their ship. Several were shot down by the soldiers remaining upon the ground, but most of them regained their ship, and entered the hatches from whence they came. Gun ports opened in her side, and she sent a salvo at the oncoming airship. The shells hit, tearing into the newcomer, but she plunged onward, intending to come to grips with her enemy.

The invader turned away slowly, still firing. The hatches closed, and then she accelerated away at a speed that startled all of the onlookers. In a few moments, she was lost to view. The other airship came to a stop, and hovered over the park. After the pandemonium of the attack, those people still left alive stared at their rescuer. Who could it be? Like the invader, this new ship had no markings, and moved soundlessly also.

On the ground wounded men groaned, and cried out in agony, and horses screamed. Both had been injured by shot or ray, or crushed in the mad rush for safety. Rifles were cautiously lowered, and uninjured soldiers began to check the wounded. I crept out from my position of safety, and looked about myself in amazement. The scene that met my gaze was like some horrific battlefield. Everywhere I looked there were dead bodies; bloody and broken. Horse, man, woman, and child, each lay on the road in the contortions of death.

The pretty girls and their old chaperone who had stood watching the parade in rapture now lay still, their fashionable bombazine dresses torn and bloody. I went up to the girl, and knelt down. Her lovely blue eyes were wide open. I passed my hand over them, and closed them respectfully. I rose to my feet, and stumbled along dazedly. I looked for my companions, and finally came upon them, all lying dead in the road. I checked all three, but life had fled. Poor Ross. His young life had been cut short. Flint and Barrett lay near him. They had all been riddled by the black invader's weapons.

"Ere, George," a voice said, "Ave a look at this."

I turned to see two soldiers standing over the body of one the invaders. I went over to them, and looked down at it. The armour was all black, and the helmet was fitted with breathing tubes that went back over the shoulder to a small pack. A mask covered the face, in the form of a stylized skull, and two round glass lenses hid the eyes from view. They were like the ports of a ship. A larger pack was the rocket pack that the invader had flown with. It was like no battlesuit that I had ever seen before.

"Rum bit 'o' gear, innit?" One of the soldiers said, holding the dead man's weird firearm. It was made of a dark metal, and had some sort of cylinder mounted below the barrel.

"Don't look like nuffink I ever seen before. What d'you fink that is, Bert?"

I looked closer. "I think it's a battery."

They regarded me. "A batt'ry? Nah, it carn't be," George said.

"Ave a look, then," he said, and handed the weapon to me. I turned it over in my hands. It was surprisingly light. Then I thought that that would make sense, because troopers who flew through the air could not be encumbered with a weapon of much weight. Forward of the trigger was the magazine. As I inspected the gun, the magazine rattled. I shook it, and the sound came again. Puzzled, I wondered if there was something wrong with it. Could it have been damaged when its owner had been shot down? I sniffed the barrel, and found a strange scent;

not that of gunpowder, it was more like the smell that was in the air before a thunderstorm. A glint of reflected light caught my eye, and I looked down.

On the road lay hundreds of small metal spheres. I knelt down, and picked one up. It was like a ball-bearing, its once shiny steel like surface streaked with blood. I gazed about me at the others that lay scattered on the road. They were all bloody. Suddenly, it hit me. I rose to my feet.

"It's some sort of electric gun," I said to the two soldiers. I held the sphere out for them to see. "This is what it fires. This magazine is full of them." I shook the weapon, and it rattled again.

"Eh?" said George. "Garn, that can't be righ.'"

"Electric gun?" added his comrade. "Nah, mate. You're barmy."

"Here, you men!"

We turned to see an officer of the Honour Guard approaching. He stared at me. When he came up to us, the two soldiers came to attention, and saluted him.

"I would ask you to give that weapon to the corporal, sir. It could be dangerous."

The corporal was George. I handed it to him.

"Thank you, sir. Corporal?"

"Yessir?"

"I want you and your companion to go about collecting these weapons. We don't want anyone to hurt themselves, do we?"

"Nossir! Righ' away, sir!" He nodded to me, and then he and Bert left to carry out the officers order.

"Interesting looking breathing gear," said the officer. He was inspecting the corpse. "And I've never seen armour of this type before. No insignia, or unit symbol. I wonder where these chaps came from?" He knelt down, and tried to remove the helmet, but met with no success. He rose to his feet. "I suppose we'll have to leave that to the boffins. Thank you for your cooperation, sir." He saluted me, and strode off towards another group of soldiers.

I still had the metal sphere in my hand. I took out a handkerchief, wiped the blood from it, and put it in my jacket. I tossed the bloody handkerchief on the road, and took out my pad. I put down all of what I had seen, typing quickly. I added my conjecture of the weapon and its unusual properties.

I put my pad away and wandered into the park. My throat was dry, and I needed to drink. I reached one of the ornamental pools, and knelt down. I cupped my hands in the water, and brought it to my lips. The soothing water was cool as I drank. Refreshed, I looked up, and saw the airship hovering above me. I got to my feet, and began to walk towards it.

A large crowd of people had gathered beneath it. I joined them, peering up at our rescuer. She was like no airship that I had ever seen before, and that was a marvel, for over the course of my employment for *The Chronicle*, I had been a war correspondent, and as such had seen all of the war equipment that all of the nations on earth had at their disposal in many theatres of conflict. I wondered who it could be who could create such a craft. I ran my eyes over her smooth lines, and searched vainly for an engine pod. None met my gaze. I shook my head in bewilderment. At that moment, a bell was heard, its pure tone coming from the massive craft. The crowd moved nervously, and a sense of apprehension fell upon us. The people began to move back, backing away from the vessel.

A hatch opened in the lower part of the airship, and a platform was lowered by cables. Standing upon the platform were three figures, regarding the carnage below as the platform descended. The crowd scattered, but only went a short distance away, their curiosity forcing them to see what these newcomers were all about.

At the order of an officer, surviving members of the Honour Guard had formed up in a line, and made ready their weapons. The platform reached the ground. The men opened a small gate, and stepped out onto the grass. They advanced towards the awaiting soldiers. In the lead was a man; perhaps middle aged, wearing a long brown leather coat festooned with gold buttons. A captain's cap was upon his head, and long leather gloves were upon his hands. He was a short and stout individual, and a large brown moustache adorned his upper lip. His feet were shod in shining black boots. His companions were dressed in a similar fashion, but it was obvious he was their leader.

"You have no need of your weapons, gentlemen," he said. "I am on your side, as I am sure you can see." His voice was smooth and cultured, like that of a Britannic gentleman.

The officer commanding the soldiers regarded him for a moment, and then ordered his men to stand down. They lowered their rifles. At this the man thanked him with a nod and a smile, and then advanced and introduced himself.

"I am Captain Zorn. I am here to offer my assistance. Please take me to Her Britannic Majesty."

The officer gave an order, and the men formed up around the newcomers and shouldered arms. At another command, the group marched forward. He smiled to himself at this, but knew that they were still uncertain of him, due to the circumstances of the unprovoked attack. The captain allowed them to escort him across the park.

I followed at a short distance. I wondered who he was, and why he had come to our aid. I glanced back once at the vast ship hanging over the park. Was there some sort of connection between this man and whoever had committed this senseless assault upon us? I took my pad from my jacket, switched it on, and began to type some more notes. I must interview him.

We came to the road. The captain looked about himself at the carnage and I saw his face grow grim. He scowled to see such wanton destruction, and waste of life. Soldiers and civilians both were helping those who had been wounded, and there were parties of doctors and nurses who had been called from the nearby hospital. They hurried about, tending to the suffering.

The officer led them over to the steamcoach. Doctor Mansfield, the Queen's Physician Royal was there, examining the Queen and the Prince. The soldiers came to a halt, and Captain Zorn stepped forward.

"I am Captain Zorn. I have come to help."

The doctor regarded him for a moment, and then introduced herself.

"My name is Mansfield. Thank you for stopping this outrage."

Zorn nodded, accepting her thanks.

"What is their condition?" he asked, indicating the Queen and her consort.

"I am at a loss; I have never seen such symptoms before. They are in a deep swoon." She looked around at the scores of wounded. "There are at least two hundred others who were struck down by that ray. They must all be taken to hospital immediately."

A group of officers arrived. I knew them all, and had interviewed them each at one time or another. They were Airlord Gray, the Airlord of Her Britannic Majesty's Dirigible Service, Captain Nathaniel Smith, the commander of the flagship *Glorious* of that service, General Crompton, the Warlord of Her Britannic Majesty's Ground Forces, and

Councillor Reading, the head of the Emergency Council.

Airlord Gray went up to the steamcoach, and peered in at the unconscious occupants. He turned to the doctor. "Thank god they are alive. Can you help them, doctor?"

"I do not know, sir. I did not see this ray that struck them down, and am quite unfamiliar with its effects. I will do my best."

"I have seen the ray before, and have experienced its awful power myself," Zorn said.

"Will they all die?" Mansfield asked.

"I am unsure," Zorn replied. "The ray affects each person differently. It affected me with only depression, but others..." he trailed off, and for a moment, his gaze became unfixed. Then, he shook his head, as though ridding himself of a particular unpleasant memory. "Others," he continued softly, "died horribly."

"Who are you, sir?" General Crompton demanded.

"I am Captain Zorn. I have come to render assistance to the Britannic Empire." He gestured towards the ship hovering over the park. "That is my ship, the gravship *Vengeance*."

"Then we owe you our thanks, sir," Captain Smith said. "If it were not for your timely intervention, the invader would have killed us all." He came forwards, and offered his hand. Zorn shook it firmly. "A gravship?" Smith said. "I've never heard of that."

"Her motive power is the same force as that which allows us to stand upon the surface of the earth. It is the same power that demands any object to fall if it is dropped."

"You mean *gravity*, sir?" Airlord Gray said doubtfully.

"I do," Zorn replied. "By manipulating gravity using magnetic fields, I can sail her to any part of the globe at thrice the speed of your fastest airship. I call it the 'Gravitic Drive."

"Can such a thing be?" General Crompton scoffed. "It sounds impossible."

"But there she is, gentlemen," Captain Zorn said, gesturing again. "It may interest you to know that the ship that attacked you was of a similar design. Her propulsion also utilises the same principle. She is called the *Lucifer*. Her captain and I are mortal enemies."

"The *Lucifer*?" Airlord Gray echoed.

"What a fitting name for a craft that has unleashed Hell upon us," Captain Smith said.

General Crompton looked unconvinced. "A hard thing to believe, sir," he said.

"Remember how swiftly the invader appeared, sir?" offered Captain Smith. "And when Captain Zorn arrived and drove her off, she certainly showed she could put on an amazing turn of speed."

"Captain Smith is correct, General," Airlord Gray added. "We saw it ourselves. These ships are much faster than anything we have."

General Crompton regarded Zorn sourly. "Then both of them constitute a threat to the Britannic Empire."

"Not so," Zorn said. "I told you I have come to assist. I am no threat to you."

"Prove it," Crompton said. "Allow us to inspect your craft. Will you give us the secret of this 'Gravitic Drive?'"

Zorn gave him a thin smile. "Yes. That is one of the reasons why I have come to you. Without my Gravitic Drive, your craft are no match for the *Lucifer*."

"I'd love to have a look at the *Vengeance*, sir," Captain Smith said. "What a marvel!"

"I would be pleased to show you her marvels myself, sir," Zorn replied.

Four orderlies arrived with two stretchers. Queen Aurelia and Prince Henry were lifted carefully from the steamcoach, and lowered onto them. With Mansfield attending, they were carried towards the hospital.

As they departed, Zorn said: "Councillor Reading, can it be arranged to have the Emergency Council meet?"

"I was about to suggest such a meeting," Reading answered. "Indeed, it is standard procedure when such an event as this befalls us, and the Queen and Prince are incapacitated, and cannot lead the Empire. These gentlemen are all part of it."

"Who carried out this attack?" Gray asked.

"I will explain all to the Council," Zorn replied.CHAPTER II

II

The Emergency Council

Three hours later, in a special chamber within Buckingham Palace, the Emergency Council was meeting. It consisted of Airlord Gray, General Crompton, Captain Smith, Commander Symes, and Councillor Reading and his dozen Councillors. They were seated at a large oval table in the centre of the large room. Captain Zorn and his officers were also present. A dozen vidscreens filled one wall of the chamber. They were watching one of them, whereupon Doctor Mansfield was speaking. At her side stood Professor Graves, waiting patiently. The body of one of the black clad soldiers was laid out on a table in front of them. The armour had been removed.

The doctor's face was pale, and the stress of the last few hours of her untiring work showed itself in the dark shadows under her eyes, and the exhaustion displayed in her stance.

"Gentlemen, at least half of the victims, including the Queen, has been afflicted with some unknown sickness that mutates healthy cells in the body, and turns them upon the others. The other victims displayed symptoms that ranged from slight depression, to shattered nerves like that of soldiers who had been shell-shocked. This sickness has no known cure. Most victims will eventually be eaten alive by their own diseased tissue."

"My god!" Airlord Gray said. "The Queen!"

"Are you certain that there is no cure for this malady, doctor?"

General Crompton asked.

Mansfield rubbed her tired eyes with a weary hand. *"I don't know, general. I've tried everything, but have not met with success."*

Captain Zorn rose to his feet. "It is called *The Blight*, and it *does* have a cure."

"How do you know this?" Councillor Reading said.

"Because I myself have been exposed to its deadly power, and yet here I stand before you."

"This ray did not affect you, sir?" Airlord Gray said. "How can that be?"

Zorn shook his head. He gave them a grim smile. "I did not say that I had remained unaffected."

"What then do you mean?" Crompton said. "Explain yourself, sir."

Zorn looked down, and stared at the table top. He was casting his mind back; back to the days when he had become involved at the beginning of a long chain of events that had led to this morning's attack. His face became clouded, as he remembered all that had befallen him and his unfortunate family. The gathering waited for him to speak.

"Captain Zorn?" Crompton prompted.

Zorn raised his head, and regarded the council, his eyes filled with suffering. He shook his head as if to clear it.

"I shall tell you how I experienced firsthand the ray and its power, gentlemen. I am an inventor, as you may have guessed. I had discovered the Gravitic Drive, and was working on the design of the *Vengeance*. I am a rich man, coming from a family line that has been blessed with great riches. Suffice it to say that I had all the monies I needed to fund my research." He paused, thought for a moment, and then continued.

"As I said, the drive had been perfected, and now it only remained for me to complete building the *Vengeance*." He smiled sadly. "She did not have that name in the beginning. No, she was to be called the *Hope of Man.* That name was my wife's idea. She thought that I could share the drive's discovery with all mankind, and therefore improve the lot of millions with the advantages that such swift transportation would bring. I agreed with this idea. And so I laboured with the intention of giving the world a great gift. However..." He trailed off.

"However?" Commander Symes said.

"However," Zorn continued, "there was another intellect that had made the same discovery that I had made. An intellect that belonged to a man who did not share my outlook. I was unaware of his existence, but somehow he discovered me and my work. And he was enraged. For he did not want to share such a discovery with the world. No, he wanted to keep the secret of the drive to himself, and therefore rule over such lesser beings than himself; meaning all of humanity." He paused, and picked up a glass that was set before him that contained water. He drank it all down, placed the glass back on the table, and went on.

"The first inkling I had of his existence was almost fatal. I was in my workshop. My wife and two sons had come to me there, and Mary was telling me that they were going into the city for the day. I was only half listening to her; my attention was fixed upon my work. She noticed this, and turned to leave. She and my boys said farewell, and I said something in response as they left the workshop. Suddenly, there was an explosion, and I was thrown to the floor.

"As I dazedly struggled to my feet, I cried out; "Mary!" Perhaps the steamcoach had exploded, and they had been injured. I rushed out of the door, to be met with an appalling sight. The mansion was afire, tall flames leapt into the sky. Hovering above the blazing wreckage was a huge airship, of a design I had never seen before. Yes, it was the *Lucifer.*

The gunports in her side were open, and as I watched in horror, the guns turned towards the workshop. With a blue flash and the sound of cracking whips, they fired a salvo. I was blown off my feet as the workshop disintegrated under the impact of the shells. 'Father!' a voice cried, and I looked about and saw my sons, and my wife.

" She was lying on the ground, and they were desperately trying to move her to safety. I got up and ran towards them. I knelt down, and saw that Mary was unconscious. I picked her up, and searched about myself for shelter. Nothing was left. The house was gone, along with the workshop.

"Then, the sound of a hatch opening came to us. We looked up, and saw one opening in the belly of the invader. The projector that you saw this morning began to lower. We watched in trepidation. An unfamiliar sound came to us; the sound of the weapon being charged. The energy vortex formed at the projector's tip. Then the violet ray was unleashed, and it struck us down. We fell, and all of us were rendered unconscious.

"Sometime later, I awoke. I sat up, and shook my head groggily. I had thought that it had been a dream. But my eyes met the appalling destruction around me. With the realisation that the awful event was real, I sought my wife and sons. They lay sprawled about me, and I searched them for signs of life. All of them breathed, but were in some sort of stupor. No matter what I tried, I could not wake them. I got to my feet, and searched to see if any of my workmen or house servants were alive. Save for myself, there was no one. All had been slain in the unprovoked attack. I heard several steamcoaches, and saw three of them enter the main gates and come up to the house. They had come to render assistance. We put Mary and my sons into one of them, and rushed to the hospital."

"What did they discover, captain?" Mansfield asked.

"They were baffled, doctor. As no doubt you are. The finest doctors and physicians were at a loss. And our symptoms were different, too. Mary and my oldest son, Victor, were afflicted with The Blight, but Andrew and I were seemingly lesser affected. The doctors insisted on examining me, even though I protested that I felt fine. Andrew displayed the nervous condition that you described, doctor, but I felt nothing."

"How long did it take. . . . " Crompton began, and then halted. He looked embarrassed.

"How long did it take for them to die?" Zorn said.

"I apologise, Captain," Crompton said.

"No need to, general. I was going to tell you, in any case. Mary and Victor slowly wasted away, consumed by The Blight. They endured three long weeks of suffering and agony before they finally passed away. It was awful to see."

"Dear god," Gray said. "What an awful death. You have our deepest sympathies, Captain Zorn."

"Thank you, sir."

"What happened to your other son, captain?" Mansfield asked.

"As I said, he and I did not suffer the same fate as Mary and Victor. However, the nervous condition that now affected him worsened, until his mind was gone. He became quite mad, and had to be confined to an asylum. There he lingers still. That was three long years ago. When I had seen to my wife and son's funeral arrangements, and had them carried out, I returned home, and rebuilt the workshop. I gathered together another group of workers, and we toiled night and day. The house remained a shattered ruin, ignored in the frenzy of the work into which I threw myself. I worked and slept in the workshop, working feverishly on the *Vengeance*. Yes, gentlemen, she now had that name. For I had vowed vengeance upon he who had destroyed my family. I would seek him out, and kill him without mercy."

"How did you find him?" Commander Symes asked.

"Once again, he somehow knew that I had survived, and was working on my gravship. One day, when she was almost completed, I was working on her bridge with several of my workmen. The vidscreen had been installed, along with most of the other instruments. As we stood there examining some charts, it was activated. We all turned our attention to it. The figure of a man appeared, clad in a red battlesuit. He wore a mask fashioned in the likeness of a skull. 'Greetings, Captain Zorn,' the man said. 'I am The Wraith.' I stepped up to the screen, my fists clenched in hatred. 'You are the one responsible for the attack that claimed my family's life,' I said angrily. 'That is so,' he replied. 'I will hunt you down and have revenge for that act,' I said. He laughed. 'I have allowed you to complete your work so that we can meet in combat, captain. We will see which ship is victorious, eh? I will send you the coordinates where we will meet. Do not worry, I will allow you to finish work on your vessel. It would not be much of a competition if we fought now.' So saying, he closed the connection, and his hateful image vanished."

"Did he do as he said?" Gray asked.

"Oh yes, he kept his word. When the work on the *Vengeance* had been completed, he appeared on the vidscreen again, and told me where to meet him. My workmen had become my crew. We took off, and made our way to the rendezvous. The *Lucifer* appeared, and we both attacked. Damage was done to both gravships, and we had to retire. As we retreated, he appeared on the vidscreen again. 'I must congratulate you, captain. You have constructed a fine vessel. I will contact you again once our damage has been repaired, and we will continue our little competition.' Since then, he has done so three times over the past three years. We have met again and again in combat, but neither of us has been the victor. Our ships are evenly matched."

"Why would he allow you to finish your work and then challenge you to a fight?" Crompton said. "It makes no sense."

"It makes perfect sense to me, sir," said Captain Smith.

"And why would that be, captain?" the general said.

"Well, you see, gentlemen, this Wraith fellow feels the need to defeat Captain Zorn in combat; both to prove that his ship is the better of the two, and also to crush the captain's spirit further. I believe it is his intention to destroy the *Vengeance*, and her captain. Once he has achieved that aim, he would have the only gravship in existence, and so would outclass every other airship on the planet." He turned to Zorn. "Would you agree with that assumption, captain?"

Zorn nodded. "I would indeed, sir. It would also stroke his massive ego were he to succeed."

"Who is this Wraith?" Airlord Gray asked.

"I do not know," Zorn replied. "I have searched everywhere for some hint of his identity, but to no avail. He is always masked. The Wraith is a shadowy figure, who only strikes from the darkness. The violet ray is his most deadly weapon. The only fact that I am certain of is that he is a confederate of Chancellor Falkenberg. He speaks with a Germanian accent, of that I am sure."

"Falkenberg?" Councillor Reading echoed. "Are you certain?"

"I am, councillor."

"The Chancellor of the Germanian Empire?" Crompton said. "What does that mean? Are you suggesting that Falkenberg wants - "

"War, gentlemen," Zorn said curtly.

"That is preposterous, sir!" the general said indignantly. He rose to his feet. "The treaty between our two nations - "

"Is worthless, general. I am convinced that The Wraith is Falkenberg's tool, and as such, he is supplying the Germanians with weapons and gravships that are far superior to those of any other nation. They will be unstoppable."

"*Nonsense!*" Crompton cried. "Show us proof, or cease your ridiculous accusations!"

"Gentlemen, please," Councillor Reading said, standing. "Let us have order."

Crompton subsided, and returned to his seat. But his gaze burned into Captain Zorn. He sat there and fumed.

"Perhaps the general is correct, Captain Zorn," Reading continued. "Sir, if you could provide us with proof of the connection between The Wraith and Falkenberg, and their intention to plunge us into another war - "

"It will be too late. They will have already struck. Remember the Third War? They never announce their intentions, they just attack without warning."

As if Zorn's words were a signal, Mansfield's image on the vidscreen wobbled, broke up, and vanished, to be replaced by the image of the bridge of a large airship. A giant windscreen showed a view of clouds sweeping by as she forged through the air. Several men manned different stations in the view, each turned away from the council. A figure stepped into the centre of the image.

It was a tall man, clad in red battle armour. He wore a metal mask upon his face, which was in the shape of a skull, as Captain Zorn had described. Breathing tubes were connected at the cheeks of the mask, and trailed over his shoulders, to his back. Two eyeholes in the mask resembled the portholes of an airship. The eyes that looked out of them were bloodshot and lit with fervour. A black hood covered his head, and a long black cape swept to the floor behind him. His voice rang out, metallic and ominous, altered by some kind of electronic device within the mask.

"Slaves of Britannia, attention. I am The Wraith. It is I who am responsible for the attack upon your queen. By now you must be aware that she and many of those who were exposed to my ray have contracted a wasting sickness. Your physicians have no doubt told you that there is no cure for it. They lie. I *have the cure. I* alone *have the cure. I will give this cure to your physicians so that the lives of your queen and her loyal subjects can be saved. But, in order for this to happen, the council must make me the Emperor of Britan. Refuse, and they will all die a terrible death. I give you three days to decide what you must do."*

The transmission ended. The image of the doctor returned.

"Does he speak the truth about the cure, captain?" she asked.

"Yes. He is the only one who has it," Zorn replied.

"He wears the same kind of armour and breathing apparatus that his soldiers wore," Commander Symes said.

"I have something to say about that, gentlemen," Mansfield said. She indicated the corpse on the table. *"Professor Graves and I have examined this body, and have discovered some interesting things about it. This was a dead man, somehow reanimated by a system of clockwork devices, his breathing provided by a pack, and his heart replaced with a mechanism. When we opened up the skull to examine the brain, we only found a small transmitter connected to another device that we believe controls the body. The professor and I both agree that The Wraith's soldiers are somehow controlled by a radio signal."*

"Good lord," Reading said.

"How extraordinary," Crompton added.

"An army of undead soldiers," Symes said. He shook his head in amazement.

"That would explain how they all departed at the same instant when the *Lucifer* retreated," Airlord Gray said.

"That broadcast must have gone out all over the Empire," Reading said.

"What does he mean about making him emperor?" Captain Smith said. "Does he really believe that we would carry out such a ridiculous notion?"

"It must be a bluff," Crompton said. "Surely he would not allow Her Majesty and His Highness to die if we would not agree to make him ruler of the Empire."

"No, general," Zorn said. "He is not bluffing. The Wraith is without mercy. He will kill anyone to achieve his goals."

"I am concerned about his alleged involvement with Chancellor Falkenberg," Reading said. "Are you sure that what you have told us is true, Captain Zorn?"

"It is, sir. You must believe me. I am absolutely certain that he is supplying the Germanians with weapons and ships that will far outclass anything that you have."

"*Gentlemen, may I say something?*"

They all turned their attention to the vidscreen, where Professor Graves was holding up one of the invader's unusual guns.

"*This is one of the weapons that Captain Zorn refers to. It is electromagnetic in nature. That is to say, it doesn't use the explosive power of gunpowder to fire its projectiles.*" He picked something up from the table, and showed it to them.

"*This small metal sphere is like a common ball-bearing. It has been given a negative magnetic charge. Inside the rifle is a small but powerful magnet, which is covered by a plate. This magnet is also negatively charged. When the trigger is pulled, the plate is lowered, the two like magnetic fields contend, and the sphere is hurled away at a velocity unobtainable by our firearms. Let me show you."*

He took up the rifle, and walked a short distance. He raised the weapon, and sighted at a large wooden barrel that was thirty feet away. He pulled the trigger, and they heard the whip cracking sound as the rifle discharged. A storm of pellets ripped into the barrel, shredding it. The professor ceased firing. They all regarded the destroyed barrel in awe. Professor Graves walked back to the table, and placed the rifle on it.

"As you can see, gentlemen, these rifles are far superior to our own. Any army that was armed with such weapons would be impossible to defeat with ordinary firearms."

"Not if they were faced with the same weapons," Zorn said.

"Are you offering to supply us with them?" General Crompton asked.

"I am, sir. Gentlemen, I offer my service to the Empire. My ship, my men, and I will not rest until The Wraith and all of his soldiers are dead. To achieve this aim, I will give you not only the secret of the Gravitic Drive, but also the electromag rifles that you have seen demonstrated here. Plus, I have the specifications of small gravflyers that will outperform any of your autogyros. Your fliers will no doubt be pleased to take delivery of them."

"If they perform like your gravship, captain, we'll be happy to take them," Commander Symes said.

"Why would you do this?" Gray asked.

"Because this has gone far beyond my own personal vengeance, sir. The Wraith and Chancellor Falkenberg would drag the world into another war; a war that would make the horrors of the Third War pale into insignificance by comparison. The weapons that they can wield have far more destructive capabilities than anything the world has ever seen. Do not forget the violet ray. He would unleash that upon millions. "

"We cannot allow that to happen," Reading said.

"Indeed not," Crompton said.

"What about the *Lucifer*?" Smith said. "Surely if she is a match for your own ship, wouldn't they build other ships like her? If they intend to go to war, they would make sure that they had plenty of these gravships, so they could wipe out any airship that was sent against them."

"You are correct, Captain Smith," Zorn replied. "I have reliable information that that is indeed what they are doing. At this very moment, hidden dockyards are constructing warships that use the Gravitic Drive."

"And their guns, captain?" said Graves. *"Are they larger versions of the electromag rifle we have here before us?"*

"Yes, professor. The *Vengeance* also has similar weapons. I will provide you with all of the necessary technical details so that you can construct these cannons and the gravships that will deploy them. My crew will assist and train crews for them. You will be able to face the Germanians on equal terms. I only pray that we are not too late. Who knows how long they have been preparing for war? Well, gentlemen, do you accept my offer?"

"We do, sir," Councillor Reading replied, knowing that it was imperative for them to do so.

"But what about this cure, sir?" said Crompton. "We must save the

Queen, the Prince, and all of those who suffer. How do you suggest we obtain it from this Wraith?"

"I have considered that, general," Zorn said. "I have a plan."

"Please enlighten us, captain," Gray said.

"There are scientists in The Wraith's employ who are responsible for the ray projector. They are the men who know the secret to its energies, and as such, they also know of the weapon's affect upon its victims. I recommend that we capture one of these fellows, and obtain the cure from him."

"And how do you propose to do that, sir?" Crompton said.

"By boarding the *Lucifer*, and taking him captive. To do this, we must use the Air Commandos. I understand that they have conducted such hit and run missions before. They rescued you from a mountain prison during the War, did they not, Airlord Gray?"

"You are correct, sir. Major McKinnon and his men are the perfect choice for such a mission."

"They will need air support," Captain Smith said. "You cannot expect them to carry the day alone."

"I have thought of that also," Zorn said. "The *Lucifer* carries a complement of gravflyers that far outclass anything that you have. As such, we must use gravflyers of our own. Only their speed and manoeuvrability will ensure that this mission is a success. They could provide the air support that the Air Commandos require."

"But we have no gravflyers," Commander Symes said. "Do you propose to use your own craft and fliers in this capture?"

"No. My fliers have limited combat experience. We need someone who is a veteran; someone who has a squadron behind them."

"We have no fliers who can operate these gravflyers of yours, sir," Gray said, "We had not even known of the existence of such craft until today."

"May I make a suggestion?" Zorn said.

"Of course," Reading said.

"I propose that we enlist some help in the fight against the enemy."

"Go on," Gray said.

"I have in it mind to seek out a flier and her squadron. They would be the quickest to adapt to the new gravflyers. Time is against us. We must get our forces up to combat readiness as quickly as possible." Captain Zorn looked over at Commander Symes. "No offence, sir, but your fliers would take too long to adapt."

Symes raised an eyebrow, and looked indignant.

"Who is this person?" Gray asked.

"She is Captain Louise Deville, a former French aviatrix. She was highly decorated during the War. I believe she and her squadron are who we must have to be prepared in time. They are the finest fliers in Europa."

"I've heard of Captain Deville and of her exploits in the Third War," Symes said. "Hasn't she become a mercenary, selling her squadron to the highest bidder?" His voice was sour.

"That is correct, commander. Deville has been seen all over the world, flying and fighting wherever there is any sort of conflict. She and her squadron of all female pilots, who are called Le Rouge Chats, are without peer in the air. Without their help, we cannot defeat The Wraith and the might of the Germanian war machine."

"Do you have such a low opinion of Commander Symes and his fliers, captain?" Airlord gray said. "He and his men are the most decorated and skilled of Britannia's fliers, and all are veterans of the War. Surely they could master these flyers that you speak of?"

"I said I meant no offence to Commander Symes and his fliers, sir,"

Zorn said. "But the simple fact of the matter is that Captain Deville and her squadron are better fliers, and as such we must have them if we are to face the enemy in time. If we take the time to instruct Commander Symes and his men in the usage of my gravflyers, we will be too late to stop The Wraith and his Germanian allies."

"Gentlemen, I believe that Deville cannot be relied upon." Symes said. "I have also heard that she had renounced France, and hated the Britannic Empire for what France had seen as our failure to assist them in the War. Her own people turned upon her and cast her out. France had suffered much, and had needed a scapegoat. Deville was that scapegoat. She had been that country's heroine, but when several important missions failed, it was she who was blamed and they exiled her."

"All of this is true, gentlemen," said Zorn. "Her misfortunes have come about due to Britannia's under utilisation of her forces. Her star has fallen, and after the war, France turned away from her. There is still bad blood between France and Britannia."

"We do not need you to tell us that, sir," General Crompton said.

"Can we rely on someone who has no country, and will only fight for money?" Airlord Gray said.

"Most soldiers only fight for money," Zorn said.

"I resent that remark, sir," Crompton said indignantly. "The Britannic Army is well known the world over for the prowess of her fighting men. They are loyal to the Queen and the Empire. They are not mercenaries."

"That may be true of the officer class, sir, but if you asked the question of the men in the ranks, you would receive a different reply."

"Are you suggesting that our enlisted men are only interested in fighting for *pay*?" Airlord Gray said. "That's an offensive opinion."

Captain Zorn turned his attention to him.

"I am afraid that however offensive it may be to you, sir, it is quite correct. Most enlisted men only fight for pay; there are exceptions, of course. There are those who have made whichever service they joined their lives. But in the main, the average enlisted man has no other interest in his position other than that of the money that it provides."

"What a cynical outlook," Commander Symes said. "How can you justify such a statement?"

"By using yourselves as an example, commander." He spread his arms, to indicate all of the officers present. "Would you be such staunch supporters of the Britannic Empire if you did not hold such lofty positions? Such positions are the result of your family and class. The money that you can draw on ensures that you may enter the finest universities, and enrol as officer cadets. The enlisted man, however, comes from the lower strata of your society. Bakers, painters, fitters, etc. They do not have the money or connections that you have, and the privileges that you take for granted are unknown to them."

"I don't like your tone, sir," Crompton said. His face was red. "How dare you demean the officer class! We serve the Empire without thought of monetary gain!"

"I am not condemning the officer class, sir. I merely state a simple fact. The enlisted man of every nation is the same. The great majority has no stomach for the fight. His loyalty is sealed within his pay check. You may not like it, but this is the truth."

"My *god*, sir!" Airlord Gray leapt to his feet. He pointed a shaking finger at Zorn. "You come in here, and offer us assistance, and then in the next breath, you degrade our men!" His face was purple with rage.

"Gentlemen! *Please!*" Councillor Reading rose to his feet. "Such disagreements are of no importance in the face of the situation in which we find ourselves. The salvation of the Queen, the Prince, and all of those who are suffering must be our highest priority. We must answer the threat of The Wraith's ultimatum." His gaze swept over them sternly. "I will not allow such dissention to distract us from our purpose. Captain Zorn, I must ask you not to air your views at this time. We respect your opinion, sir, even if it is not shared by us. But I will not hear another word. I have been given supreme executive power as Her Britannic Majesty and His Britannic Highness are incapacitated, and as such, it is my duty to ensure that the Empire runs smoothly until this crisis is over, and they are returned to lead us."

"I apologise, gentlemen," Captain Zorn said.

The officers continued to regard him with angry faces, but they held their peace. Airlord Gray sat down. After a few moments, Zorn sat down as well.

Councillor Reading sighed inwardly.

"Thank you, gentlemen," he said. "Despite the differences between us, I believe that we will accept Captain Zorn's offer of assistance. To do otherwise would be madness. However, I must ask you to accept a compromise that I will suggest, captain."

"What would that be, sir?"

"The Council agrees to all of your suggestions, but we would ask that when you have located this Captain Deville, you will ensure that Commander Symes and his squadron are also trained in the operation of these gravflyers."

Commander Symes straightened in his seat.

"I will agree to the Council's terms," Zorn said. He nodded deferentially to Commander Symes, who sat back with a satisfied smile.

"Thank you, captain," Reading said with relief.

"And now I will depart to seek out Captain Deville. I will leave my officers with you with the plans for the gravships and flyers, so that you may begin to construct them. Doctor Mansfield. Gentlemen." He turned and strode out of the chamber.

III

Aboard The Vengeance

As Zorn left the building, he was met by a horde of newsvidmen, all waiting for the opportunity of a picture and a word with Londinium's saviour. Captain Zorn forced his way through the crush, and ignored all of them. Cameras flashed, and pads were furiously typed upon. I managed to get close, and stopped the enigmatic figure by taking his arm. He turned his gaze upon me.

"Who are you, sir? What are your intentions regarding Her Britannic Majesty and the other victims of this assault? Are you a friend of the Empire?" I released his arm.

The captain smiled at me. "I would think that my actions have shown you that I am indeed a friend of the Empire." He regarded the gathered journalists as their pads continued to flash. "I have just met with the Emergency Council. They and the heads of the armed services have accepted my assistance. I have promised to aid Britannia by giving them the technical details of the ships and weapons which are at my disposal so that they may construct such devices and use them in the fight against The Wraith."

"*The Wraith*?" Connors of *The Tempus* asked.

"It is he who is responsible for this attack," Zorn explained. "He and I are bitter enemies, and have fought many times before."

"What about this sickness that has fallen upon the Queen, the Prince, and the others who were exposed to the invader's weapon?" Grimes of *The Standard* asked.

Zorn nodded. "It is known to me. This sickness is called *The Blight*. It mutates healthy tissue, and that tissue then attacks the body. It finally devours the host, and when dead, the corpse breaks down into a black dust."

"*Devours?*" Connors echoed, a disgusted look upon his face.

"Yes. It literally eats the host alive."

"Bloody hell," Grimes said softly.

"Is there a cure for this sickness?" I asked.

"Yes," Zorn replied. "The Wraith has it, and also those scientists who are in his employ. I propose to capture one of these scientists, and get the information required from him. To do this, I must seek out an aviatrix who leads the greatest fliers in Europa."

"Do you mean Captain Louise Deville?" I asked.

"I do indeed. I will go in search of Captain Deville, and obtain her assistance."

"Do you know where she and her fliers are?" Connors said.

"No. Only that they are somewhere in Espania."

"I can take you to her," I said.

"Do you know her?" Zorn said.

"I do. I met her during the War, and interviewed her for *The Chronicle*. She and I have maintained a close correspondence ever since." How close, I did not wish to say at that time.

"Very good," Zorn said. "What is your name, sir?"

"Alastair Fussell, of *The Chronicle*."

"Well then, Mister Fussell, I invite you to come aboard the *Vengeance*, and take us to Captain Deville. Do you accept my invitation?"

"I do, captain. I'd be delighted to see your marvellous ship." I grinned.

"Come then. Please allow us to leave, gentlemen. You have quite enough to satisfy your respective news services. Good day."

"Lucky bugger," Grimes muttered. I gave him a wink.

I joined Captain Zorn as the crowd of journalists parted like the Red Sea at the command of Moses, and we strode down the steps. A storm of voices broke out behind us as the reporters used their wristphones to call their employers with the amazing news.

A steamcoach waited for us at the foot of the steps. We climbed into it, and the steamcoach headed off, making for the park, where the gravship remained hovering high above. The platform was still sitting on the ground.

A large crowd of citizens surrounded it, peering up at the *Vengeance* in fascination. We alighted from the steamcoach, walked up to the platform, and Zorn closed the gate behind us as we stepped onto it. The captain pressed a button that was located on a panel on the platform's frame, and when a voice answered, he gave the order to bring the platform up.

The platform ascended into the belly of the ship, the hatch closed, and in a few moments, the *Vengeance* got under way. I looked about myself. We stood in a vast hanger, much larger than any airship that I had been on. The captain beckoned to me. I went over to him, and he showed me a vidscreen, which he activated. The view displayed was of the park and the crowd below. As I watched, the gravship slowly moved over the park, and then we turned to the West. We picked up speed, and the park and Londinium fell behind at a startling rate.

"Well, Mister Fussell," Zorn said, deactivating the vidscreen, "Would you like a tour of the ship?"

"I would indeed, captain. Lead on."

I followed as he led the way across the hanger bay. He opened a hatch, and stepped through. I did the same, and continued down a long corridor in his wake. I looked around, marvelling at the ship's construction. She was built unlike any other vessel that I had ever seen. Hexagonal shaped panels interlocked in a complex pattern of creation unfamiliar to me. The bracing supports were like nothing so much as the ribs and bone structure of some unimaginable animal. When I pointed out the unusual design to Zorn, he smiled.

"All of my designs come from nature, Mister Fussell. If we take the time to look, the universe has created some of the finest planners and builders. The bees, the ants, all of them have unique ways of building their abodes. I have taken inspiration from them, and also from the many skeletal and microscopic wonders around us."

I ran my hand over the hull.

"I've not seen this metal before, captain. What is it?"

"The *Vengeance* is constructed of the lightest alloy on earth, Mister Fussell. I call it *Carbonium*. It is a hardened metal that is not only extremely light, but it can bear much more weight than the steel hull of any ocean going ship. Plus, it is many times stronger."

"Impressive."

He led the way down the corridor.

We came to another hatch. The captain opened it, and inside was a galley, the likes of which one would expect to find in only the finest Parisian hotel. It was fitted out with an amazing array of equipment designed for the culinary arts. A dozen cooks laboured there, preparing and cooking. One of them came over to us. He was a short individual, with dark hair and eyes. He smiled, and bowed deferentially.

"Sir?"

"This is Mister Fussell, Marcel. Mister Fussell, my head chef, Marcel."

I shook the proffered hand.

"I'm pleased to meet you, Marcel. Your galley is impressive."

"Thank you, monsieur. Will you be taking luncheon with the captain?"

"He will," Zorn said.

"Eh, bien. Then I will hope to impress you further with our food, monsieur."

"I do not doubt it. Merci, Marcel."

He gave us another bow, and returned to his work.

"Take a picture, Mister Fussell. I imagine your readers would be interested to see our galley."

"Of course, captain. Thank you." I took my pad out of my jacket, turned it on, and took several pictures.

"Shall we continue?"

"By all means, captain."

He closed the hatch, and I followed him down the corridor. We came to another hatch. Below us, the deck vibrated to the power of the engines, and a humming sound came to my ears. Zorn opened the hatch, and the sound immediately became louder. He stepped inside, and I followed. As he closed the hatch behind us, I gazed about. We were in a small compartment. Hanging from a series of hooks were what looked like coveralls. Boots were arrayed on the floor in a neat line against the bulkhead. Across from us was another hatch. A desk was situated on the other side of the compartment, and a man rose from the chair behind it as we entered.

"Captain."

"Macklin, This is Mister Fussell. I am taking him to see the engine room. Please fit him out."

"Yes, sir. This way, sir." He gestured at the coveralls.

I went over, and he looked me up and down. He turned to the coveralls, and took a pair down and handed them to me.

"Try those, sir."

"Thank you." I opened them up, unsnapping the little metallic studs on the front of the garment. I stepped into them, and Macklin helped me do them up. They were a perfect fit.

"There you go, sir."

"You have a good eye, Macklin."

"Thank you, sir. Now for some boots." He looked at my shoes. "Seven, sir?"

"Correct."

Macklin went and fetched me a pair. He took my shoes, and put them in the line. I tugged the boots on. They were also a good fit.

"Ready?"

I turned at the sound of Zorn's voice. He was already wearing his gear.

"Of course. Thank you, Macklin."

"You're welcome, sir."

"Won't we need hearing protection, captain?" I asked.

"Not in my engine room, Mister Fussell." he smiled enigmatically.

He turned and opened the other hatch. The humming sound intensified. Zorn stepped through, and when I followed, Macklin closed the hatch behind us. Before us was a set of steps, leading down into the engine room. Zorn began to descend them, and I went after. The engine room was unexpectedly cool. I had been on many ships, and this was a welcome surprise.

We reached the bottom of the steps, and stood upon the deck. The space was like a vast cathedral. Huge beams crisscrossed the overhead in an intricate interweaving of *carbonium.* I took out my pad, and began taking pictures. As I snapped away, I gazed around the chamber; my fascinated eyes were met by all manner of intricate and unfamiliar machinery. Everything was constructed in a way that was hitherto unknown to me. We were dwarfed by such devices. I felt like an ant next to their gleaming hugeness. The engine space was spotless. And then another thing occurred to me. The humming sound I had heard was indeed louder here, but it was in no way uncomfortable, like the sound of an engine room in a conventional vessel would be. It was if we stood in a vast beehive. I stood and listened, surprised at the harmonious sound.

"Calming, isn't it?" Zorn said. He was watching me with a bemused expression on his face. "I sometimes like to walk here at night when I cannot sleep. I find the sound relaxing."

"It's amazing. It's like nothing I've ever heard before. Is this the sound of your gravitic drive?"

"No. Merely the vibrations given off by the shield that contains the energies of the drive."

"I see. There's another thing, captain. I'm amazed at the coolness of the engine spaces. I was anticipating the unbearable heat that one has to endure on ocean going vessels."

"And why should that be, Mister Fussell? The *Vengeance* is a ship of the air, not one of the sea. Surely you have flown in other conventional airships. Their engine rooms are not hot either."

I gestured at our coveralls.

"I suppose it came into my mind when we put these on, sir. I was expecting a blast of heat. Why then should we wear such clothing, if these spaces are so clean and cool?"

"A good question. These coveralls are worn not to protect us from heat, but from the build up of magnetic forces from the drive. It is shielded, but there is always the possibility of such forces escaping containment." He brushed his hand down the front of the garment. "There are special fibres sewn into this clothing that are designed to protect us should such an event occur."

"What would happen if someone were not wearing these, and the forces that you speak of were unleashed?"

"They would turn that unfortunate inside out."

"Good lord. Has it ever happened before?"

Zorn nodded, his face sombre.

"Yes. Once when we were testing the drive, containment failed. I lost ten men. It was a horrible way to die." He became thoughtful, and I held my questions, knowing that the horrific accident that he had described was playing itself out in his inner vision. We stood there for a moment, and then he shook his head as if to clear it of such an awful scene. "Shall we go on?"

"Certainly."

"Come, let me show you the real power of the *Vengeance*."

He proceeded down the catwalk, and I followed, taking pictures all the while. We walked along, two insects crawling through an immense space. We finally came to a control room. Zorn opened the hatch, and stepped inside. I followed, and as I took in the room and its equipment, he closed the hatch behind us. Four men were in the room, and one of them came over to us.

"Captain." He was tall and rangy, blonde, with blue eyes. He and his companions wore the same coveralls as we did. The others were busy monitoring the workings of the engines, their gaze fixed upon several screens.

"Mister Mercer. This is Mister Fussell. He is my guest. Show him the core. Mister Fussell, Mister Mercer is the Chief Engineer."

"Of course, captain. This way, Mister Fussell."

He led the way to the opposite bulkhead. A large hatch covered half of it. I guessed that it was in the very heart of the ship. I stood in front of the hatch, excited at the prospect of seeing the core and the amazing energy that powered the wonderful ship around us. Mercer grinned. He could see that I was excited. He pulled a lever that protruded from the bulkhead, and the hatch rose slowly. A gleam of whirling many hued light burst into the room, and as the plate rose higher, the spinning colours became more intense, filling the compartment. A rushing sound, like that of an immense waterfall accompanied the visual lightshow. The ever present beehive hum faded away as this new sound reverberated around the control room. The hatch came to a stop, having reached the full extent of its open position. A glass pane at least three foot thick stood between us and the ravening forces beyond. I thanked god that it was there. I gazed into the inferno.

Two immense magnetic poles faced each other in a vast compartment. Copper wires were wrapped around them, at least a foot in diameter. The gravitic forces whirled and spun, changing colour from moment to moment. They formed a huge ball of energy that rotated furiously in midair in the magnet's grip. A larger ball, barely seen, enveloped all; obviously the shield that Zorn had spoken of.

I stared open mouthed at the kaleidoscope of riotous hues that whirled and spun before me. It was like a restless beast, chained and confined, ever seeking to break its bonds. I shivered at the sight, recalling the horrific deaths of those poor men.

"It's quite safe, sir," Mercer said, noticing my sudden discomfort.

I nodded dumbly, still staring at the maelstrom of gravitic force. Such power! It was incredible. It was surely enough power to light up a city.

"Mister Mercer is correct, Mister Fussell. The accident of which I spoke of cannot occur again."

I turned to see Zorn standing beside me. He spoke while keeping his attention fixed on the core.

"I have ensured that there are safeguards in place. The core cannot break containment."

"What would happen if the ship were damaged in battle, and your safeguards were lost?"

"In that event, the core would be ejected, for if they were to be released, the energies unleashed would destroy the ship utterly."

I returned my gaze to the inferno.

"It's like a beast, captain. A monstrous creature that is chained, and hates its captivity."

"Indeed, Mister Fussell. That is how I think of it also. But the beast will not escape, rave as much as it does. Thank you, Mercer."

"Sir."

The engineer raised the lever, and the hatch lowered again, blotting out the unnerving sight. In a moment, the sight and sounds that had assailed me were no more, safely contained. The pleasant hum returned, soothing after the cacophony that had accompanied the viewing of the core.

"You did not take a picture, Mister Fussell," said Zorn.

"I was - *overwhelmed* - by the experience, captain." I took out a handkerchief, and wiped my sweaty brow.

"Perhaps later?"

"Yes, yes. Later."

"Would you care to see our electromagnetic cannon?" Zorn asked.

"Oh, yes. Yes, please."

"Come then. Thank you, Mercer."

"Captain. Mister Fussell. It was a pleasure to meet you."

"And I you. Thank you, sir."

We left the control room, and proceeded back the way we had come. The image of the core was still in my mind. What awful destruction would occur should it be released. We came to the steps that led to the deck above.

"You are quiet, Mister Fussell."

"I was thinking of the core, captain. I had not expected to see such violence."

"*Violence?*" Zorn echoed. He stopped and turned to me.

"Forgive me, it was a poor choice of word."

"No, sir. You are correct. The gravitic forces within the drive *are* violent. For them to escape would be a catastrophe. But, I ask you, are not the boilers on a steamship filled with violent force also? Just because you cannot see them, it does not mean that they are not as potentially destructive as the energies that you have just seen. Steam under great pressure is also quite dangerous."

"Of course you are right, captain. It was just a shock to see it."

"I understand. My own reaction upon seeing it for the first time was the same. Please believe me when I say that I have created the drive for the benefit of all mankind, not for any destructive purpose."

"Unlike The Wraith?"

He frowned.

"Yes. He is only bent on one thing. World domination. He would keep the secret to himself, and make all men his slaves. But enough. You wanted to see our cannons. Come."

He started upward, and I followed. In a time that appeared to be much shorter than our descent had been, we reached the compartment where we had donned our coveralls. As Zorn closed the hatch behind us, Macklin came over, and started to help me out of my boots.

"Well, sir, what did you think of the engine room?"

"I am amazed, Macklin. The complexity of the machinery is incredible. The *Vengeance* is a marvel."

He unfastened the snaps on my garment, and I stepped out of it.

"Aye, she is that, sir. She's a grand ship."

He went and hung up the coveralls, and brought me my shoes.

"There you are, sir."

"Thank you, Macklin."

I put on my shoes, and stood ready to go.

"Now let me show you our cannons," Zorn said. "Good day, Macklin."

"Good day, captain, Mister Fussell."

"Good day, Macklin."

We stepped out of the compartment. Zorn closed the hatch, and we went along the corridor. We came to another hatch, and as Zorn opened it and stepped inside, I saw a control room, filled with vidscreens. There was only one man in there, and he jumped up from his chair and hurried over.

"I wasn't aware that there was an inspection, captain. I'll call the lads."

Zorn held up his hand.

"There is no need for that, Mister Kennedy. This is Mister Fussell. He is my guest. He wanted to see our cannon."

"Very good, sir. I'm pleased to meet you, Mister Fussell."

He was an older man than the other crew members that I had met so far. He had thinning blond hair that was going grey, and the lines around his blue eyes spoke of much experience. He was sturdy, but not fat. However, his young lean years were far behind him.

"Thank you, Mister Kennedy."

I looked over at the wall of screens.

"This is fire control, sir," Kennedy said. "Come over here."

There was a large screen in the middle of the displays. He activated it. An image swam on the vidscreen, and resolved into a view along a barrel. A giant crosshair appeared at the middle of the screen. At the end of the barrel were a series of large rings.

"You can see that she's no conventional cannon, sir. Those rings are the accelerators. The electromagnetic energy flows up the barrel, and the projectiles are sent along the barrel by the magnetic force that's released at the breech. As the shell reaches the end of the barrel, the accelerators give it a final push, and away it goes."

He pointed at a console.

"That's where the energy is created. There are generators in the engine room that supply us with it. That lever there controls the amount of energy that's fed to the cannon."

"Very impressive, Mister Kennedy," I said. "I have seen your cannon in operation. They are devastating."

"It's the velocity, sir. Our shells travel at a much faster speed than that of conventional shells." He was very proud of his weapons. "Perhaps the captain would allow me to show you them in operation sometime?"

"You will have the chance soon, Mister Kennedy. Mister Fussell is a friend of Captain Deville. I imagine that when we find her, she will be in the thick of a fight. Mister Fussell will then possibly see your cannon in a combat situation."

Kennedy grinned. "That's what they're here for, captain."

"Thank you, Mister Kennedy. Come, Mister Fussell. Luncheon awaits."

"Good day, captain; Mister Fussell. Come back anytime, sir."

"Thank you. Good day, Mister Kennedy."

We left the compartment, and walked down a corridor. We came to a hatch, and when Zorn opened it, I gazed in amazement at the opulent compartment that was revealed beyond. He ushered me through. I stepped inside, staring at the lush carpeting, the highly polished woodwork and brass fittings, and the huge table with accompanying chairs set in its centre. Soft yellow light came from a large chandelier that was suspended above the table. I turned to him as he closed the hatch.

"This is unexpected, captain."

"Did you think we would dine in a mess hall, Mister Fussell?" He smiled.

"Well, no. But this - "

"Excess?" He prompted.

"I wouldn't use that word, captain."

"You need not be modest, Mister Fussell. I know that this compartment is much more luxurious than is necessary. Such splendour is hardly what you would expect to find aboard the *Vengeance*. It would be more in place in the palace of some Eastern potentate. You must forgive me. This dining room, and my own state room are the only rooms that are furnished so. The crew's quarters, while comfortable, are not as splendid as this. However, I am captain, and I am accustomed to such finery. Actually, it was more for my wife's benefit. I wanted her to have nothing but the best."

He became silent. Once again, his face became clouded, and I stood there mutely, not wishing to interrupt his thoughts, dark as they were. I looked around the sumptuous room. The table and chairs were made of some dark wood that was unfamiliar to me, gothic in their design.

There were several portholes on either side of the compartment, each frame being constructed of gleaming brass. The carpet beneath my feet was thick and luxurious, deep red in colour. I could imagine Zorn and his devoted wife and children dining in such splendour, sailing high above the world. Once again, I was exposed to the depth of this amazing and mysterious man's great love for his lost family.

"Shall we?"

I came out of my musings at the sound of his voice.

"Of course, captain."

He gestured to the chair situated on the right of the table. I went and sat down. He took the chair at the head of the table. He pressed a button that was in front of him.

The hatch opened, and a crewman entered. He was carrying a silver tray, upon which was set a bottle and two glasses. He came up to us, and put the glasses on the table. Then he poured from the bottle, filling up the glasses. He put the bottle on the table, and stood awaiting Zorn's command.

"You appreciate fine wine, Mister Fussell?" Zorn asked.

"From time to time I do, captain." I picked up my glass and sniffed. I then took a sip. It was indeed fine. I put down the glass, as I was not a drinker. "French?"

"Of course. This is Mister Horton. He is my personal steward. Horton, this is Mister Fussell."

"Good day, sir."

"Good day, Horton."

"What do we have for luncheon today, Horton?"

"Veal cooked in brandy and cream, with snow peas, chat potatoes, and honeyed carrots. Dessert is creme brulee, followed by Grand Marnier."

"Excellent. You may serve us."

"Yes, captain." He went out.

"Now you will see if Marcel was boasting." He picked up his glass and drank.

"I have no doubt that his food will far surpass any expectations I have, captain. Everything about your wonderful ship is incredible. I have run out of superlatives. The *Vengeance* is a wonder. I congratulate you. You have created something unique and impressive." I raised my glass and saluted him.

He returned my toast, and put his glass down.

"Would you believe me if I said that it means nothing to me without my wife and children? All of my work; the Gravitic Drive, the electromagnetic cannon, The *Vengeance* herself, all of these things used to fill my every waking moment. I toiled like a stevedore, never once acknowledging the love of my family. I have discovered wonders, it is true. But at a terrible cost. I would give it all away in a second, if it meant that my wife and sons would be returned to me whole and healthy." His face was dark.

"How - " I began.

The hatch opened, and Horton, followed by three other stewards, brought our repast in. They set down the plates of food, and arranged the cutlery for us. When they had finished, Zorn dismissed them with a wave of his hand. Used to his black moods, they departed, and the hatch closed with a clang.

"I shall tell you how my family was taken from me. Eat, Mister Fussell, and listen to how my life was forever changed."

I began to eat. The meal was excellent. I should have expected nothing less.

"I am an inventor, as you know, Mister Fussell," Zorn began. "I come from a family that is very wealthy, so my experiments did not lack the money required to carry on. I had discovered the drive, and was designing a small ship for trials. During this time, I buried myself in my work; nothing or no one was allowed to interrupt me. Not even my wife. Mary was very patient with me. She could see how important the work I was doing was. It would be of great benefit for all mankind. Transport would be revolutionised; gravships would cut travel time down, unite the entire world, and would one day even take us to the stars." He paused, and regarded me closely. "Do you think that an impossible dream?"

I put down my knife and fork.

"No, captain. I do not. From what I've seen of this wonderful vessel, I wouldn't wonder if that would be your ultimate aim. Please continue."

"As I said, I was working day and night, my whole attention fixed on the drive. Mary came to me, with my sons, Victor and Andrew. She told me that they were going into the city. I was only half listening, and made some reply. Seeing how engrossed I was in my work, they left. Eat your meal, Mister Fussell."

I continued my repast.

He picked up his glass, drained it, and refilled it from the bottle.

"Suddenly, there was a huge detonation, and everything in the workshop crashed to the floor. I staggered to my feet, and stumbled to the door. My first thought was that there had been some kind of accident with the steamcoach. Mary and my boys could have been injured, even dead. I raced outside into bedlam. The mansion was afire, and a giant ship hovered above. It was The *Lucifer*. She fired at the workshop, and it disintegrated in an explosion that hurled me to the ground. A voice cried out, and I looked and saw my sons trying to move my unconscious wife. I ran to them, and took her in my arms. As

I cast about desperately for shelter, a hatch slowly opened in the belly of the ship above us. The projector that you saw in operation during the *Lucifer's* attack lowered, and a hum came as it powered up. It fired, and we were all struck down."

He stopped speaking, reliving the awful event in his thoughts. I continued to eat, the scrape of my cutlery the only sound in the compartment. I knew that I should not interrupt his black thoughts. In a few minutes, I had finished, and lay my knife and fork down.

"I regained consciousness," Zorn continued, his voice raw. "Mary and my sons were in some kind of stupor. I could not wake them, try as I must. Some neighbours came in their steamcoaches, and we rushed my family to hospital. Mary and Victor showed signs of The Blight, but Andrew and I seemed unaffected, save for some nervous shock, and mild depression. The doctors were baffled. "

"Why did it affect you in different ways?" I asked, puzzled.

"I do not know. Perhaps it is because every human being is an individual, as different to each other as snowflakes. We know that drugs and alcohol cause a variety of maladies on their users. Perhaps the ray is the same."

"What happened then?"

"There is little to tell. Mary and Victor lingered in agony for three weeks. The Blight ate them alive."

"My god. And your other son, Andrew? What happened to him?"

"The nervous condition that he was afflicted with became steadily worse, until he went mad. I had to confine him to an asylum. He is there still. That was three years ago."

"I am so sorry, captain."

"Thank you, Mister Fussell." He raised his glass to his lips, and drank it all down. He refilled the glass from the bottle. I noticed that he had not touched his meal.

"So after this, you created The *Vengeance?* How? Your workshop was destroyed."

He regarded me with his steely eyes.

"I rebuilt it. I now had a different purpose. I worked harder than before. Days, weeks, months, all went by in a blur of feverish activity. I replaced my dead workmen, and together we toiled around the clock. Finally, she was nearly finished. My gravship was almost complete. It only remained for the drive to be tested, and for some equipment to be fitted. Then, one day, I was on the bridge. The vidscreen was activated, and I gazed upon he who had destroyed my former life. I stared at the masked and armoured figure with my blood boiling in my veins. He challenged me to a trial by combat between our two vessels. I accepted gladly. He gave me the location to meet. When I had completed the work on the *Vengeance*, we took off and made our rendezvous with the *Lucifer*. We both attacked. Damage was inflicted on both ships, so we retired. He appeared on the vidscreen again, and said that we would continue to meet until one ship was destroyed. Over the last three years, we have done so several times, but neither of us has managed to defeat the other."

"He calls himself The Wraith," I said. "I saw the network broadcast that he made also. But who is he? Where does he come from? Why should he target you and your ship?"

"He is a mystery," Zorn acknowledged. "I only know that he is Germanian. That much can be identified just by his accent. But any other information about him is sorely lacking. I have tried, without success, to discover his real identity. His motives are clear, however.

He is jealous of any other who possesses the secret of the drive. Both he and I discovered it, but he wishes to be the only one to have such power. And he would destroy both me and the *Vengeance* to ensure that he is indeed the only one to have it. He would make all of mankind his slaves." He emptied his glass.

"There is something you should know, Mister Fussell. My name is not Zorn. My real name is known only to my crew, and they have been sworn not to reveal it."

"Why then do you call yourself that name?" I asked.

"It is a message to my enemy. The name Zorn is Germanian. It is an old family name, which means *wrath*. In this way, I have let him know that I will have my revenge upon him." Once again his eyes blazed. "I have left my old life behind. My family, my estates and titles; all are gone. I am a man without a country. The *Vengeance* is my home."

The hatch opened. Horton returned, with the other stewards. They brought the dessert. As they set the plates before us, Zorn waved them away irritably.

"You haven't eaten your food, captain," Horton said.

"Take it away," Zorn growled, "and bring me another bottle of wine. No, leave Mister Fussell's dessert."

"As you wish, sir." Horton and his companions cleared the table, except for my creme brulee, and left the compartment.

"Now you know why I hunt this man," the captain said. "I will pursue him to the ends of the earth. I almost had him once when we fought off Cape Horn. But a huge storm blew up, and we were separated. I will follow him into Hell." He clenched his fist angrily.

His eyes were red, and his face was showing the affects of the wine that he had drunk on an empty stomach. He fell silent, brooding over his glass. As I ate my dessert in the uncomfortable silence, I realised that the captain was a vengeful and bitter man, driven not by his unparalleled knowledge of science, but by the most primal instinct that mankind had felt ever since he sat around the fire in his cave: revenge. I saw that Zorn would give his life, even his very soul to destroy the man who had changed his life forever, and stole his love away from him: The Wraith. The *Vengeance*, instead of being a wonder of scientific creation, was nothing more to him than the instrument of justice.

Zorn finally spoke, asking: "How will you contact Captain Deville?"

"I have a number that I can call her on," I answered. "I will call her and tell her that *The Chronicle* is interested in an interview."

"I am not convinced that she will agree to meet," Zorn said.

The hatch opened, and Horton entered, bringing another bottle of wine. He came up to the table, and set it before the captain.

"I assure you that she will, captain," I said. "We were once great friends."

He regarded me sceptically for a moment. It was clear that he doubted my ability to contact the French aviatrix.

"We will see if your confidence will be rewarded. Horton."

"Yes, captain?"

"Please show Mister Fussell to the cabin aft of my cabin. There he may rest until we reach Espania." He picked up the other bottle, opened it, and poured himself another drink. He eyed my unfinished wine. "You did not finish your wine, Mister Fussell."

"Forgive me, captain. I am not a drinker."

He smiled sadly. "I see. Well then, there is more for me. Horton, take Mister Fussell to his cabin."

"Of course, captain. This way, sir, if you please."

I rose to my feet.

"Thank you for your hospitality, captain. Please tell Monsieur Marcel that luncheon was excellent."

He nodded. I followed Horton across the deck. As we reached the hatch, Zorn's voice rang out.

"Mister Fussell!"

I turned. He had raised his glass in a toast.

"Welcome aboard the *Vengeance*."

I bowed to him, and then Horton and I left the compartment. We left Zorn to his wine and bitter memories.

IV

Meeting Captain Deville

Doctor Mansfield took off her spectacles, and rubbed her tired eyes. She had been inspecting another blood sample that had been provided by the Queen under a microscope. She had gazed futilely at sample after sample; all were the same. They showed the rapid mutation of healthy cells as they transformed and attacked the remaining cells. It was always the same result. In a few moments, all of the blood had changed, and destroyed itself. Then there was only a black dusty residue left on her slide. Mansfield sighed. She and her assistants had worked around the clock, desperately trying to find a cure for The Blight. Nothing worked, but they continued on with their task doggedly. A third of those who had been afflicted were dying slowly. The Queen was one of them.

The door opened, and one of the nurses from the contamination ward came in. She walked up to the doctor. Her face was pale and drawn.

"Yes, Ellen?" Mansfield said. She knew that the nurse bore bad news.

"One of the patients has died, doctor." Her voice was soft. There was a tremor in it.

"I see," Mansfield said. "Which one?"

"The old man... He - " The blood drained from her face.

Mansfield grabbed the nurse as she fainted.

"Aaron!" She cried.

One of her assistants raced over, and helped her take the stricken nurse to a nearby empty bed. They laid the poor girl out, and Mansfield rubbed her hands between her own.

"Aaron, fetch some water, please."

"Yes, doctor." He hurried away.

"Ellen. Ellen." The doctor gently slapped the unconscious nurse's cheeks.

"Oh." The girl snapped awake. "What?" She stared about, her eyes wide. Then she saw Mansfield standing over her. Her face reddened, and she covered it with trembling hands.

"Oh, doctor. I feel so stupid!" Her voice was muffled, but Mansfield could hear the shame in it.

"Now, now, Ellen. You've had a bit of a shock, haven't you?" She took the nurse's hands, and slowly lowered them to reveal the girl's white face.

Aaron came back with a glass of water. He handed it to Mansfield wordlessly.

"Here you are, my dear," the doctor said. "Drink it all down."

Ellen took the glass and drank hurriedly. Aaron took it from her gently.

"What did you see?" Mansfield said.

The girl's face screwed up in horror.

"Oh, doctor. It was *awful...*" She grabbed Mansfield's hands and held them tightly. Her eyes were brimming with tears.

"Easy, easy. Just try and tell me what you saw."

Ellen took a deep breath, and then spoke in a rush.

"I was doing my rounds, and I came to Mister Creedie. He was breathing shallowly when I checked him, but he seemed to show no change from the night before. But then..." She paused, and then went on. "Then, he groaned, and began to pant. Black lines appeared on his face, as though something terrible and unnatural was growing there at a frightening speed. It looked like fungus, or something. In a shorter time than it takes me to tell you, it had covered his mouth and nose. He struggled for air, his eyes staring at me horribly. He scrabbled at the covers in agony. I wondered what to do. I quickly put on my rubber gloves, and ran to an instrument cart that was nearby. I picked up a scalpel, hoping to clear the substance from his mouth so that he could breathe. I hurried back, but the awful stuff had covered his entire face. He was still. I knew that he was dead. As I stared in horror, his entire upper body turned black, and he - *crumbled* - into dust. God, it was horrible." Tears ran down her face.

"*Bloody hell!*" Aaron gasped. He glanced at Mansfield. "Sorry, doctor."

Mansfield ignored his outburst and apology.

"Oh, Ellen. What a terrible thing to see." She stroked the girl's hair.

The nurse blushed furiously.

"And then I go and faint like a little girl. I'm so ashamed."

"Don't you dare beat yourself up like that," Mansfield said sternly. "You're an excellent nurse, my dear. And you've seen plenty of awful things. Remember the casualties that you cared for during the War? You performed your duties then admirably, surrounded by such horror."

"Yes," Ellen replied. "But I've never seen anything like that before."

"None of us have. But I fear that this death is but the first of many. If we cannot find a cure soon, then the Queen, and all of those who suffer will die horribly."

"I feel like we're fighting a losing battle," Aaron said. "Nothing works."

"We *must* win," Mansfield said, determination in her voice.

The nurse made as if to rise from the bed. The doctor grabbed her shoulder.

"Are you sure you're all right, Ellen? Why don't you rest for a while?"

The girl shook her head.

"No, thank you, doctor. I'm all right now. I won't lie about while everyone else is working so hard." She looked embarrassed. "Please don't tell anyone what happened."

"Not a word," Mansfield said. She met Aaron's gaze.

"Did something happen?" He said lightly. "Must have missed it." He gave the nurse a reassuring smile.

"Thank you both." She got to her feet. "Back to the fight. I'll report if there are any other…"

"Losses?" Mansfield prompted.

"Yes. Losses. Thank you, doctor, Mister Parker." She gave them a wan smile, and went out.

"Now *there* is real courage," Aaron said.

"We will all need it in the days to come," Mansfield said.

They returned to their work.

Prince Henry wiped the Queen's brow with a damp cloth. He sat back in the chair that was next to her bed. He had stayed by her side since she had been admitted to the hospital following the *Lucifer's* attack.

"Thank you, my dear," she said. "Could I have some water?"

The Prince rose and went to a little bedside table. Upon it was a glass carafe and a glass. He picked up the carafe and filled the glass. He took it to the Queen. She gulped it down.

"Better?" he asked.

"Much. Thank you." She gave him the glass. The prince returned it to the bedside table, and resumed his seat by her bed.

Queen Aurelia returned her attention to the others present in the room. They were: Airlord Gray, General Crompton, Captain Smith, Commander Symes, and Councillor Reading.

"Please continue, Councillor. You had told me of the timely arrival of Captain Zorn's ship, and how he drove off the invader. You then held an Emergency Meeting that he attended. This Captain Zorn offered to assist us in the fight against this Wraith." She lay back.

"Yes, Your Majesty. He said that to help you and the others who were struck down by The Wraith's weapon, he would need assistance in capturing one of the scientists who had developed the weapon. They possess the knowledge that is needed to cure everyone. Zorn proposed a raid, using the Air Commandos. They are experienced in these type of lightning raids. But he said that the air support they need is beyond our capabilities. He has flyers that operate on the Gravitic Drive, the power that drives his ship, and The Wraith also has flyers that use this motive power. None of our conventional craft have the speed that they possess. As such, no machines that we have are fast enough to escape The Wraith's craft. He told us that he would seek out a French aviatrix; her squadron are supposed to be the best in the world. They would use his gravflyers, and thus give the Air Commandos a fighting chance. Zorn insists that this is the only way for this desperate mission to succeed."

"The best fliers in the world?" The Queen said sceptically. She looked over at Commander Symes.

"I disagree, Your Majesty. Our chaps are certainly better fliers than this Captain Deville and her squadron." He looked sour.

"Deville?" she echoed. "I seem to remember hearing this name before."

"She was a highly decorated veteran of the War," Airlord Gray said. "But then she was cast out. She became a mercenary, selling her squadron to the highest bidder."

"I do not believe that this Deville is the best choice for such a vital mission, Your Majesty," General Crompton added. "We should insist that Commander Symes and his men are the ones to go. Britannic fliers, for a mission that affects the Britannic Empire; not some French aviatrix who sells herself for money." Sarcasm dripped from his voice.

"Do you believe that your fliers could be trained to operate these new machines, Commander?" Queen Aurelia said.

Symes stepped closer to the bed.

"I'm certain of it, Your Majesty."

"And you have no faith in this French woman and her squadron?"

"I did not say that, Your Majesty. Obviously they are top-notch; all veterans of the War. They call themselves 'Le Rouge Chats.'"

"The Red Cats?" The Queen smiled. "An interesting name."

"I believe the name refers to Captain Deville's hair, Your Majesty," Airlord Gray said. "She has long red hair that can be seen for miles in an open cockpit."

"I think the name actually refers to the fact that they are all women," Your Majesty," Symes offered. He glanced at Gray. "Perhaps both opinions are correct."

Queen Aurelia raised her eyebrows.

"A squadron of women fliers? Now that is interesting. There are no women in our Royal Air Service who are fliers, are there, Commander?"

"There are none serving as combat fliers, Your Majesty," he answered. "There are some transport fliers, and also air ambulance fliers."

"I see. I should like to meet this Captain Deville and her Red Cats," the Queen said.

Airlord Gray stepped closer to the Queen's bed.

"I am not convinced that this French woman and her squadron are our only hope, Your Majesty. Surely Commander Symes and his elite squadron could be trained to operate these - " He searched for the word.

"Gravflyers, sir," Symes said.

"Yes, these gravflyers. I think that it would be a grave error to hand the safety of yourself and the Empire into the hands of a mercenary. How can we trust someone who has been cast out of their own country? Someone who fights only for money?" He was obviously disgusted.

Queen Aurelia regarded him.

"You do not believe that she can help us, Airlord Gray?"

"I have grave doubts about her, Your Majesty."

"I see. And what are your feelings regarding this Captain Zorn?"

The Airlord frowned.

"He is an enigma, Your Majesty. We don't know who he is, or where he comes from. We don't know anything about him."

"We do know that he appeared and saved Londinium from destruction," Prince Henry said.

"I accept that, Your Highness. But *why*? Does he have some ulterior motive for helping us?"

"I'm afraid I agree, Your Majesty," General Crompton added. "This Zorn fellow could be a danger to us. He might be lulling us into a false sense of security, and then he will make his move against us."

"Why then would he provide us with the plans to construct our own vessels equipped with this Gravitic Drive?" Queen Aurelia said. "And also leave two of his officers with us to help us in their construction?"

"Perhaps that is part of his own plan, Your Majesty," Gray said.

The Queen pondered for a moment, and then she turned to

Captain Smith.

"What is your opinion, captain?"

"I am uncertain, Your Majesty. But it is true that Captain Zorn did drive off the invader. I think we should see what he does. I don't believe that he will turn on us."

"You think he can be trusted?" Airlord Gray said.

"I'm not sure, sir. But we should at least give him the benefit of the doubt."

"You would put the fate of Her Britannic Majesty and her subjects in the hands of a man we know nothing about?" General Crompton said roughly. "Perhaps give him power over the whole Empire?"

"I did not say that, general. I only said that we should allow him to carry out his plan. I don't see that we have any choice."

"Of *course* we have a choice," Crompton said, his voice rising. He turned to the Queen. "Your Majesty. We have these two men and the plans to make our own ships. Why do we need to put our faith in this mysterious stranger? We should construct these craft ourselves, and Commander Symes and his fliers should learn to fly them, and accompany the Air Commandos in this raid."

"Perhaps the general could tell us where The Wraith's hidden base is?" Captain Smith said. "Without Zorn's knowledge of its location, we are foiled in our attempt to kidnap the scientists that we need to save Her Majesty and all of those who have been afflicted."

General Crompton rounded on Captain Smith.

"Are you certain that even *he* knows where this base is? We only have his word on it. This comes from a man who appears from nowhere, and expects us to trust him with Her Majesty's life, and also the lives of all of those who suffer. Can we trust him? I say *no*; we must build these machines, and use them for ourselves."

"General Crompton."

Crompton turned back to the bed.

"Your Majesty?"

"I have heard enough. It is my wish that we accept the help of this Captain Zorn, for he seems to be genuine. I believe that he and his ship appear to be the only defence we have against this Wraith and his advanced science. Sometimes allies are to be found in the most unlikely circumstances. "

Airlord Gray stepped forward.

"Your Majesty - " he began.

Queen Aurelia held up an imperious hand. Gray closed his mouth with a snap. The Queen sat up, and fixed them both with a commanding gaze.

"Gentlemen. It is my command that Captain Zorn is to carry out this mission in whatever way he wishes. He is the only one who is familiar with the enemy's ways. You will assist him in any way possible."

"Yes, Your Majesty," Gray and Crompton chorused.

"However, I am not a tyrant. I have listened to your - *suggestions* - and I agree with them. We will build these craft, general, and I will insist that Commander Symes and his squadron be trained in their operation. He will choose several of his best men, and they will accompany Captain Zorn and the Air Commandos on the mission. Does this meet with your approval, gentlemen?" She lay back in the bed.

Somewhat mollified, Gray and Crompton both bowed to her.

"It does. Thank you, Your Majesty," Gray said.

"I am also satisfied with your decision. Your servant, Your Majesty," Crompton said.

"What of The Wraith's demand, Your Majesty?" Reading asked. "If he has the cure for this disease, we must somehow obtain it from him."

"Are you suggesting that we bow to him, and make him emperor?" Gray said scornfully.

'No, of course not," Reading said. "But we could seem to be acceding to his wishes, get the cure, and then deny him."

"No, Councillor Reading," Queen Aurelia said. "We will do no such thing."

They all turned to regard her.

"If I and my subjects are to die, then so be it. We will not submit to him."

"But, Your Majesty - " Reading began.

The Queen held up her hand. Reading became silent.

"Hear my command, gentlemen. This Wraith is to be denied his outrageous request. If I am to die, that is fate. We will not give Britannia to this man. I have confidence that Doctor Mansfield and her companions will find a cure. You must have faith that it will be so."

The door opened. Doctor Mansfield entered. She came up to the bed, and took up the Queen's wrist. As Mansfield checked her pulse, she stared at Aurelia's face, and was relieved to see no evidence of any foreign substance there. She lay the Queen's arm back on the coverlet, and applied her stethoscope to her chest. She listened intently for a moment, and then removed it.

"Could you sit up, please, Your Majesty?"

Prince Henry stood, and helped the Queen sit up.

"Thank you, Your Highness," Mansfield said. She put her stethoscope on Aurelia's back, and listened. Then she removed it, and tapped here and there with two fingers. She nodded to herself.

"Is there any change?" Prince Henry asked.

"No, Your Highness. The lungs are clear." *So far,* she thought to herself. She faced the others in the room. "Gentlemen, I must ask you all to leave, Her Britannic Majesty has to rest."

They all bowed to the Queen, and filed out. The only exception was Prince Henry. He resumed his seat, and his vigil.

Mansfield took a small bottle out of her coat, and removed the stopper. She shook two small pills out onto her palm. She offered them to the Queen.

"To help you sleep, Your Majesty."

"It seems that that is all I do nowadays," she said wryly.

As Aurelia swallowed them, the doctor filled the glass, and gave it to her. The Queen washed down the pills. Mansfield received the glass from her, and replaced it on the table. Aurelia lay back, and was asleep in moments.

"Thank you, doctor," the Prince said.

Mansfield bowed to him, and went out, closing the door quietly. Prince Henry sat staring at his wife's pale face.

Councillor Reading sat at the desk in his office, laboriously going over the ubiquitous reports that came with his position. He sighed. He had been sitting there for four hours, and was growing tired. He made to rise, but was interrupted by the sudden activation of the vidscreen that sat upon his desk. The councillor resumed his seat, as an image swam on the screen, and then resolved itself into the giant armoured figure who they had seen when the Emergency Council had met.

The Wraith regarded him for a long moment. Neither of them spoke. Then, the giant addressed him.

"Councillor Reading. Have you come to a decision regarding my request?"

Reading stared at him in distaste.

"Yes," he said.

"And that decision is?" The Wraith prompted.

"Defiance."

"Defiance?" The figure echoed. *"Do you think that you can deny me what I ask? Remember the condition of your queen, and all of those who were affected by my ray. If you do not accept my terms, they will all perish. Will you be responsible for that?"*

"I am well aware of Her Majesty's condition. She herself has given the command that you are not to be given what you ask."

"Fool. How long do you think she can survive without my cure?"

"I do not know. But she has made her decision, and that is final."

The Wraith stared at Reading, and the councillor could almost sense the hatred that filled him. They sat staring at each other for what seemed an eternity.

"Very well," The Wraith finally said. *"I hope she will enjoy the awful death that is coming to claim her."* With an angry stab of his gauntleted finger, he closed the connection.

Reading rose to his feet, and walked across the floor. He went to a coat and hat rack that stood near the door. He took up a coat, and put it on. He picked up a hat, and went out of the office in search of a steamcoach to take him to the hospital. He must report The Wraith's message to the Queen.

The Wraith stood looking out of a window that gave onto a view of the Hartz mountains. He was in a large room that had been carved out of the rock by a team of his engineers. It was within the secret base from which he had operated for years. Hidden deep in the mountains, this base was filled with the advanced scientific apparatus that he had surrounded himself with. In a giant hanger several levels below him was the *Lucifer*, herself surrounded by smaller gravships, and dozens of gravflyers. The base was a hive of bustling activity; men went to and fro, engaged in the many tasks that filled each of their days. They were all fanatics, devoted to the Wraith's cause. They would all give their lives without question in his service.

He was listening to someone who was speaking to him via vidscreen. The speaker was a spy that he had planted deep within the Britannic Empire; someone who was privy to secret information of the highest level. The image was dark, and the spy's face could not be seen. His voice was also modulated by some electronic device. This was to ensure that if the transmission was intercepted by the Britans, his identity would not be discovered. The spy had just informed him of the discussions that had taken place both at the meeting of the council, and also in the Queen's hospital room.

"*Good work,*" The Wraith said. "*I am well pleased with this. You have done well. Where is Captain Zorn going to?*"

The electronic voice hummed from the speaker.

"*He is on his way to Espania to meet Captain Deville. She is fighting for the Revolutionaries.*"

"*I see. I will send some of my gravflyers to deal with them.*"

"*Do you think that they will be able to do so? I mean, this Deville, she is quite - capable.*"

"*Are you questioning the skills of my fliers?*" The Wraith growled.

"*No, no, of course not, master. But her reputation as a combatant has been well earned. During the War, she was a highly respected officer; by both sides. Our own men respected her abilities, and considered her a worthy opponent. Many of them fell to her guns.*"

"*I am aware of this,*" The Wraith said testily. "*However, that was years ago. Surely she doesn't possess the same quick reflexes that her younger self had. Age, my friend, it catches up to all of us. Now that she is older, she will not react so quickly, and my younger fliers should make short work of her and her Red Cats. They will be easily skinned."*

A harsh grinding sound came from the mask. The spy knew that his master was laughing. It was an awful sound; nothing human or humorous could be heard in those metallic tones. It was as though a machine was attempting to mimic a normal person's mirth. There was silence on the vidscreen, for the spy knew that if he interrupted his master, he would pay for it at a later date.

The sound finally came to a halt.

"There is another thing you are forgetting," The Wraith said.

"What is that, master?"

"My fliers are equipped with gravflyers, and this French woman and her squadron only have older, conventional machines. They would have to be the best fliers in the world to be able to overcome the technical advantage that this gives my men over them. Their ancient craft will be no match for my elite squadron."

"Zorn is of the belief that Deville and her squadron are the best fliers in the world, master. He told this to the Emergency Council, and Councillor Reading told this to the Queen."

"And she believed it?"

"She is inclined to allow Captain Zorn to attempt the mission, and see if he is right about their capabilities."

"Ridiculous! You will see; Deville and her witches will be shot from the sky. All this talk of them being the 'best fliers in the world' will cease when they are lying in smoking wreckage upon the ground."

"Surely you are right, master."

"Of course I am. Have there been many deaths?"

"Only a few, master."

"How disappointing. I shall have to get Finke to increase the output of the projector. Keep me apprised of the Queen's condition. Contact me when you have other information."

"Yes, master."

The communication ended.

The huge armoured figure stared out of the window at the snow-capped mountain range. The Wraith stood there like a statue, his thoughts whirling through his brain.

Now we shall see how Zorn reacts when his ally is destroyed. I wish I could see the look on his face when he realises that he has no chance against my forces. And when their queen dies, those Britannic fools will blame everything on him, and they will cast him out. I will challenge him to meet in combat. Then, we will see if the Vengeance *or the* Lucifer *is the victor.*

He turned away from the window, and pressed a button on the communicator on his desk.

"Sir?" A man answered.

"Get me Hauptmann Schenk."

"At once, sir."

A few moments later, the communicator chimed. The crimson figure pressed the receive button.

"Yes?"

"Hauptmann Schenk here, sir."

"Ah, Schenk. I have a job for you. You are to take your squadron into Espania, locate Captain Deville and her Red Cats, and destroy them. You should have no problem achieving this, as they only have older autogyros."

"Yes, sir. Thank you, sir. To remove such an enemy to Germania will be a pleasure."

The Wraith closed the connection. He imagined the carnage that

Schenk and his much faster machines would cause amongst the slower flyers. Why, it was no competition at all. *The Red Cats will be red; their blood will cover Espania!*

The metallic grinding tones rang out again as he laughed.

The *Vengeance* arrived at the scene of a battle. The giant gravship hovered over the field of conflict as the massed forces of Espania faced off against their Revolutionary opponents. Zorn and I stood on the bridge, looking out of the huge window and down at the combat below us. Hovertanks and soldiers of His Espanish Majesty moved forward, firing as they advanced. The Revolutionary hovertanks rushed forwards to meet them, and their ground troops followed behind them. Carnage ensued as the two forces met.

High above the battlefield, Captain Deville and her Red Cats had engaged the Espanian Air Force. The little autogyros whirled and zipped about as each tried to shoot the other down. I pointed out one of them, showing Zorn the image of a crimson feline in an attacking posture that was painted on the gyro's side. My gaze leapt from one ship to another as I sought out Deville's flyer. I finally saw it, and showed Zorn.

"There she is."

As we watched, one of the Espanian machines got on her tail. She seemed not to notice. As we looked on, my heart was in my mouth. How could she not know she was a target? The Espanian bore in, lining Deville's ship up in his sights. I made as if to cry out. We must call to her, get her to take evasive action! Suddenly, just as the Espanian was about to open fire, the French aviatrix kicked her flyer to starboard, spun her on her axis, and then sprayed her pursuer with a hail of lead from stem to stern as he rushed by her. The Espanian flyer broke up under the impact of the shells, and fell burning towards the ground. I exhaled, not realising that I had held my breath. Deville's little gyro whirled away, seeking out another target.

"She *is* good," Zorn said. He turned towards me. Seeing my pale face, he said: "Are you all right, Mister Fussell?"

"Yes, yes. It's just the shock of watching the combat." I took out my handkerchief and wiped my sweaty face.

He smiled and returned his attention to the fight. There were dirigibles of either side slightly below us. They moved slowly towards each other, and then opened fire. Several of them suffered hits, and fell away burning. Each side had inflicted losses upon the other. They continued to fire, and the flyers wove in and out around them, continuing their deadly dogfight. As more craft were hit and plunged towards annihilation, I became aware of something. We were not involved in the fight. Zorn had us holding station at a distance. If either side had noticed us, they had not considered us a threat, and so we hung there unmolested while death and devastation raged below us.

"Captain?"

"Yes?" He replied without looking at me. His attention was fixed upon the conflict.

"Why do we not join the fight?"

"We are not here to fight. Our purpose is to meet Captain Deville, nothing more. This clash between Espainia and the Revolutionaries is of no concern to me. "

"But the Revolutionaries are fighting for a just cause. The Espanian king is a tyrant, and must be deposed."

"I have no intention of becoming involved. The politics and strife that engulf all nations is of no import."

I grabbed his arm. He fixed me with a burning gaze.

"But if we don't act - " I began.

He angrily took my hand and removed it from his arm.

"Mister Fussell - " His voice was furious.

A klaxon sounded, drowning out our voices. Instantly, he stepped away from me and looked into the main vidscreen.

"Battle stations!" He cried. The bridge crew rushed to their stations.

I went to his side, and stared at the viewscreen. I was baffled by the multitude of icons that were displayed there.

"What's happening?"

"We are under attack, Mister Fussell. Strap yourself into that chair." He went and sat in his command chair. I did as he said.

"They are The Wraith's gravflyers," he said to my unasked question. "You have your wish, Mister Fussell. Now we are involved." He pointed.

I looked out of the window, and saw a new group of jet black flyers entering the fight. They moved with incredible speed, and manoeuvred like swallows. They engaged Deville's flyers, and a group of them broke off to attack the *Vengeance.* They hurtled towards us, and opened fire. Their bullets rattled against our hull like a deadly rain. In seconds, they had passed us, and were turning for another strafing run.

The Espanian dirigibles, seeing the *Vengeance* come under attack, turned their attention to us. They came towards us, believing us to be in league with the Revolutionaries. They began to fire.

Zorn stabbed a button on his chair's arm.

"Main guns. Engage the Espanian airships." He looked over at me. "I hope you are satisfied, Mister Fussell."

My comment was drowned out by the sound of bullets hammering against our hull. I stared out of the window at the approaching dirigibles. The electromagnetic cannons were making short work of them. A single shot, and the speeding projectile would tear right through them. Still they came on, firing upon us. I gritted my teeth as the *Vengeance* rang like a bell as their shells hit us. The Revolutionaries, heartened by our entry into the fray, ordered their airships to attack them from the rear, and soon they were pinned between us. Under such withering fire from both sides, they couldn't stand a chance. In a few moments, the pride of the Espanian fleet was annihilated. Their burning hulks exploded in midair, or fell away blazing. The Espanian flyers, demoralized by their destruction, scattered like startled birds and fled. The Wraith's gravflyers, seeing that they were now vastly outnumbered, beat a hasty retreat.

The Revolutionaries now turned their attention upon the surviving Espanian ground forces. Their dirigibles added their firepower to the hovertanks below. Deville's flyers strafed them without interference. Without air cover, they were slaughtered. In a few moments, it was all over.

But was she still alive? I released the safety catch on my belt, and rose from my chair. I walked up to the window, and looked out. The French machines hovered over the battlefield. I searched for her ship.

Then I was aware that Zorn was at my side.

"Can you see her?"

"No," I said.

"Call her."

I punched her number into my wristphone. I listened to the ringtone, desperately hoping she would respond. She had been in many battles, and had faced death a hundred times or more. Surely she was still alive? The call went on and on with no response. Had she really been killed?

"Fussell?" Her voice came tinnily from my wristphone. I looked at the screen, and was overjoyed to see her face.

"Patch that call up on the main screen," Zorn ordered.

"At once, sir," a bridge officer replied.

The main screen was suddenly filled with Deville's face.

"What are you doing here?"

"I'm Captain Zorn's guest," I said. "*The Chronicle* has asked me to interview you. Would you like to come aboard?"

"Who is Captain Zorn? Why did he join the combat?"

Zorn stepped forward.

"*I* am Captain Zorn, madam. We can talk about that when you come aboard. And many other things as well. Do you accept our invitation?"

She smiled.

"You have a fine ship there, captain. I've not seen anything like her. I accept your invitation."

"Good. I look forward to meeting you. Land in the main hanger. I will have it opened for you." He turned, and indicated his wish. A bridgeman nodded, and pressed some buttons on his console.

"Bon. Here I come."

The call ended.

"Now it is up to you to convince her of the seriousness of our mission, Mister Fussell," Zorn said. "Follow me. We shall welcome Captain Deville aboard."

I followed him out of the bridge. We proceeded along the corridor, and entered the elevator that led to the main hanger. As the door closed, he turned to me.

"Do not touch me again." His eyes burned into me. Then he looked away and ignored me.

We rode the elevator down in silence.

The elevator doors opened, and we stepped out into the main

hanger bay. I followed Zorn as he walked towards the main hatch. As we approached, it opened, and we could see Deville and her Red Cats hovering outside. They moved forward and entered the bay, their engines roaring loudly. We advanced towards the captain's flyer as they were landing. They were painted green, and the pouncing red feline symbol was emblazoned upon every hull. Those hulls were worn and marked with the signs of battle. I wondered how many of her fliers she had lost in the fight. They shut off their engines, and the thunder turned into a whine that descended in pitch as the propellers slowed to a stop.

Deville alighted from her cockpit. She removed her flying helmet, and shook out her long red hair. She tossed her helmet onto her seat, and walked towards us with the grace of a cat. She was still blessed with the slim figure that she had during the War.

Zorn bowed to her.

"It is an honour to meet you, captain. I am Captain Zorn. Welcome aboard the gravship *Vengeance.* We are here to ask you for your assistance in a mission of utmost importance to the Britannic Empire."

Deville nodded deferentially to him.

"Thank you, captain. Mission? What do you mean?" She turned to me. "I thought you said that *The Chronicle* wanted you to interview me. What is this talk about a mission?"

"I'm sorry," I said. "It was the only way I could think of that you would agree to meet. If I had told you the real reason we wanted you, you might not have agreed to come."

"You are correct. Why should I help the empire that was responsible for my exile? Explain."

I took a deep breath.

"Several days ago, during the ceremony honouring the fallen of the

War, Queen Aurelia was attacked by an unknown ship that appeared out of nowhere. A weapon was used that had not been seen before; a type of ray that struck many Britans down. Captain Zorn appeared with the *Vengeance*, and drove the attacker off. After the attack, those who had been exposed to the ray showed symptoms ranging from paranoia and depression, to an awful wasting disease that mutates the body and consumes the victim alive. It is called The Blight."

The captain was listening dispassionately. Her fliers had all exited their craft, and were standing behind her. I could see several that I remembered from the War. Among them was Marguerite, Deville's daughter. Her hair was as red as her mother's. She gave me a smile.

"Go on," Deville said.

"Captain Zorn told us about the invader. He is called The Wraith, and they are sworn enemies. Captain Zorn informed the Emergency Council that the only cure that was to be found was in the hands of this Wraith, and he proposed that the Air Commandos lead a capture mission to bring one of the scientists with this knowledge to Britan so that Her Britannic Majesty, and all of those who suffer could be saved."

"And where do I come in?"

"I was just getting to that. The Wraith's machines operate upon the same drive that his ship, and the *Vengeance* use. It is called the Gravitic Drive, and uses the power of antigravity. Because of this, these gravflyers are much faster than anything we have. Captain Zorn has offered to give us the secret of the drive, and to help train some fliers in their operation. Without their speed, the mission is doomed to failure. Those black flyers that engaged us at the end of the battle were the gravflyers I speak of. You have seen for yourself how fast and agile they are."

"And I suppose that I and my squadron are the fliers to be trained that you speak of?" Her voice was cold.

"Yes. That's why we've come to ask for your help. Without your assistance, the Queen and many of her subjects will die."

"What is that to me? As I have said, I owe nothing to Britan. Why should I come to her aid?"

I stepped forward.

"I know you, Louise. I remember the great courage that you showed during the War. I know that you are a woman who can be depended upon to do the right thing."

She laughed scornfully.

"That woman no longer exists. The only thing that concerns me now is that we are paid well for our skills. This is what I have become. I have no country. My only loyalty is to my squadron."

"I'm sure that you will be well paid," I said reasonably.

"There is not enough gold in all of Britan to repay the wrong they did me." Her eyes flashed. "The wrong that they did to *us.*" She indicated with a backward stab of her thumb her companions who stood at her back. While she stared fixedly at me, she said over her shoulder: "What do you think, mes amis? Should we help the Britans?"

"*Non!*" came the cry from their lips. Only Marguerite refrained from joining in. Her face was troubled.

One of them advanced a step. I recognised her. Lieutenant Yvette Delacroix. She was an excellent flier, and well known for her hot temper. It had gotten her in trouble many times. Despite that, she was one of Deville's much valued officers.

"Mon Capitaine, let their own fliers do their dirty work. We want nothing to do with them." She spat upon the deck. A murmur of angry agreement came from her comrades. All but Marguerite. She looked upset.

Deville smiled. "You see? My companions agree with me. We decline your offer."

"There is something more," I said hopefully.

"And what would that be?"

"We have intelligence that proves that The Wraith is in league with the Germanians, and that Chancellor Falkenberg is preparing for war. All of Europa is in danger. Even if you don't join us, you'll find yourself fighting against them. Why not accept the Queen's offer, and bring your people to Britan?"

"There are always such rumours," she scoffed. "Falkenberg would not dare to make war again. He does not possess the weaponry."

"I told you, he would be assisted by The Wraith's science. He has weapons that you have not dreamed of. They will wipe out any nation that tries to stand in their way. France will fall, as will all of Europa."

"What is that to me? France cast me out. I go where the money is. I am not interested in joining you."

Zorn had remained silent through all this discourse. Now he spoke, saying: "That is your final answer?"

"It is."

"Louise - " I began.

She held up a hand.

"Not one word more. We are leaving. I must ensure that my fliers are paid. And I must see if we can retrieve the bodies of those who we lost today. Four of my fliers were shot down. Au revoir, gentlemen." She spun on her heel, and she and her squadron turned away, and proceeded towards their craft. Marguerite gave me a look that said she did not agree with her mother's decision, and that she was sorry, and then she followed them. They all climbed into their cockpits, and started up their engines. Deville looked over at us impatiently.

Zorn activated his wristphone.

"Open the main hanger doors."

"Yes, sir."

The huge door slowly opened. Deville nodded once to us, and then they took off and departed. One by one, they exited the hanger bay, the thunder of their engines echoing loudly. In a moment, they had all gone. Zorn and I watched them as they flew away, and in a few moments more, they had disappeared from sight amongst the clouds.

"Close the doors."

"Yes sir."

"I didn't think she would refuse," I said.

Zorn regarded me.

"There is much anger and bitterness within her, Mister Fussell. She has no love for the Britannic Empire. You cannot blame her." He thought for a moment. "Perhaps Commander Symes and his fliers will be good enough to bring the mission to a successful outcome." But the look on his face was doubtful.

"Perhaps," I said.

The hanger door closed with a boom.

V

Captain Deville Reconsiders

Captain Deville and her two escorts flew low over the fields of Espania. They were going to obtain their pay for the recent battle. She looked ahead to the mountains that they were approaching. El Magnifico, the leader of the Revolutionaries had his base there. *A fat fool*, she thought. *Why do they follow him? Is he any better than King Fernando? Neither of them inspire my confidence.* She smiled. *But at least he pays well.*

She glanced in her mirror at her two companions. *Good fliers, both of them. Much better than any that the Britans could put in the air. How dare they come to me and make me an offer after what they did. I would spit in Queen Aurelia's eye before I flew for her.* She checked her instruments. *Getting low on fuel. I'll be glad to get back, refuel and then stand down and relax.*

The three autogyros reached the mountains, and flew into a large canyon. They followed its winding progress along, coming dangerously close to the canyon walls. *But such flying is child's play*, Deville mused. She was grinning. She loved to fly, and to fly in such close quarters made her blood race. It was almost as good as combat. *Or sex.*

Ahead of them was a structure that they called The Ring. It was a natural rock formation, forming a large ring that an autogyro could just fit through. There was no margin for error. Deville grinned, and raced towards it. She hurtled through, and glanced in her mirror. Her comrades shot through the centre of the formation, and formed up behind her. They sped on, racing towards the Revolutionary base. They would arrive in a few minutes.

Then the base was suddenly below them. They throttled back, and swept over the landing field. Deville pulled the throttle lever back, and engaged her landing gear. As it lowered, she brought the craft down towards the ground. The wheels touched, and she cut off her engine. As it whined down, her escorts landed near her. She took off her helmet and gloves, and stepped out of the cockpit. She put her gloves in her helmet, tossed the helmet onto her seat, and waited for her companions to exit their machines. The rotors above her head slowed to a stop.

Deville looked about. There was nobody around. *Strange,* she thought. *They usually meet us.* She shrugged. They were probably still drinking to their success. Her companions walked over to her.

"Captain!"

They turned to see four men walking towards them. In the lead was a fat man with black hair and a moustache.

"Ricardo! How are you?"

"Very well, captain." He held up a bottle. As he came closer, she could see his face was red with drink.

"Still celebrating?" She asked with a smile.

Ricardo grinned. "But of course! Such a victory!"

He offered her the bottle. She took it and had a swig. Wiping her mouth, she handed it to one of her fliers. She drank, and passed it to the other one. She also took a drink, and handed it back to Deville.

"How is your master? In fine spirits, I imagine." She gave the bottle back to him.

"Ah! It would be more accurate to say that the spirits are in him!" He laughed at his own wit. "Come! He is waiting for you."

He put his free arm around her shoulder, and they headed towards the camp. As they got closer, they could hear music. It was wild Espanian guitar, accompanied by shouts and drunken singing.

They arrived at a cliff face. In front of them was a tarpaulin, with two guards posted on either side. One of them grinned and rose from a chair when he saw Deville and her companions, showing a mouth filled with dirty yellow teeth.

"Ah! Capitano! Welcome, welcome!" He pulled back the tarp with a flourish.

"Enrique. Good to see you."

They went inside. The music and sounds of drunken revelry hit them in the face like a blow. They had entered a large cave. The Revolutionaries were gathered there, dancing and drinking in celebration of their victory. A large table filled with food and wine was against the far wall. Ricardo and his companions left them, and went over to it, helping themselves to its bounty. El Magnifico was seated on a huge chair, with two young Espanian girls at either side. One of them played with the beard that swept to his waist, and the other stroked his ear. At the sight of Deville and her fliers, he beamed. His eyes opened wide, and he struggled to rise. The girls helped him up. He shouted something, but it was lost in the bedlam. He shouted again, but once again, it was lost in the tumult going on.

El Magnifico frowned. He pulled a pistol from his belt, cocked it, and fired several times into the ceiling of the cave. The shots rang out and echoed in the cavern. The music halted, and the singing and dancing ceased. Everyone looked around, and hands went to weapons. When they saw it was their leader who had fired, they relaxed, and waited for him to speak.

"That is better," he said. "Look, here is Captain Deville, our saviour.

Make her welcome!" He grinned.

The gathering cheered. Shots were fired. Bottles and glasses were held aloft in salute.

Deville bowed to them. She went forward, and stood before El Magnifico, who had collapsed back into his chair.

"Thank you," Deville said. "I have come for our payment."

The fat man peered at her.

"Payment?" He laughed. "You should be honoured to fight for us. That should be payment enough." He accepted a glass of wine from one of the girls, and drank deeply.

Deville regarded him. She would have to be careful. She knew that here, his word was law. And in the state that he was in, anything could happen.

"Pardon me, Your Excellency, but you agreed to pay us should we help you. King Fernando's forces have been eliminated. Now you can march on the capitol, and make yourself the ruler of all Espania."

He belched. "True, true. And we have you to thank for that."

"In that case, you should pay us, and we will be on our way."

El Magnifico's eyes blazed.

"Did I not just tell you that the honour of fighting for us was payment enough?"

"You did," she said carefully. "But that was not what we agreed to. We are mercenaries. We fight for payment."

The fat man leaned forward. His piggy eyes glared at her.

"You should take care how you speak to me, woman." He spread his arms. "Look around you. These are my people. One word from me, and you will all die."

With a lightning swift move, Deville drew her sidearm, and aimed it at him. A gasp of astonishment rippled through the crowd, even as guns were drawn. Deville's companions drew their pistols, and moved closer to her.

"Pay us," she gritted, "or I will shoot you like the pig you are."

El Magnifico sneered.

"You will not do it. They will tear you apart." He grinned suggestively. "Maybe they rape you first."

She stepped closer.

"Maybe. But I will kill you first."

He stared at her. Surely she was not so stupid! He met her icy gaze, and knew immediately that she was not bluffing. The witch *would* shoot him.

"Go then," he hissed. "Get out. You will get nothing more from me." His face was like stone. The mirth with which he had greeted her had gone.

"You have not seen the last of me," Deville said coldly.

She and her companions backed away. Her pistol was still aimed between El Magnifico's eyes. They reached the tarpaulin, and several of the fat man's men stepped in their path.

"Let them go," he said.

One of the men grabbed the tarpaulin, and held it open for them. Deville and her companions exited, her eyes still fixed upon El Magnifico. They left the cave, and when they were out of sight, he activated his wristphone.

"They are here. Come now."

"Good. We are on our way."

El Magnifico closed the connection.

Now we will see how good you really are, he thought. He smiled wickedly. He grabbed the girl on his right, and kissed her deeply.

Outside, Enrique rose from a battered old chair as the fliers swept past him.

"Capitano! You are leaving already?"

"Yes. I need to get back to base."

"But the celebration - "

Deville stopped. Her companions halted. She turned.

"You should go home to your family, Enrique."

The Espanian stared at her.

"Goodbye," she said. She turned and strode away.

Enrique scratched his head in perplexity.

Deville and her fliers arrived back at the landing field.

"See you back at base, captain," one of them said.

She nodded absently, still furious at El Magnifico's cavalier treatment.

Her companions walked towards their machines. Two shots rang out, and they both fell to the ground. She reached for her pistol.

"Don't," a voice warned.

The Revolutionaries appeared, rifles pointed at her. Enrique stepped up, and took her firearm. They surrounded her, and regarded her in deadly silence.

El Magnifico's laughter broke the stillness. She saw him approaching, the two girls struggling to help him heave his massive bulk along. They stopped in front of her, and he gave her a superior smile.

"You are not so high and mighty now, eh? I no longer have need of your services." He gestured back the way he had come.

A black clad flier appeared, and walked slowly towards them. Deville realised that he was one of the men who had piloted the black flyers that had appeared over the battlefield and engaged them and the *Vengeance*. The flier stood before her, and looked her up and down. He was wearing his helmet, and his breathing mask. Black gloves covered his hands. He folded his arms.

"I have new friends now," the fat man said. "He would like to see how good a flier you are."

"I will give you a two minute head start," came the flier's voice from the mask. His accent was Germanian.

"No, no," El Magnifico said. "Make it three." He grinned at Deville. "For all the help you gave me. Good luck."

Deville looked at her dead companions. She glared at El Magnifico once, and then leapt into her cockpit. She tugged her gloves on, rushed through the autogyro's start up sequence, and threw her helmet on. The crowd backed away as her machine rose into the air. The black flier was watching impassively. She knew that his craft was much faster than her own was. Her only chance was to make a run for it. As her landing gear retracted, she saw him activate his wristphone. She cursed, and as she rose above the field, she scanned the sky. Four black gravflyers were hovering above the cliff. As she threw her craft into a turn and sped away, they gave chase.

Now began a deadly race. Deville pushed the throttle into combat overdrive. The canyon walls flashed past in a blur as she hurtled past. Something sparked against the rock, and she was showered with debris. She glanced in her mirror, and saw all four of her pursuers closing in, their gunports winking. Bullets tore at her as she threw her craft into an evasive weave. But here there was no room for error. The canyon was narrow, and dangerous to fly at the best of times. But in a combat situation...

"Merde!" She cried, as a hail of bullets ripped into her flyer. The little craft staggered under the impact, and she hauled at the control column in desperation as the canyon walls rushed at her. Just in time, she avoided colliding with them. Her machine began to smoke. One

look in her mirror showed the white trail behind her. She suddenly had an idea.

Deville threw her flyer towards the rock wall. Her closest pursuer rushed in, sure of a kill. She bit her lip as the wall rushed towards her. The smoke from her craft billowed out towards him. As her enemy fired again, she skimmed the wall at the last moment, and pulled up hard. Her pursuer peered through the smoke that suddenly enveloped his sight. He pulled back on the stick. Too late! The flyer smashed into the rock, and exploded in a fireball.

"Take that!" Deville cried. One down, three to go. She dropped down, and flashed over the rocky ground. Bullets ripped past her, and kicked up dirt. She looked quickly in her mirror. Two of them this time, closing in. *So fast!* She thought.

She looked ahead. *The Ring!* She gained height, and raced towards it. Her enemies were closing, and they fired. Her flyer was hit again, and she barely recovered before she plunged through the centre of the formation. Her pursuers both attempted to follow, but got in each other's way. They collided, and their interlocked craft clipped the inside lip of the rock. They exploded, and tumbled away, scattering burning wreckage everywhere. The third black machine gained height, and left the canyon.

Deville was coaxing her little craft along. She was adjusting power levels, and desperately trying to keep her engine going. It was overheating, not meant to sustain overdrive for long. She glanced in her mirror. No sign of pursuit. The black cloud of the destroyed flyers rose into the sky. *Three for one! Not bad, Louise!*

A hail of bullets whipped past her. She zigzagged.

A moment later, she raced out of the canyon. A glance in the mirror showed her final enemy closing for the kill. Her craft was badly damaged. To run was out of the question. She would be shot down like a wounded bird. She turned and sped towards him. As his gunports flashed, Deville released the stop on the trim wheel, and spun it hard. Her autogyro skidded in a slide to starboard. As her pursuer's bullets passed harmlessly by, she turned her flyer around, and as he whipped past, she mashed her thumb down on the trigger. A hail of bullets ripped into the black craft, and it bucked and fell away burning. As she watched, it plunged to earth, and disintegrated in a massive explosion.

She exhaled. *That was too close!* She checked her instruments. Everything was in the red, and she was almost out of fuel. She throttled back, and limped towards home, trailing smoke that was turning black.

The crash alarm howled as Deville approached the landing field. Her flyer staggered through the air, trailing black smoke. She hauled back on the stick as the field rushed up to meet her. Activating the landing gear, she dropped the revs on the engine, and the little machine dropped swiftly. Deville gave the engine one last boost, and then killed it. The flyer came to earth with a bump, she undid her harness, and leapt out. She ran from the burning machine as the fire truck screeched to a halt. The fire crew jumped out, and deployed the hose. They approached the stricken flyer and sprayed it with foam.

Her fliers rushed up to her.

"Capitaine! Are you all right?"

"What happened?"

"Where are Julie and Martine?"

"They are dead. El Magnifico betrayed us," she said coldly. "He is in league with The Wraith. I fought with some of the black gravflyers, and barely escaped with my life."

"Cochon!"

"Bastard!"

"Fussell told me that we would become a target," she gritted. "He said that The Wraith and Falkenberg are planning another war, and that we would become involved whether we liked it or not. He was right."

"What do we do now?" Margeurite said.

Deville thought for a moment. Her wristphone chimed.

"What is it?"

"Mon Capitaine, there is a group of flyers approaching. I do not recognize their configuration. They are very fast."

Merde! "How far away are they?"

"Twenty minutes, and closing quickly."

"All fliers, scramble!"

As her fliers rushed towards their craft, she spoke into her wristphone, giving the order: "Sound the evacuation alarm!"

"At once, Mon Capitaine!"

The alarm hooted. The firecrew had put out the burning machine. Their chief ran over to Deville.

"What is happening, Mon Capitaine?"

"War!" Deville cried. "Get the ground crews out of here, Etienne! Head for Calais. I will arrange to have you picked up. Leave everything!"

He gaped at her, his mouth hanging open in shock.

"Get going!" She shouted.

The chief threw her a salute, and raced away to carry out her order. The base was suddenly in chaos; people and vehicles rushed here and there.

Deville ran towards a flyer. It was a spare machine. She leapt into the cockpit, and hurried through the launch sequence as bedlam erupted around her. As she took off, she looked out over the field. Her squadron was in the air, hovering over the field and waiting for her orders.

She activated her comm.

"All flyers, close up and follow me!"

The squadron closed up around her. She pushed the throttle forward, and the little autogyro sped away. Her squadron followed suit.

Hauptmann Schenk's gravflyers came in low over the base, guns hammering. Only a few vehicles remained, filled with ground crew that had been slow to evacuate. Flyers sitting on the ground were destroyed, sending fireballs into the air. The workshops and barracks were strafed, and the ammunition dump went up with a roar. The trucks, scattering everywhere, were riddled with bullets, and their occupants were torn apart. The fuel dump was hit, and a huge explosion scattered blazing fuel everywhere. It was all over in a few minutes.

"Where are the fliers?" Schenk wondered as he circled the scene of devastation.

"Herr Hauptmann, there is a group of flyers heading for the coast."

So! "Pursue and kill!"

The gravflyers turned towards the coast, and rushed in pursuit.

Ten minutes later, a call came to Deville.

"Mon Capitaine, they are on our tail."

Deville glanced in her mirror. The black gravflyers were coming up fast. There was no way to outrun them.

"It has been an honour flying with you, Mon Capitaine. Three section, turn and engage the enemy."

Four of the flyers broke off, and turned to race towards their pursuers.

"No, Marie! I order you to rejoin the squadron!" Deville cried.

"I am sorry, Mon Capitaine, my headset is dead. I cannot hear you. Am attacking now."

There was a click as Marie turned off her communicator.

Tears welled up in Deville's eyes as the rest of the squadron ran. She glanced in the mirror, and watched as Marie and her section closed with the enemy. She turned her attention forward.

Minutes later, they crossed the French coast, and headed over the channel. *Where is that damned airship?*

"Mon Capitaine. The enemy is upon us. It has been an honour to serve with you. Four section, turn and engage."

Four section split away, and hurtled towards the oncoming gravflyers. Now only One and Two sections remained.

"Bon Chance, Juliette," Deville said. She closed the communication. She sobbed. Her squadron was being eliminated, and there was nothing she could do about it but run away. Tears spilled from her eyes, filling her goggles. She pushed them up onto her helmet angrily, and wiped them away with the back of her glove as the slipstream tore at her face.

The *Vengeance* flew high over the channel, heading for Britan. Zorn and I were looking out of an observation port in the main hanger. I gazed at the water far below us, my thoughts roiling in my brain. What were we to do now? Could Symes and his men operate the new machines as well as we had hoped Louise and her fliers would have?

"Do not be disappointed in Captain Deville's decision," Zorn said, breaking into my reverie. "It is a waste of time to think of her refusal. We must put our hope in Commander Symes and his fliers."

I turned to him.

"It is time we are running out of, captain. The Queen and those who suffer must have the cure. How do you intend to proceed?"

As Zorn made to answer, his wristphone chimed. He activated it.

"Captain, there is a large group of flyers approaching from France. They are in two groups; one is running, the other is pursuing. The craft in pursuit outnumber their quarry by three to one."

"Battle Stations!" Zorn cried. "Come, Mister Fussell."

We raced to the elevator as the alarm klaxon sounded.

"Could it be Deville?" I said.

"I do not know. We will see."

"And the pursuing machines?"

"Perhaps they are The Wraith's gravflyers."

The door opened, and we hurried down the corridor to the bridge. Zorn took one look at the main vidscreen and nodded to himself. The cluster of small specks that were displayed there meant nothing to me.

"Captain," the communications officer said, "the first group of machines are Captain Deville's squadron. The other craft chasing them are gravflyers."

"Magnify visual."

The picture on the screen rapidly zoomed in, until we could see the green autogyros clearly. There were only eight. Where were the others? I suddenly felt cold. Surely -

"Show me the gravflyers."

The image zoomed again, to show the jet black gravflyers that had attacked us in Espania.

"Those are The Wraith's gravflyers," I said.

"They are closing on the French craft, captain," the communications officer said.

The vidscreen chimed.

"Captain, incoming call. It is Captain Deville."

"Put it on the main screen."

The image of predator and prey vanished, to be replaced by Louise's face.

"Captain Zorn. I have reconsidered your offer. We would like to come aboard and discuss this mission of yours."

I grinned. She was as cool as always.

"We would be delighted to have you aboard, captain," Zorn said. "First we must dispose of those uninvited guests." He turned to the communications officer. "Launch the dragonflies."

"At once, captain."

"Split the image," Zorn said.

The vidscreen broke up into two images. One was of Louise. The other showed a score of sleek gravflyers exiting the *Vengeance's* main hanger bay. They hurtled towards the oncoming craft.

"Captain Miller."

Another image popped up on the vidscreen. It was of the leader of Zorn's gravflyers.

"Captain?"

"Destroy all but one of the pursuing craft. We must allow The Wraith to know who it was who disposed of his elite."

Miller smiled.

"It will be a pleasure, sir. Engaging now."

His image disappeared. Zorn's gravflyers sped past Louise's craft, and plunged towards The Wraith's machines. They scattered like frightened birds as Miller and his companions opened fire. Three of them were hit, and spiralled down out of control, burning all the way. A savage dogfight ensued. Gravflyers twisted and turned, each trying to get on his enemy's tail. Bullets flew in a hail of destruction, and one by one, The Wraith's flyers were shot from the sky. In moments, only two of them were left, desperately avoiding the massed fire from Zorn's dragonflies as they harried them mercilessly.

"Captain Miller."

"Yes, sir?"

"That will do. Let them go."

"Yes, sir. Break off, men, and return to the Vengeance."

The two survivors fled, no doubt amazed that they had escaped destruction. Miller and his companions closed up around the French aviatrixes, and escorted them towards us.

"Your fliers are very good, captain," Louise said. She had watched the combat along with us.

Miller pulled up alongside her. She looked the craft over. An armoured bubble shaped cockpit flowed into a sleek slim lined body. Two ball shaped objects sat on the end of the stubby wings just aft of the cockpit. They were obviously housing the Gravitic Drive. The fuselage tapered away, becoming thinner at the aft end. Another drive ball was there, smaller than the other two. *For stability, no doubt,* Deville thought. The resemblance to a dragonfly was plain to see. Four deadly guns were mounted below the cockpit, and she could see some missile tubes as well.

"Thank you, madam. But I bet my lads aren't as pretty as your ladies are."

She smiled at the compliment. But then her smile vanished.

"Did you suffer many casualties, captain?" Miller asked.

"Almost half of my squadron. And I do not know how many of our ground staff and support crews."

"I am sorry, captain. Please excuse my flippant comment. It was a bloody stupid thing to say."

"Not at all, captain. You and your men are in high spirits from your

success in the fight. I understand completely how you feel."

"That's no excuse. Please accept my apology."

"Accepted. Your craft are very manoeuvrable. Very nice flyers. Very fast. Captain Zorn?"

"Yes, Captain?"

"These amazing flyers are powered by this Gravitic Drive that you spoke of?"

"They are indeed. It is the same type of drive that the *Vengeance* is powered with."

"And these are the machines that you want my companions and I to fly?"

"That is correct."

"I think I would like to see these marvellous gravflyers up close."

"Bring your machines into the main hanger, and I will have Captain Miller show them to you."

"Thank you, captain. Landing now."

The image on the screen changed to show the main hanger door opening. Louise and her squadron came in to land, followed by Miller and his fliers.

"Let us go down and greet them," Zorn said. "Helm, continue on course for Britan."

"Yes, sir."

Zorn and I headed towards the elevator. I wondered which fliers Louise had lost. *Not Marguerite,* I hoped fervently.

The elevator deposited us at the main hanger. We alighted, and walked towards Louise and her fliers, who were gathered around Miller's gravflyer. He was sitting in the cockpit, explaining the controls to the French aviatrixes. I searched the group for Marguerite, and was relieved to see her.

"Well, Captain Deville," Zorn said as we came up to them, "do my machines meet with your approval?"

Louise turned.

"They are incredible, sir. So far in advance of our old craft. It was a miracle that we escaped destruction at the hands of The Wraith's gravflyers." She shook her head. "Non. It was not a miracle. Two sections of my fliers, my friends, gave their lives so that we may reach you. We must not let their sacrifice be in vain."

"And it will not, madam, I assure you," Zorn said. "We will honour them."

"Thank you, captain."

"Captain Miller."

"Sir?"

"These ladies are surely tired and hungry. Take them up to the mess, and when they have dined, show them to the guest quarters. I will have Mister Bannon prepare them in advance."

"Yes, captain." He climbed out of the cockpit.

"Thank you for your hospitality, Captain Zorn," Louise said.

"Thank you for reconsidering your decision, Captain Deville."

She nodded to him.

"This way, ladies," Miller said, and led them towards the elevator. Marguerite hurried over to me, and gave me a hug and a kiss.

"I'm so glad you're alive," I said.

"Thanks to Marie and Juliette and their sections. We owe them our lives. It was awful, Alistair. We had no choice but to run. I know that mother is devastated by their loss. Can you speak to her?"

"I will."

"Merci. I must go." She kissed me again, flashed me a huge smile, and then ran after her comrades.

"Well, well, Mister Fussell. I think that young lady likes you very much," Zorn said.

I coughed in embarrassment.

"Do you have feelings for her?"

"It's - *complicated*," I answered.

"Matters of the heart always are. Come, we shall also dine."

We walked over to the elevator.

VI

The Price of Failure

The Wraith sat in his chair. Before him stood two fliers; Hauptmann Schenk, and Leutnant Eckhardt. They were the two survivors that Zorn had allowed to escape from the battle over the channel. He was listening to Schenk's description of the fight, and of how their comrades had been bested and shot down in flames by Zorn's fliers. He did not interrupt, he just sat listening passively to Schenk's account.

"And so, master, Leutnant Eckhardt and myself are the only survivors," Schenk finished. He licked his lips nervously.

"*I see,*" The Wraith said evenly. He rose from his chair, and walked slowly around the two fliers, until he stood behind them. The two aviators began to sweat, knowing of their master's mercurial and unpredictable nature.

But instead of berating them, he put them at their ease.

"*Do not be concerned, my friends. It is not your fault that Deville and some of her fliers escaped. You are not to be held responsible for the annihilation of your squadron, Hauptmann. Why, even though you had numerical superiority, Zorn's fliers displayed superior skills, and won the day. You cannot be blamed if they were better than you.*" His tone, as far as his mask could make it, was soothing; indifferent, even.

Eckhardt heard sarcasm there, but Schenk seemed to be unaware of it, because his relief at not being reprimanded blinded him.

"*It is regrettable that so many men and machines were lost, but they can be replaced, no? Thank you for your report, gentlemen. You are dismissed."*

The two fliers clicked their heels together, and their right hands shot out in salute. They turned to go.

"One moment, Hauptmann."

Schenk stopped, and turned.

The Wraith's right hand shot out, and he took Schenk by the throat. He lifted the unfortunate flier off the ground. From the wristband of The Wraith's armour an electrical current passed into Schenk's body. As Eckhardt watched in horror, Schenk was electrocuted in a shower of sparks, screaming and burning. It was all over in a moment. The Wraith dropped the smoking corpse on the floor. He fixed Eckhardt with a manic gaze. His bloodshot eyes pierced the Leutnant through.

"Such is the price of failure," he said icily. *"You will not fail me, will you,* Hauptmann *Eckhardt? The squadron is yours."*

The sickened Eckhardt shook his head mutely. The stench of burnt flesh filled the room. He almost vomited.

"Good. You may go."

Eckhardt glanced once at his comrade's remains, and then hurriedly walked towards the door, every nerve in his body screaming at him to run. He reached the door, and one of the two guards standing there opened it for him.

"Hauptmann."

Eckhardt halted, and turned. Sweat beaded his face. He swallowed nervously.

"Do not forget," his master said ominously, and pointed at Schenk's body. *"Do not fail me."*

Eckhardt merely nodded, unable to speak after witnessing such horror. As he departed, the two guards came forward as The Wraith beckoned imperiously.

"Dispose of that."

Wordlessly, they took up the corpse, and carried it out of the room.

The Wraith crossed the floor to his desk, and pressed a button on the communicator. A voice answered.

"Finke? Come to my office."

"Yes, master."

The huge figure walked around the desk, and looked out of the window. He clasped his hands together behind his back. A few minutes later, the door opened, to admit a small man wearing a lab coat. He wore thick glasses, and his face wore a tired expression. His fair blonde hair was beginning to go gray. The Wraith turned away from the window.

"Ah, Finke. How go the repairs to the ray projector?"

"Slowly, I'm afraid, master. The damage was extensive. It will take a long time to repair it."

A metallic growl escaped the mask. Finke knew that meant that his master was displeased with this information. Unlike many of his other subordinates, however, Finke was adept at reading The Wraith's moods, and had made plans that would mollify his master's anger.

"I have had an idea that we can put into action that does not require the projector."

"Continue."

"We could irradiate some water with the ray, and introduce it into Europa's water supply. This would make certain that the population would be exposed to the effects of the weapon. We need only ensure that Germania's water supply is not contaminated. In this way, we could be in no doubt that any force that would oppose us would be struck down and any resistance would be swept away."

"Very good, Finke. Proceed without delay. Inform Chancellor Falkenberg of your plan."

"I thought you would agree, master. I have already made the necessary arrangements. By noon tomorrow, most of Europa will be infected."

"Excellent. You are to be congratulated for your initiative. You may go."

I walked down the corridor towards the guest quarters where Louise and her fliers had been accommodated. I stopped outside the cabin that had been assigned to her. I knocked hesitantly.

"Come in."

I opened the hatch, and stepped inside. Louise and Marguerite were sitting at a small table. They had been deep in conversation, but now looked over at me silently.

"Marguerite," Louise said, "Leave us." Her voice was raw.

"Yes, mother." She rose from her chair, and walked across the room. As she passed me, she smiled, and opened the hatch. As it closed with a clang, I pulled out a chair and sat down. I noticed that there was a bottle of brandy on the table. It was half empty. There were two glasses.

"It's good to see you, Louise."

She smiled wanly.

"I wish it were under better circumstances," I added hastily.

"As do I, mon ami."

"Captain Miller says that you and your fliers are quick studies. It shouldn't take you very long to master the gravflyers."

"Ah, oui. They are pretty little craft."

She subsided. An uncomfortable silence fell.

"How do you feel? Are you all right?"

"Non. I am heartbroken. To lose so many of my fliers." She looked down at the tabletop. "My friends. I have failed as a leader."

"No, you haven't," I said. I reached across the table and took her hands. "You did what had to do. They did their duty also. They knew you had to escape."

She looked up. Tears welled in her eyes.

"Oh, Alistair. It was horrible. They went back and faced the enemy, knowing that they were going to their deaths. I ran away, and they fought and died for me. I am not worth such a sacrifice." A tear spilled over, and ran down her face.

I reached out and wiped it away gently.

"No, Louise. You are one of the best fliers I have ever seen. You've lost comrades before. Don't blame yourself."

"But I do. How can I expect the others to still follow me? I should make Yvette squadron leader, and step down."

"That's not the answer. Yvette is a good flier, but her temper would get the entire squadron killed. *You* are the leader of Le Rouge Chats."

"There are not so many of us now. That was my fault."

"If you want to blame someone, blame The Wraith. He was the one who attacked the Britannic Empire, and as a result of that, you and your squadron were brought into this. He sent his fliers to assist El Magnifico, and that traitor betrayed you. They hunted you, and destroyed your base. Then they pursued you across France, and over the channel. All of that was The Wraith's doing."

At the mention of the Revolutionary leader's name, a fire was lit in her eyes. Her lips skinned back to reveal her teeth in a grimace.

"El Magnifico," she said coldly. "I will deal with that fat pig."

She reached out, and took up the bottle. She poured it into both glasses, and handed me one.

"To the lost fliers of Le Rouge Chats." She held out her glass.

I clinked mine against it.

"To the lost fliers," I said.

We both tossed the fiery liquid back in one gulp. I coughed.

"Still not used to it, eh, mon ami?"

"No," I wheezed. "I don't drink at all. Tea is my beverage."

She gave me another wan smile.

"Thank you for your company. I would like to be alone now, please."

I looked at the holster at her hip.

"Do not worry, I will not do anything foolish," she said, seeing where my gaze rested.

I rose to my feet. I held out my hand.

"I know. But give me your weapon."

"You doubt my word?"

"No, Louise, but you are drinking. You know what you can get like when you drink."

She nodded.

"Eh, bien."

She stood, and took off her pistol belt, and handed it to me. I walked over to the hatch as she sat down and poured herself another drink. I opened the hatch, and closed it.

"Well, Alistair?"

Marguerite stood there, her face pensive. She had been crying.

"She will be all right, mon cherie. She's drinking to her comrades."

She looked at the pistol belt.

"That was a good idea." She sniffed. "Merci."

"Not at all. I hold your mother in the highest esteem. This has been a bitter blow to her. To lose so many of her friends is terrible. I know that many of them had flown with her since before the War. Keep an eye on her."

"I will. And you, Alistair, how is your life?"

"Much the same. I write, and write." I laughed.

"No woman?" She raised one eyebrow.

"No."

Marguerite stepped closer. She was shorter than I. She reached up and put her arms around my neck.

"It is not good for a man to be without a woman's touch," she said, her voice husky. Her eyes glowed.

"Marguerite - "

She pulled my face towards her, kissed me deeply, and brought our bodies together. It seemed to last for a delicious eternity. She broke off the kiss, and looked me deep in the eyes.

"You know how I feel about you. We should be together." Her voice was soft, pleading. She stroked my neck. I was on fire.

"I'm twice your age, Marguerite," I said.

"I don't care. Mother was nineteen when she married Papa, and he was forty two." She smiled. "I love you, Alistair."

"I know. But it would be impossible - "

"Nothing is impossible. I have missed you. Even though years have passed since we last saw each other, I have thought about you all the time."

"I'm flattered. But what about your mother? I know she is against the idea of us being together."

Marguerite gave me a grin.

"She *was*, but I have convinced her otherwise. It took me a long time, but I did it. She thinks highly of you, Alistair. She will agree to a match between us."

"I think it would be more accurate to say that you've worn her down with your persistence, and forced her to accept your proposal."

"Proposal?" She grinned. "Are you proposing to me?"

"You little minx. What I meant was - "

"I know what you meant. I am teasing you. But I tell the truth. Mother has agreed that we would make a fine couple."

She saw my reticence.

"You do not like the idea of being with me?" She pouted.

I chucked her under the chin.

"It would be wonderful. But this crisis means we can't think only of ourselves. The world is on the brink of war."

"Then we must ensure that we both survive it. Will you talk to mother?"

"Yes, after all this is through, I'll speak to her."

She squealed with delight.

"Kiss me."

She didn't have to ask me twice.

The *Vengeance* arrived over Londinium. She took up station over St James Park, as before. Standing in the main hanger were Captain Zorn, Louise and I. We were to go and see The Queen, and introduce Louise to her. We stepped onto the platform, and Zorn pressed the button. The platform began to descend towards the ground. A large crowd had gathered below us, and cheered when they saw us. Hats were tossed into the air.

"A fine welcome, captain," Zorn said.

"Perhaps they know of our mission," Louise said.

"I doubt it," I replied. "But they know that Captain Zorn defended them against the *Lucifer,* and so that makes him a friend."

"And a friend of his is also a friend of theirs?" She smiled.

"That seems logical to me," I said.

The platform touched the ground. Zorn opened the gate, and we stepped out. Six guardsmen and an officer were waiting for us. They fell in around us as the crowd cheered on.

"This way, if you please," the officer said, saluting us.

We proceeded towards a steamcoach that stood at the edge of the park. We walked through the ecstatic crowd, pressed on all sides by happy, smiling faces. I grinned, and saw Louise smiling also. Even the usually dour Zorn managed a smile.

We arrived at the steamcoach, and were helped into it by two servants. The officer saluted us again as we set off. We rolled along, surrounded by the exulting populace, who were held back from the road by guardsmen as we swept past.

Finally, we reached the hospital. We alighted, and were met by an orderly.

"This way, please."

We followed him inside and along the corridors until we reached Queen Aurelia's room. The orderly motioned for us to enter. We filed inside, and went over to the bed. The Prince was still sitting at her side. We all bowed.

She had visibly deteriorated since Zorn and I had seen her last. But there was still strength in her eyes; determination too.

"Your Majesty, here is Captain Deville," Zorn said. "She has come with her squadron to help us in this time of need."

"As you promised, Captain Zorn. You have my thanks, and my congratulations for succeeding in your mission. Welcome, Captain Deville. I thank you for agreeing to come."

"Your Majesty."

At that moment, Admiral Gray, Captain Smith, and Commander

Symes entered, accompanied by another officer that I didn't know. They bowed.

"Gentlemen," The Queen said, "here is Captain Deville, the squadron leader of Le Rouge Chats. Captain, this is Airlord Gray, Airlord of Her Britannic Majesty's Dirigible Service, Captain Smith, of Her Britannic Majesty's Dirigible Service, Commander Symes, of the Royal Air Service, and Major McKinnon, of Her Britannic Majesty's Air Commandos, Highland Regiment."

Airlord Gray regarded Louise with undisguised distaste, and Smith and Symes wore blank faces, and looked as though they would rather be somewhere else. It was plain to see that these officers had been talking about Louise, and were united in their distrust of her. An uncomfortable silence fell.

Which was broken by Major McKinnon. He stepped forward, and offered his hand to Louise with a grin.

As they shook hands, he said: "I'm verra pleased to meet ye, Captain Deville. I've heard soo many tales of yer exploits in the War. I'm lookin' forward to meetin' yer lovely lassies."

"Merci, Major McKinnon. I have also heard of your daring missions behind enemy lines." She gave him a smile.

Gray and his companions watched this interchange, obviously unimpressed. I gave the Airlord a mock salute. He scowled in return. Queen Aurelia noticed, and smiled to herself.

Doctor Mansfield and Professor Graves came to the door. They entered, and bowed. Their mood was sombre.

"What news? Prince Henry said.

"Bad news, I'm afraid, Your Highness," Graves said. "The Wraith has infected all of Europa's water supply. Millions have been affected. Almost all of the population has taken ill."

"How can that be?" Captain Smith said. "Captain Zorn destroyed his weapon."

"That's true, sir," Graves said. "However, during the night, small canisters were introduced into Europa's reservoirs. These canisters contained contaminated water that then went on to spread the contagion throughout those reservoirs. France, Italio, Greece, Espania; all have reported the outbreak of symptoms that we have already seen in The Wraith's attack upon the Queen and her subjects. Only Germania seemed to be exempted."

"Why would Germania not be affected?" I said.

"Perhaps Chancellor Falkenberg is in league with The Wraith," Zorn said.

"We have had this discussion before, captain," General Crompton said. "We have no proof that Germania has joined with our enemy."

"On the contrary, general," Airlord Gray said, "It would seem we *do* have proof, and most damning proof at that."

"You can't seriously be suggesting that because Germania is the only unaffected region, that means that they are on The Wraith's side?" Crompton scoffed.

"I do, sir. How else can we explain her immunity?"

"Well, we know that Germanian security is second to none," Crompton offered. "Maybe they caught the culprits before they could use these canisters."

"That is highly doubtful, sir," Smith said. "I think the Airlord is correct; Falkenberg is in league with the enemy."

"I don't think - " Crompton began.

"General."

All eyes turned to the bed. Queen Aurelia sat up.

"We do not have time for such discussion. Perhaps you are

right, or Airlord Gray and Captain Smith are. It does not matter. What *does* matter is that The Wraith has struck a devastating blow against our allies. Do not forget that we have a treaty with France and Espania. If they are attacked, we are duty bound to go to their aid."

"But, Your Majesty," Crompton said, "what aid could we give? We do not even have a cure for yourself and your subjects."

"It does not matter. We must go to their aid. Doctor Mansfield, have you had any success? How are my fellow patients faring?"

"Your Majesty, there have been fifty more deaths, and others are suffering badly, certain to die. I have tried everything I know. Nothing seems to halt the contamination."

"I know that you are doing your best, doctor."

"Thank you, Your Majesty." She came up to the bed, and took Queen Aurelia's pulse. She listened for a moment, and then peered into her eyes. she turned and addressed all of us. "Her Majesty needs to rest. I must ask you all to leave."

"I always do what the doctor orders," Queen Aurelia said. "Thank you, Captain Deville, gentlemen. Please leave us."

We all bowed, and left the room.

The Wraith sat in his office in his mountain hideaway, speaking to a caller on his vidscreen. It was Chancellor Falkenberg. The Germanic leader was tall, with electric blue eyes, and dark hair that was beginning to gray at the temples.

"*Are we ready to invade?*" he said.

"*The plan to infect the water supply has succeeded beyond expectation,*" his servant said. "*We need only wait for perhaps a week or two, and there will be no armies to oppose us; many men will die, or at the very least, be so affected with depression that they cannot form an effective fighting force."*

Falkenberg smiled.

"I am pleased with the success of your plan," he said, *"but we will continue without delay. It is my sacred duty to be the ruler of Europa, and nothing is going to stand in my way. Prepare our forces, the invasion will go ahead as planned; in three days time."* His eyes flashed with manic fervour.

"What of Britannia?" The Wraith asked. *"Surely they will come to Europa's aid?"*

The Chancellor shook his head.

"They have enough to deal with, my friend. Aurelia is fading fast. Her subjects are dying. Europa's fate will not concern her."

"I would not be too sure of that, master. My spy tells me that she has ordered her High Command to render assistance. Do not forget that they also have Zorn and the Vengeance *and its gravflyers at their disposal."*

Falkenberg's eyes narrowed. His mouth turned down with displeasure at the mention of Zorn's name.

"That meddler! You will destroy him, and his ship. Once he is out of the way, Britannia will be ripe for invasion. They have no gravflyers, and once Zorn and his craft are no longer available to them, they will stand no chance against your elite fliers."

The Wraith bowed his head.

"Yes, master."

The Chancellor placed his hands on the table before him, and spread his fingers.

"Is there something more?" he asked.

His servant looked up. Despite the lack of expression upon the mask, Falkenberg could tell that he was reticent to say something to him.

"Well?"

The Wraith thought for a moment, and then replied.

"Captain Deville and her squadron were rescued by Zorn, and were taken to Londinium. They will be trained in the use of his gravflyers, and will assist the Air Commandos in their raid against us."

An inarticulate roar of fury burst from the speakers. Falkenberg clenched his hands into fists, and brought them down on the tabletop with a crash. He glared out of the vidscreen, his teeth bared.

"What!" he cried. *"How could that happen? I thought you sent your best fliers to dispose of her."* His face reddened with anger.

"I did, master. They failed."

The Wraith could see the veins standing out on Falkenberg's neck. It was well known to all that the Chancellor's rages were a thing to behold. From a distance, of course.

"Did any of them return from the mission?"

"Yes, master."

"I hope you showed them that I do not tolerate failure."

The Wraith nodded.

"I did, master."

Knowing full well what his servant meant, Falkenberg allowed himself a small smile.

"Good. You will deal with that witch and her fliers. She will join Zorn. Then it will be your task to ensure the destruction of any air power that Britannia possesses. Their old flyers will be no match for your gravflyers. Once they have been swept from the sky, the Germanic forces will cross the channel, and invade. Surely the Britannic ground forces will be no match for the might of the Germanic Army?"

"Surely you are correct, master."

"But first, Europa," Falkenberg continued. *"We will attack without warning, destroying most of the opposing flyer's on the ground. Then, with your gravflyers giving the ground forces air cover, we will sweep through Europa, facing hardly any resistance, thanks to the devastation wrought upon the enemy by the action of the contaminated water."*

"It will be done as you command, master." His right fist shot out in salute.

Falkenberg returned the salute nonchalantly, and broke the connection.

VII

Preparing for War

Biggin Hill Royal Air Service base was a hive of activity. Captain Miller, Zorn's Leader of Fliers, was instructing Captain Deville and her squadron on how to operate the gravflyers. The French aviatrix and her companions were finding it a little difficult to adapt to the speed and manoeuvrability of the craft. A crowd of onlookers were watching them go through some take off and landing procedures.

The men of the RAS shook their heads at the amazing swiftness and turning capabilities that the gravflyers displayed. Their own autogyros, like those of all other countries in the world at that time, were far surpassed by these marvels of engineering, having only engines that were still based on the explosive combustion principle.

A group of them were clustered around one of the machines that sat on the ground. They inspected the little craft with the greatest interest; peering at the drive balls, gazing into the cockpit, and also examining the light electromagnetic guns that she was armed with. The gravflyer was made of a light alloy frame, and sheathed with carbonium panels. She was much lighter than their own machines.

"That's the future we're lookin' at, lads," one of them exclaimed. A chorus of agreement met this statement. The machine's flier was there, and they pumped him full of questions.

At the edge of the field, watching Louise and her fliers as they went through their training, were Commander Symes, Captain Zorn, Air

Officer Sebastian King, and I. King was Symes's best flier, and he was speaking.

"Captain Deville and her ladies are actually doing very well, gentlemen. Don't let these shaky take offs and landings fool you. The gravflyers are a tricky little machine to handle. They're very fast, and they move like swallows. They put our old clunkers to shame." He grinned.

"I agree with you there, Sebastian," Commander Symes said. "When I took one up this morning, I found her to be a swift little craft. An absolute dream to fly, once you get the feel of her. Captain Zorn, I must congratulate you on the invention and construction of such wonderful machines, and thank you for allowing us to use them."

"Thank you, commander. Soon the Britannic Empire will be outfitted with their own gravflyers, and your squadrons will be upgraded from your old petrol driven machines, and trained in their operation. Thus they can meet The Wraith's fliers on equal terms in the air."

"Could the Gravitic Drive be fitted to the existing dirigibles that the Empire possesses?" I asked.

Zorn shook his head.

"Unfortunately, no, Mister Fussell," he replied. "The gravitic forces that power the drive would be too strong for the airframe of such craft to withstand, and they would be torn apart. However, new gravships like the *Vengeance* are being constructed even as we speak."

"That means the *Vengeance* and the *Lucifer* are the only gravships in existence at this time," I said.

"That is correct." He gestured at his vessel that was sitting on the ground behind us. "The *Vengeance* is more than a match for the damaged *Lucifer*. The Wraith would not dare to engage us until his repairs are complete."

"But we must assume that he is also constructing gravships of his own," Symes said. "And if Falkenberg is indeed involved, that means Germania will be constructing them too."

"Surely you are right, commander," Zorn said. "Technology like the Drive, once discovered, is coveted by all nations. And once it is implemented by one of them, it would be suicide for the other nations to not equip their forces with machines that use it. No race is won by a slower machine."

"Especially not an arms race," King added. "It's a sad fact that many of humanity's technological advances were discovered during times of conflict."

"It's human nature," I said. "Everyone wants to survive. I imagine the first caveman to discover how to use a club found out the advantage such a weapon had over fists."

"That's right enough," said Symes. "Look, here comes Deville."

One of the gravflyers was coming down the field. It slowed as it approached, and came down gently to a landing in front of us. The engines made a humming sound, like that of the engines of the *Vengeance*. They whined down to a stop as the flier cut them. The cockpit opened, and she alighted on the runway. Louise took off her flying helmet and goggles, peeled off her gloves, and tossed them into the cockpit with the casual gesture I had seen her make a hundred times. She shook out her long red hair, and strode towards us. A huge grin was plastered on her face.

"Mon Dieu, Captain Zorn!" she exclaimed, "what a lovely little machine you have made."

Zorn bowed to her.

"I am glad that they meet your approval, captain."

"But they are a bit hard to handle," she added. "Skittish, like a young colt."

"We have faith in your skills and that of your ladies, captain," Commander Symes said. "We are sure that you will master these craft."

Louise gave him a smile. It was obvious that the flying skills that she and her comrades were displaying had modified the commander's views of their involvement.

"Eh, Bien, M'Sieu Symes. And then it will be your men's turn, non?" She grinned.

We laughed, and King said: "Let us hope they are up to the task."

Falkenberg and The Wraith sat in a steamcoach that was taking them to inspect the amassed Germanian forces that were ready for the attack on Europa. As it rolled along, the Chancellor listened to his servant.

"Thousands of gravtanks and troopers await your command, master. My gravflyers are poised to support the assault. They will descend upon the unsuspecting flyers as they sit upon the enemy's field, and destroy them. Any enemy machine that is lucky enough to get into the air will be dealt with swiftly. No Air Service in Europa is equipped with machines that are as fast as those that we possess. We will sweep any opposition from the sky."

"Excellent. You have done well, my friend. It is time; time that I fulfilled my destiny. After this attack, surely all of Europa will fall, thanks to the successful action of infecting the water supply. Surely there will be no resistance to speak of. How has the spread of infection proceeded?"

"We have succeeded far beyond our expectations. Millions have been struck down. The opposing forces have been decimated. The Blight will kill most of those affected, and the other victims will pose no threat. It

is as you say, master. No nation in Europa can now field a competent fighting force. None, save Germania. It will be a swift victory."

Falkenberg's eyes were lit with manic fervour. He clenched his fists in exultation.

"*Victory!* Our flag will fly over all Europa, and we will take our destined place as rulers. The other inferior races will serve us as slaves."

"*And you will be the ruler over all, master. Your word will be law. You will be a god; life or death will be decided by you and you alone.*"

Silence met his words.

The Wraith glanced at his master out of the corner of his mask's eye ports. Falkenberg sat staring into space, and his servant knew that the Chancellor was dreaming dreams of conquest. As in all other times that he had seen Falkenberg lost in such reveries, he became silent, knowing that to interrupt his master would be unwise. The steamcoach rolled onward through the beautiful countryside.

They arrived at the staging area. Thousands of gravtanks were lined up in a display of armoured might. Huge flags that were marked with the Germanian armed forces symbol; a black clenched gauntlet outlined in red, rose above the mass of armour. This sigil was also emblazoned upon their metal hulls. Squadrons of The Wraith's black flyers sat upon the field, their crews standing in full flight dress before them. Hundreds of the sleek flyers were ready to take off and rain destruction upon the unsuspecting enemy. Rank upon rank of gray-clad troopers crashed to attention as the steamcoach bearing their beloved leader drove up to a podium set in front of the gathering. On their right breast, and upon their helmets was also the fist. There were thousands of them; they stretched back as far as the eye could see. A military band struck up, playing martial music as the steamcoach came to a stop. Falkenburg and The Wraith alighted, and they proceeded to the podium. The Wraith halted at its base as his master ascended the steps and stood with his gaze fixed upon his army. A giant banner with the ubiquitous black fist was raised behind him.

"All hail Falkenburg!" a voice cried, and was echoed by thousands of throats crying *"All hail Falkenburg!"* The right hands of the massed forces, clenched in fists that echoed the symbol upon flag, gravtank and troopers were thrust into the sky. The band played the Germanian National Anthem.

The band came to a stop and a silence descended. The Chancellor allowed the silence to stretch until it became uncomfortable, and then spoke, his voice thundering across the field with the aid of towering loudspeakers.

"Soldiers of Germania! Now is the time to take back that which is ours! It is my sacred destiny to rule Europa, and with your help and courage, this is what will surely happen! Your success against the weak slave nations that we face is assured! Go and conquer in our beloved Fatherland's name*! At dawn we strike!"*

He pumped his fist high in salute. A roar of approval resounded. Once again, the fists of the gathered force were raised in salute. As the Chancellor's eyes flashed, filled with the exultation of the power of his army, the voices roared again: *"All hail Falkenburg! All hail Falkenburg!" All hail Falkenburg!" All hail Falkenburg!"*

Meanwhile, in Londinium, the General Staff; Airlord Gray, General Crompton, Councillor Reading, and Captain Smith, were joined by Captain Zorn and myself in the Queen's hospital room. As before, Prince Henry sat by her side. He had never left it. We were discussing the disturbing reports that had come out of Europa. The deaths of millions due to the poisoning of the water supply was an act that had shocked all of us to the very core.

"Surely now, gentlemen," Councillor Reading said, "we must send aid to our friends?"

"Indeed," General Crompton agreed. "Whatever aid we can give must go to Europa's assistance."

"It is more than aid that we must send, general," Captain Smith said. "Europa's armies will have been stricken too. They will not be able to put any troops in the field. And their fliers would have suffered as well. It is the perfect time for Germania to attack. We must send our own forces to support France and Espania."

"I agree," Captain Zorn said. "Falkenburg will not miss this opportunity. He will strike while they are weak."

"But can we be sure that Falkenberg is even involved?" General Crompton said. "I think it would be dangerous to assume his complicity, without absolute proof."

"I agree," Airlord Gray said. "We cannot act without certainty of his involvement. We do not want to make Germania our enemy."

"I think that he *is* our enemy, sir," Captain Smith said.

"We still should wait until we have confirmation of his participation in this attack," General Crompton said. "We cannot just go ahead and send our forces into - "

"If we wait, it will be too late," Zorn said. "It will be chaos."

"Perhaps this is what The Wraith's intention was; create chaos so that his forces can attack without fear of resistance," I said.

"That sounds right to me," The Prince said.

"But, Your Highness, it would be - " Airlord Gray began.

"It is imperative that we send our own forces to Europa," the Queen interrupted. "France has never forgiven us for not supporting them enough in the Third War. Such an oversight must not be allowed to happen again."

Gray and Crompton make to speak, but she forestalled them by holding up her hand.

"I know what you think, gentlemen. This is not the time to argue about such matters. It is my order that you arrange our forces for immediate departure for Europa. You may leave us."

We all bowed to her, and left the room.

The Wraith was listening to his spy via the vidscreen in his office. He had returned to make some last minute adjustments to the invasion plan, and had received the call.

"The Queen has commanded The General Staff to send aid to Europa, master. Not only that, she has ordered them to send an expeditionary force comprised of elements from all of the services. Ground troops, supported by hovertanks and artillery, and gravflyers will cross the channel and support the enemy."

"It is too late. The attack will take place on the morrow as planned. The Britans will be of no help. Our forces will sweep away any opposition. But that will be negligible, thanks to the success of the contamination of the water."

"Captain Deville and her aviatrixes have successfully completed their training on Zorn's gravflyers, and in turn they have been training the fliers of the RAS. Hundreds of the machines have been constructed, and they will join the forces coming to Europa's aid."

The Wraith's bloodshot eyes hardened.

"It is of no matter. My own gravflyers, and those of Germania, outnumber the Britannic flyers by a ratio of four to one, and they will send them down in flames. Surely my fliers, who have had years of experience, will overmatch the hastily trained RAS fliers?"

His spy made no reply. The Wraith knew that meant that he was hesitant to say something that he may not approve of.

"You may speak. What are you thinking?"

The agent cleared his throat. When he went on, he spoke cautiously.

"Well, master, you may be right about the RAS fliers. They do not have the experience that your men have with the gravflyers. Your elite fliers should make short work of them."

"But?" The Wraith said tersely. *"I sense there is something else."*

The image on the vidscreen was still and silent. The spy was obviously thinking of how to give his opinion without enraging his master. Finally, he spoke.

"There is the added complication of Deville and her squadron, master. They are very good fliers. They may prove to be more of a challenge than the RAS."

The Wraith leaned back in his chair. This was to show his spy that he was relaxed, and was not concerned with his opinion. It was a psychological ploy to make his agent relieved that he had not reprimanded him for having defeatist thoughts.

"They will be dealt with. Some casualties are to be expected. They may shoot some of our fliers down, but I assure you, at the end of the day, Deville and her witches will be nothing more than burning wreckage."

"Surely you are correct, master."

Once again the spy ceased to speak.

"What else is there?" The Wraith demanded. *"I am not happy with this indecision. You may tell me what you think without fear. I put you in your position so that you may provide me with intelligence regarding the enemy. Your information is valuable, and whether I like it or not, you must report it to me immediately without fail."*

The spy nodded in agreement.

"Of course, master. I apologize. I only wanted to tell you that Zorn has given the plans of his gravship to the Britans, and they are hurriedly constructing their own even as we speak."

"We already knew that. We too are constructing gravships. It will be a while before they are completed. Then we will match them against the Britan's machines."

"Of course, master."

Once again, The Wraith sensed the vacillation in his spy. He was growing tired of this.

"And?" he said irritably.

"Zorn is bringing the Vengeance *to Europa along with the expeditionary force. Our dirigibles will be no match for her. And as you say, our own gravships will take too much time to complete to be put in the air against her. The* Lucifer *is damaged, and would be no match - "*

The Wraith's metallic fists crashed down upon the table top. His eyes flashed fire. He sat forward, and his image loomed large in the spy's screen.

"The Vengeance *will be destroyed,"* he hissed. *"Do not concern yourself about the* Lucifer's *condition. She will meet Zorn in battle, and he will fall."*

"But the repairs, master? Her main weapon is disabled. Without the ray projector, the outcome of such a fight would be doubtful."

"Doubtful?" The crimson figure echoed. *"You do not believe that we can be victorious?"* His voice was menacing.

"I didn't say that, master, I only meant - "

"Your opinion has been noted. Do not make remarks about matters that do not concern you. Leave the Vengeance *to me."*

Chastened, the agent nodded again.

"Yes, master."

"Continue your work. Contact me when you have other information."

"Yes, master."

"One more thing."

"Yes, master?"

"Do not speak to me like that again. Your task is to supply me with intelligence. It is not necessary to give your opinion. You will remember this, and not speak in such a manner again. Am I clear?"

"You are, master. I will obey."

"Good."

The Wraith stabbed the button, and terminated the call.

VIII

The War Begins

Dawn in Europa. The sun rose through the morning mist. All was peaceful; the morning chorus of birds was the only sound in the hush. Suddenly, the calm was shattered by the sound of thousands of flyers as they hurtled through the sky. At an airbase in France, the ten men who had escaped the worst affects of the tainted water ran out of their huts and stared skyward at the massive armada that was bearing down on them in amazement. Flyers filled the sky above them, all gray and marked with the black fist of Germania. The Wraith's black flyers escorted them. A wing of fighters and bombers broke off from the main formation, and plummeted towards the base.

Coming out of their stupor, three of the Frenchmen, fliers all, sprinted towards their craft that were sitting on the runway. Their ground crew rushed to assist them, and two of their number raced over to an anti-flyer gun, and frantically tried to get it ready for action. The wing of fighters rushed in low over the runway, guns hammering. The flyers on the ground were obliterated in a fireball as the deadly hail of metal shredded them. The fliers and their ground crew were cut down by the storm of bullets. The two men manning the defences fired desperately at the strafing flyers. One of them was hit, and spiralled in to explode. But then one of his comrades fired at the gun pit, and the valiant defenders were killed.

The bombers flew over the base, and released their deadly ordnance. With a thunderous roar the bombs destroyed the airbase completely. The fighters and bombers, their destructive work done, formed up and rejoined the main body of flyers, and the aerial armada continued on, leaving the shattered remnants of the base burning behind them. In a few moments, the roar of their engines had disappeared along with them.

The same result was repeated all over Europa. The bases, manned with only skeleton staff due to the affects of the contaminated water, were destroyed swiftly by Falkenburg's forces. On the ground, the gravtanks and troopers met hardly any resistance as they advanced. Such resistance was crushed without mercy by the assistance of the gravflyers, and by noon that day, the majority of Europa's armies and air forces lay dead and broken. The victorious Germanians pushed onwards towards the channel.

In Londinium the news of the Germanian invasion was met with astonishment. The success of their forces against the demoralised and weakened forces of the other nations of Europa was received with shock. The scenes of devastation that were broadcast on the Imperial Network stunned the watching populace. As before, Germania was the aggressor, attacking without warning, or declaration of war. War had once again come to ravage Europa.

The General Staff had met in the Queen's room at the hospital to discuss the matter. Captain Zorn and I had joined them, for it was evident that the time that Zorn had warned about had come, and Her Britannic Majesty had wanted us to be involved in the meeting. Zorn made no comment, but we both knew that they were all embarrassed and ashamed that they had not heeded his advice. Now everything would have to be done in a rush in an attempt to stem the Germanian advance.

"Your Majesty, we have made preparations to cross the channel, and give our assistance to the beleaguered continent," Airlord Gray said.

"The army is also ready, Your Majesty, and will depart as soon as possible," General Crompton added.

"Your Majesty, the *Glorius* and the fleet under my command is ready to sail," Captain Smith said.

Queen Aurelia nodded.

"Will the new gravflyers be ready?" she asked.

"Your Majesty, the training program is not finished. Only ten squadrons have made the changeover to the new machines," Commander Symes reported.

She went into a coughing fit, and Prince Henry rose and took her a glass of water. The Queen drank it, and lay back against the pillows. She looked drawn and haggard. How much time she had, we did not know.

"They will have to be enough, commander," she said weakly.

"The rest of the RAS officers will continue to train, while the squadrons who are ready will go to Europa along with the rest of our forces. When the remaining fliers have successfully completed their training, they will join their comrades." Symes stopped speaking, and his face was thoughtful.

"What is it, commander?" The Queen asked.

"I fear that the two hundred flyers available will not be enough to halt the advance of the Germanians," he said. "The French have taken so many losses that they cannot put anything into the air. Putting two hundred machines against hundreds, perhaps thousands of enemy craft is suicide."

Louise stepped forward.

"My aviatrixes will make up for the lack of numbers, Your Majesty. Each one of my girls are worth at least ten of the Germanian fliers. We have faced such numbers before."

The Queen smiled.

"You see, commander? Captain Deville will be there with you."

"Perhaps the captain can tell us how to engage such a large force with only a small number of flyers?" Symes said archly.

"Not head on, commander," Louise said.

"How then?"

"You must fight like a mercenary, commander. Hit and run. Dive into the formation, destroy a bomber, and then run."

"Run?" Symes echoed, aghast.

"That is what I said. We all know that the Germanians outnumber us. We will neutralise that advantage by such attacks."

"By running away?" Symes looked disgusted."The RAS does not fight using such tactics, captain. We have tried and true methods of attack; formations that have served us well for many years of conflict."

"Oui," Louise said. "I have seen such formations. They are pretty to see at air shows, but are useless in combat, and will get your fliers killed. Is that not what happened during the last war?"

The commander's face reddened. She was right, and we all knew it. Symes was mortified.

"We have modified our attack formations, captain," he said, his voice raw. "It might amaze you, but we actually did learn a thing or two from the losses we experienced. We have adjusted our methods accordingly."

"I did not mean to upset you, commander," she replied. "I only tell you what I would do against such overwhelming odds."

Symes was silent.

"Perhaps you and the captain could work out some formations that will be to our advantage, commander?" The Queen said.

Symes bowed in acquiescence.

"As you command, Your Majesty."

"The addition of the *Vengeance* to the Britannic forces should also help to turn the odds in our favour," Zorn said. "Apart from the *Lucifer*, the Germanians have no gravships. Their air fleet is composed of the older airships that are powered by internal combustion engines, and are much slower and more lightly armed than my ship. Plus, it is possible that the damage to the *Lucifer* has not yet been repaired. If she has not been put into combat, we have the only gravship in the air."

"We have managed to construct and make ready three new gravships with Captain Zorn's help, Your Majesty, Airlord Gray added. "The crews have been working hard, training and making themselves familiar with their new ships with the help of Captain Zorn's crew. They are more than a match for Falkenburg's out of date airships."

"Very good, gentlemen," She said. "I am pleased with your information. It appears that Britannia is ready for the fight. Go with my best wishes, and good luck to you all."

She gave us leave. We bowed to her, and departed to put our plans in motion.

The Wraith sat in the command chair on the bridge of the Viktor, the flagship of Falkenburg's airship fleet. She sailed high above the battlefield. The Lucifer was still undergoing repairs, but her speed and armament had not been needed; the Germanian forces had outmatched every attempt at resistance. He looked at the vision displayed in the main vidscreen of the carnage that the Germanian advance had wrought upon the helpless city of Amiens.

Large columns of black smoke ascended into the sky. Buildings had been levelled, and here and there were destroyed vehicles and out dated hovertanks, smashed and burning. There were hundreds of corpses, men and horses alike. The gallant French cavalry had attempted to stop the armoured advance of the Germanian gravtanks in a valiant but hopeless charge. They had been mown down like wheat by the Germanian machine guns. Now the column of Germanian ground troops was advancing past their broken bodies. Flyers passed by overhead, going on to destroy the next target.

A bridge officer walked up to The Wraith.

"Sir, there is a communication for you."

The Wraith activated his personal vidscreen with the push of a button. It rose up from the side of his chair, and unfolded itself in front of him. An image swam on its screen, and resolved itself into a familiar figure. It was his spy.

"Master, the Britannic forces have departed." He held up a datacard. *"This will give you the numbers and strength that the enemy has sent."*

"Good. Transmit the information."

"Yes, master." The spy put the card into his terminal and pressed a button. An overlay of streaming figures and images covered his face as the information was sent to the *Viktor*. The crimson figure on her bridge watched it all with satisfaction. The Britans had only committed a small force. It was laughable. The combined strength of the Germanian and his own forces would ensure their destruction.

"Very good. You have done well. Where and when will the Britans land?"

"They will land at Cherbourg, master, in three hours time."

"Good. Keep me up to date on their deployment. I will make ready a

reception for them. Call me again when you have anything further."

"Yes, master."

His spy broke the connection. The Wraith pressed another button on his chair arm. After a moment, Falkenburg's image appeared on the screen before him.

"How is the attack proceeding?" The Chancellor asked.

"We have destroyed all of the pitiful opposition, master. They have nothing that can oppose us. Our advance has exceeded your expectations."

Falkenburg clapped his hands together. *"What are our casualties?"*

"They are light, master," his servant replied. *"In all, only one hundred and twenty troopers have fallen, eighty six of them wounded. Twelve gravtanks have been destroyed, with another five damaged. Of the flyers, fifteen have been shot down; eight of these were bombers, and the others fighters, with nine of the fliers safe. In contrast, the enemy's ancient hovertanks have been obliterated, and his flyers either destroyed on the ground by our surprise attack, or shot down in their hundreds. Their burning wreckage litters the countryside. Their ground forces have ceased to exist. They are either dead, or our prisoners."*

Falkenburg rose from his chair. His face was ecstatic. He was almost dancing with excitement.

"This is wonderful news, my friend. Now we can see the superiority of Germania's fighting men. To sweep through Europa, and destroy all opposition while only suffering such light losses, is proof that we are the master race."

"Yes, master," The Wraith replied. He did not dare to mention that the success of their attack had relied more upon the contamination of Europa's water supply, than of the strength of their forces.

"There is something more, master," he said.

The Chancellor resumed his seat.

"*And what is that?*"

"*I received a communication from my spy. He told me that the Britans have sent a force to assist the enemy. They will land at Cherbourg in three hours. He gave me the strength and numbers of their disposition.*"

Falkenberg's eyes thinned to slits. He clenched his fists.

"*They will suffer for their interference.*"

"*Yes, master. I will have them met on the beaches. We will throw them back into the channel. Not one soldier will set foot in Europa.*"

The Chancellor shook his head.

"*No,*" he said. A crafty expression appeared upon his face. "*Allow them to land, and advance. We will lull them into a false sense of security, and then we will strike. They will be destroyed, but at a time of my choosing.*"

The Wraith thought that this was unwise, but he knew better than to contradict his master.

"*It will be as you say, master.*"

"*You are to be congratulated on the success of our plan,*" Falkenberg said. "*Make sure you send that information to all of our forces.*"

"*Yes, master.*"

Falkenberg terminated the call. The Wraith pushed a button, and the vidscreen folded itself up, and returned to the side of his command chair. He returned his attention to the devastation that was still being displayed upon the main vidscreen. The *Viktor* sailed on.

Captain Zorn and I were summoned to the hospital. When we arrived, we were met by Major McKinnon, who was waiting for us at the entrance.

"Guid mornin', captain, Mister Fussell."

"Good morning, major," Zorn replied. "Do you know what this is about?

"I canna say, sir. His Highness will inform ye when ye see him. Shall we?" He made a gesture for us to follow him.

We proceeded inside, and walked along the corridor until we met an orderly.

"This way, gentlemen."

We continued on in his wake, until we reached an office. Doctor Mansfield's name was displayed on a sign that was fixed to the door. The orderly knocked.

"Enter."

The orderly opened the door, and ushered us inside. He went out and closed the door. Sitting at the doctor's desk was Prince Henry, and Councillor Reading stood by his side. We bowed to His Highness.

"Ah, gentlemen. Thank you for coming. Please sit down."

We each took one of the seats that were facing the desk. Prince Henry glanced at Reading, and nodded. The Councillor spoke.

"Gentlemen, we have received a communication from France. It is a message from Doctors Yvette and Andre Molyneaux. They have informed His Highness that they have in their possession a cure for The Blight. Patients that they have treated with this cure have shown positive results, and in some cases, have been pronounced free of the disease. But they are in Paris, and the Germanian advance is now a threat to them. They have heard of the Queen's plight, and say that if they and their research can be evacuated to Britannia, in return they will cure the Queen and all of her suffering subjects."

"This is wonderful news," I said.

"Indeed it is, Mister Fussell," Prince Henry said. "It is imperative that they are brought to us, gentlemen. The Queen is slipping away from us, and many of her stricken subjects are the same. Time is short. We must bring these doctors and their cure to Britannia."

"The plan is for Captain Zorn to take the *Vengeance* to France. Because she is a fast ship, she should evade any encounter with the enemy," Reading said. "Major McKinnon and a dozen of his men will accompany you. Mister Fussell is to go along because of his knowledge and experiences in France. If anything untoward should happen, he should be able to assist you."

"Plus," His Highness added with a smile, "he is always in search of a good story, and this adventure should provide him with one."

"Thank you, Your Highness," I said, smiling wryly.

"Do you agree to do this, captain?" Prince Henry asked.

"I do, Your Highness. But I would like to make one change to your plan, if I may."

"What would that be, captain?" The councillor said.

"It is this. I will take the *Avenger*. She is a smaller and much faster craft than the *Vengeance*. She can depart immediately."

"Can she accommodate all of you?" Prince Henry asked.

"Yes, Your Highness," Zorn replied. "She has the capacity to carry twenty people. There will be no problem."

"Excellent. We thank you for agreeing to take on this task. Good luck to you all." Prince Henry rose to his feet, and we followed suit. "You are our only hope, gentlemen. We are relying on you. The Queen's life, and those of her companions, are in your hands."

"We will no' fail, Yer Majesty," Major McKinnon said. "We'll ha' those doctors and their cure back here in a wink."

"I know you will, major," Prince Henry said. "Your men have never failed in a mission yet."

"I will send a message to the French doctors informing them that you are coming to fetch them," Reading said. "Good luck, gentlemen."

Dismissed, we bowed to His Highness, and took our leave.

The combined Britannic forces crossed the channel, and came ashore in France at Cherbourg. The troops rushed ashore, expecting at any moment to be met by a hail of bullets and shells. It did not come, and as they advanced up the beach and then signalled the fleet that the area was secure, many veterans gave each other knowing looks. Surely the enemy lay in wait for them somewhere? They should not have been able to gain a foothold in Europa so easily. The green troops among them were grinning, and saying how easy this war business was. The old soldiers ignored them gruffly. They would find out how *easy* it was when they met the enemy.

The transports landed, and started to put their cargo on the beach. As they offloaded their vehicles and gravtanks, all were surprised at the absence of enemy opposition. Not even a single flyer was seen observing their landing. Once unloaded, the gravtanks and other vehicles were assembled in their groups, and advanced inland, filled with troops. The flyers, having flown cover for the airships and ships, landed and refuelled. The fliers gathered together and wondered at the enemy's non appearance.

"We will see them soon enough, mes amis," Louise assured them.

Once they had refuelled, they took off and headed towards their respective operating zones.

IX

The Rescue

The *Avenger* hurtled over France, heading towards Paris and her rendezvous with the Molyneaux. Zorn was flying her, and I sat in the cockpit with him, marvelling at the displays and controls in front of me. Major McKinnon and his twelve men sat in the compartment behind us. She was built like the Vengeance; her hull was carbonium, and Zorn had told me that her bracing was constructed in the same manner as the larger gravship. The captain was telling me all about her.

"She was actually built before the *Vengeance*. She was the test craft to prove that the Gravitic Drive worked. Once she had passed all of my tests with flying colours, I knew I could construct a much larger vessel. The principle is the same, no matter the size of the ship." He checked a display on the panel in front of him, and keyed his microphone. "Major McKinnon, we are approaching the coordinates where we are to pick up our passengers."

"*Acknowledged,*" came the reply over the cockpit speakers.

We heard him giving orders to his men; telling them to check their gear one last time, and to make ready to disembark.

"*Look!*" I shouted, pointing ahead.

Zorn gazed out of the cockpit, and saw large columns of black smoke ascending into the air. Above them was a dark cloud, approaching rapidly. As we looked more closely, it resolved itself into a mass of Germanian fighters and bombers. Between the *Avenger* and the formation of enemy machines lay Paris.

"There are hundreds of them!" I cried.

Zorn nodded, his face grim. "We must beat them to Paris."

He pushed the throttle lever wide open. The gravship leaped forward, speeding towards the beleaguered city. French anti-flyer guns on the ground opened up on the Germanian formation, their desperate gunners firing wildly. As a squadron of antiquated French flyers rose to meet the invaders, two squadrons of The Wraith's black gravflyers peeled away and dove to meet them. In a few horrible moments, the French machines were shot down, completely outclassed by the enemy. The *Avenger* rushed onward.

"*There!*" Talbot cried.

I looked down and saw a steamcoach on the side of the road below us. Two people stood there, waving wildly. Several bags and crates that no doubt contained their vital research were stacked by them.

"Brace yourselves!" Zorn shouted.

He threw the *Avenger* downwards, and landed her close to the couple. The hatch opened with a pneumatic hiss, and McKinnon and two of his men ran over to the French doctors. As his men took up their luggage, the Major hurried them towards the gravship. Shadows flitted across the road.

"*Look out!*" Zorn cried.

I looked up and saw six of the Germanian gravflyers diving down upon us. Zorn turned and saw that the passengers were safely aboard, and were being buckled into their safety harnesses. Their luggage was hastily stowed in a locker. He punched the button for the hatch, and even as it began to close, he took off. The enemy pursued. In moments, they were firing range, and their guns opened up. Bullets riddled the fuselage, and men cried out as they were hit.

Zorn flung the *Avenger* into desperate manoeuvres, trying to dodge the enemy's deadly fire. As he turned and twisted, an enemy gravflyer crossed his bows. He flicked the safety off his guns, stabbed the trigger, and a storm of lead tore the flyer apart. She spun away, burning. Zorn rolled the gravship, turned, and then latched onto another gravflyer's tail. He pressed the firing button, and the small craft exploded as her fuel tank was hit. I cheered.

But the remaining four eluded Zorn's guns, and pressed their attack relentlessly. Bullets tore into the *Avenger's* hull, and another scream rent the air as someone was mortally wounded. Suddenly, there was an explosion. A display flashed erratically on the instrument panel, and an alarm hooted in the cockpit.

"We've lost an engine!" Zorn yelled. He fought the controls as the gravship shuddered and yawed uncontrollably through the air.

Spinning wildly, the *Avenger* plummeted towards the ground. Bullets rattled against the hull like hail as the Germanian's fired upon the careering ship. The ground rose up to meet us. A wall of trees rushed towards us.

"Hang on!" I cried.

The *Avenger* smashed into them, and tumbled over and over, before finally coming to rest. She began to burn. The enemy came down and hovered close to the wreckage, guns ready. But there was no sign of life. The Germanians, satisfied that the gravship was finished, departed.

On board the *Viktor*, The Wraith was listening to his spy via his vidscreen.

"*These two doctors, the Molyneaux by name, claimed that they possessed a cure. Zorn was despatched to bring them to Britannia.*"

"*Impossible!*" The Wraith scoffed, "*only* I *have that knowledge.*"

"*Are you willing to take the chance that they may indeed have a cure, master? It would become a danger to the plan. The threat that you hold over them would count for naught.*" He paused, and then went on. "*However, the Avenger was shot down by Germanian flyers as they attempted to rescue the Molyneaux. Britannic Command has lost contact with Zorn and his passengers. Did any of them survive the crash? It would be prudent to find out.*"

The Wraith nodded.

"*I agree. It is imperative that we find out if there are any survivors. If the enemy does indeed have a cure to* The Blight, *it will render the weapon useless. Do you have the coordinates of the crash site?*"

"*I have the coordinates where they picked up the doctors, master. They did not get far from there, for the Germanian flyers spotted and pursued them immediately. They were shot down within minutes of the pickup. Surely the crash site is close by?*"

"*You may be right. Transmit the coordinates to me.*"

"*Yes, master.*" The spy held up a datacard. He put it into his terminal, pressed the send key, and in seconds, the information was displayed. The crimson figure took a datacard from a box that was fitted to the side of his command chair. He inserted it into a slot on the side of the screen. He pressed the record button on his chair arm, and saved the information. He removed the datacard.

"*Good work,*" he said. "*Call me if you have anything of interest.*"

"*Yes, master.*"

The Wraith terminated the call, and then he pressed a button on his command chair.

"*Yes, master?*" came the answer.

"*Report to me immediately.*"

"*Yes, master.*"

A few moments later, an officer dressed in the uniform of the Germanian Flying Storm Troopers entered the bridge, and went directly over to The Wraith. He clicked his heels in salute.

"You summoned me, master."

"*I have a task for you. I have received intelligence about two French doctors who contacted the Britans, and told them that they had a cure for The Blight. The Britans sent a ship to pick them up and take them to Britannia. It was shot down by Germanian flyers just outside Paris.*"

"A cure, master? Surely that is a lie."

"*We cannot chance it. I do not need to tell you what such a thing would do to our plans.*"

"I understand, master. The threat of the weapon would be negated."

"*Exactly.*" He held up the datacard, and then tossed it to his man, who caught it deftly.

"*Oberleutnant Hartz, you are to take twenty of your best men and search for these French doctors. Bring them to me. Dead or alive. Destroy any equipment that they have with them. That datacard shows their last known whereabouts.*"

"What of the rescue team, master? If any of them survived the crash, should I bring them to you as well?"

"*No. They are of no interest to me. If any of them survived, shoot them.*"

The officer nodded, and clicked his heels again. Then he left the bridge, to assemble his team.

Meanwhile, the survivors of the crash were hiding in a barn at a farmhouse on the outskirts of Paris. I and most of the others had escaped major injury, and along with the major and his remaining men's help, we had located the barn, and had helped the wounded there. The casualties were four of McKinnon's men; shot or killed in the crash when we were shot down. We buried them at the crash site, and covered their graves with leaves. The captain had taken one last forlorn look at the *Avenger*, and then we had hurried away. The Molyneuax were unhurt, and were busy treating the others. Zorn's right arm was broken. All of the others had cuts and bruises, but no other serious injuries.

Major Mckinnon took me aside.

"Our wristphones are no' powerful enough to contact Command, and the radio on the *Avenger* was destroyed in the crash. Somehow we must get to a radio, and send a call for help so tha' Command can mount a rescue mission." He looked grim.

"Is there some way we could link the wristphones together and make that call?" I asked.

He shook his head.

"No. There's no way to interlink them."

"What about the radio set your man was carrying?"

The man spoken of had been riddled with bullets. We had brought his set with us to see if it would work. One of McKinnon's men had been trying ever since we had reached our hideout.

The major turned, and beckoned him over. The man came to up us, and saluted McKinnon.

"This is Private Halliwell, Mister Fussell."

"Pleased to meet you, sir." He offered me his hand.

"And I you, private." We shook hands.

"Well, Jim?" the major asked.

"I'm sorry, sir. She's completely had it. I can't get anything. There's a carrier signal, but it's all just static." He wiped his brow with the back of his hand.

"Damn. Keep tryin'."

"Yes sir," he said resignedly. He saluted, and went back to his fruitless task.

"How long will it be before Command misses us?" I asked.

"Oh, they'd already know somethin' was wrong," McKinnon said. "We were supposed to transmit a code tha' told them we had picked up the doctors."

"Wouldn't they send someone to see what happened to us?"

"Eventually. I canna say how long it will be before they do."

"Well, we can't just stay here," I said. "The Germanians might be looking for us. And it's vital that we get the Molyneaux to Britannia and The Queen."

"I know tha'. But we canna move in the daytime while the enemy are aboot. Maybe we can find some sort of transport, and get away."

"Where?"

"I dinna ken."

One of the men posted guard at the barn doors signalled to the major.

"Please excuse me, Mister Fussell."

"Major."

He went to see what his man wanted. I walked over to Zorn, who was lying on a pile of hay. His arm had been set with a crude wooden splint, and bandaged. I knelt down.

"Mister Fussell. Good to see you. You have a fine story to tell, eh?"

"Captain. I believe it's only just the start of it. How are you doing?"

"Well enough. I have had worse injuries. The loss of the *Avenger* pains me more than this scratch."

"I can well imagine. She was a fine little craft. I am sorry that she was lost."

He licked his lips. I picked up a canteen that was by his side, took off the cap, and offered it to him. He drank deeply, and handed it back to me.

"Ah. Very nice. Thank you, Mister Fussell. A pity it is not wine." He smiled.

"When we get back, I'll see you get a bottle." I took a drink, and recapped the canteen.

"We will share one."

"Perhaps a glass."

Zorn smiled.

"Did the major's man have any luck with the radio?" He asked.

"No, I'm afraid not. He can't seem to raise anyone."

"I thought so. I was watching him. His face told me about the radio's condition."

"Major McKinnon told him to keep trying."

"Yes. That is what the military does; never gives up, even when the situation is hopeless."

"Is that what you think?" I said. "Our situation is hopeless?"

"I have failed. The mission has failed. We will be captured and executed. And your queen and her companions will die. I would consider that a hopeless situation."

I looked into his eyes and saw the fatalism there. Dour he may be, but this attitude was not like him. Perhaps he had been drugged for the pain of his wound, and that was affecting his thoughts.

"No, captain. We aren't finished yet. Command will send someone to pick us up. We'll get out of here and back to Britannia." I reached out, and gripped his shoulder reassuringly. Unlike before, he didn't react at my touching him.

"Perhaps you are right, Mister Fussell."

"I am. You'll see."

I saw that he was fading.

"You're tired, sir. Rest. Have a sleep. You can't do anything but wait."

"Wait," he echoed. "Yes, wait. But for rescue, or capture and death? Which will it be, I wonder?"

With those discouraging words, he fell asleep. I looked about me. Halliwell was busy with the radio, McKinnon and his men at the doors were still talking, and the Molyneaux were tending to the others. I lay down in the hay, and gave myself up to slumber.

At a forward base where she and her squadron were refuelling, Captain Deville was taking a call from the Emergency Council. Councillor Reading was speaking to her via the vidscreen in the communications hut.

"*That is all that we know of the* Avenger's *fate, captain. We lost contact with her, and can only assume that she was shot down. Will you mount a search for the* Avenger, *and ascertain if any of those who were on board survive? Especially the doctors. We must have their cure.*"

"I will do this, councillor. Do you have any idea of where she was shot down?"

"*Only a vague idea. I can give you the coordinates where she was supposed to pick up the Molyneaux.*" He gestured to someone out of her view. Navigational information began to stream over the screen. A technician who was sitting at her side put a datacard into the dataport, and pressed record on the machine. In a few moments, the data had been copied, and the technician ejected the datacard, and handed it to Deville.

"That is their last known location," Reading said. *"I'm sorry, it's the best I can do for you."*

"It will have to do," she said. "I will get my fliers ready."

"Thank you, captain. I will arrange for a transport flyer to accompany you in the search. You must find the French doctors, for the Queen and her subject's sake."

"If they are still alive, I will bring them to Londinium," Deville said, as she put the datacard in her flying jacket.

"Thank you again, captain. The fate of the Britannic Empire is in your hands."

"You may count on me, councillor. I will find them."

The vidscreen blanked as the call ended.

Deville nodded her thanks to the technician, and left the hut to inform her fliers of their new mission.

A black transport flyer marked with The Wraith's insignia landed at the crash site. The hatch opened, and a dozen Fliegen Sturm Truppen dispersed, weapons ready. They were wearing battle armour, rocket packs, and full faced helmets that incorporated a breathing mask and a communicator. Most were armed with machine pistols, but every fourth man carried a heavier machine gun. Oberleutnant Hartz descended the ramp. He was clad in armour like them, but wore his helmet with the mask detached and strapped to his right shoulder. He and half of his men went over to the wrecked gravflyer, while the others formed a perimeter. While he stood and waited outside the ship, his men entered, and searched it. Moments later, they exited and a feldwebel reported to him.

"No one is aboard, Herr Oberleutnant. They must have fled."

Hartz stroked his chin, and looked about.

"Search the surrounding area."

"Jahwol." The feldwebel gestured, and the troopers began to search.

Five minutes later, a trooper called out.

"Herr Oberleutnant! Over here!"

Hartz went over to the trooper, and saw where we had buried McKinnon's men. The downdraft from the transport's engines had blown the leaves away when they landed, and had revealed the hidden graves. He smiled.

"Good work. Look for anything that shows the direction that the survivors have taken. For," he said smiling, "dead men do not bury themselves."

The troopers fanned out, and began to look for any signs. After another short search, one of his troopers called him over.

"Herr Oberleutnant! Here! Come and see."

The Oberleutnant went over, and looked down to see some bootprints.

"Excellent. Feldwebel, take six men and track these prints. Locate the survivors, and call me."

"Jahwol, Herr Oberleutnant." The feldwebel pointed out six of the troopers, and they came to him. He took one look at the bootprints, ascertained the direction that they indicated, and went in pursuit. The troopers followed him.

The Oberleutnant activated his wristcom. An image of The Wraith appeared in holographic form above it.

"We have located the crashed machine, master. There are four graves, but there were survivors, and I have my men searching for them."

"Very good, Hartz. Track the fugitives down, and bring them to the Viktor. We must know who was killed. Open the graves."

"Yes, master. And if the doctors are among the dead?"

"It is of no concern to me. Ideally, I would like to interrogate them about their cure, but if they are both dead, then that will serve my purpose also. They will no longer pose a threat."

"I understand, master."

The crimson figure terminated the call.

"You two," Hartz said, addressing two of his troopers, "open the graves."

"Jahwol!" they chorused.

As they began the grisly work, Hartz walked back to the transport, and walked up the ramp. He went over to the command chair, and sat down and waited for his feldwebel to call.

Captain Deville and four of her fliers stood waiting on the field. The sound of distant guns echoed in the air, and to the east there were columns of black smoke rising, indicating the presence of the advancing Germanian forces. Their flyers were ready to go, but they were waiting for the transport flyer that Reading had promised. Deville impatiently checked her chronometer.

"Mon Capitaine," one of her fliers said, "it is almost an hour late."

"Oui," another said. "They must have been shot down."

"Should we go, capitaine?" the first flier asked.

"We cannot," Deville said. "We must have the transport to pick up any survivors. *Merde!*" She began to pace angrily.

"If there are any," one of the fliers said.

Deville rounded on her. She was about to reprimand her, when the sound of engines intruded.

They all turned to see a Britannic transport coming in over the field. It approached them, and landed. As they hurried over to it, the cockpit's side window slid open, and a flier poked his head out.

"Sorry we're late. We got lost." He grinned.

Deville and her fliers stood there fuming, but the Britan didn't seem to see the anger on their faces.

"Lucky we are here to show you the way," Deville said sarcastically.

"Oh, yes. Good show. Shall we?"

The captain and her companions glanced at each other. *Britans!*

"Very well. Take to your machines, ladies." Deville turned and headed over to her own flyer as they went to carry out her order. She leapt into the cockpit, and put on her helmet and gloves. She activated her comm. "Ready?"

Her fliers all answered in the affirmative. She started the engine, and as it warmed up, she contacted the transport.

"Follow me," she said curtly.

"*Lead on,*" the transport flier replied cheerily.

Britans! She thought. *Merde. What have I got myself into?*

She fed power into the engine, and the flyer rose into the air. It was followed by her comrade's machines, and then the transport ascended. They formed up over the field, and then turned towards the east.

They headed towards the black smoke.

Feldwebel Grun and his troopers followed the tracks we had left and found our hiding place. McKinnon's sentry posted at the door saw them approaching, and opened fire. I sat up, startled awake by the gunfire. I looked over to the barn door, and saw McKinnon and his men returning fire. Zorn grabbed my arm.

"Give me a weapon."

"No, captain. Stay here."

I shook him off, and ran towards the major. I dropped to the dirt floor behind him.

"Give me a weapon, major," I said, echoing Zorn's words.

"There are none to spare, Mister Fussell." He fired several shots.

A hail of bullets ripped through the air, and two of his men fell. One of them was near me. I reached out, grabbed the harness on his pack, and dragged him into cover. I checked him. He was dead. His machine pistol was still gripped tightly in his dead hands. I prised it out of them.

McKinnon glanced over his shoulder.

"Can ye fire tha'?"

I ran my eyes over the weapon. It was simple.

"Yes."

"Ge' to it, then."

I crawled forward, and looked out. The troopers had spread out, and were laying down a withering fire.

"They mean to keep us pinned down here while they send for reinforcements," I said.

"Aye," McKinnon replied, "tha's what they're doin'. We ha' to ge' oot of here." He snapped off a couple of shots. One of the troopers fell.

I saw another of them preparing to move. His position was exposed. I checked my weapon, and selected single fire. No use wasting ammunition. I sighted on the trooper, and breathed out. As he rose, I fired, and drilled him through the head.

"Guid shot!" McKinnon exulted.

One of his men shot down another.

"That's three!" He cried.

 While his troopers kept us pinned down, Grun called Hartz.

"Herr Oberleutnant, we have found them. We have them pinned

down."

"Good work. Send me your location."

The feldwebel held up his left arm. On it was a communications unit that ensured he was in contact with his squad at all times. It also contained a tracking device that could send his location to any other unit. He pressed the button, and Hartz received the coordinates on the screen that was mounted on his command chair.

"Good. Keep the fugitives from escaping. We will arrive shortly."

"Jawhol, Herr Oberleutnant."

The feldwebel's image disappeared from the screen.

Hartz addressed the flier at the controls. "Take off, and go to this location." Hartz sent the coordinates to the flier's screen.

"Jawhol!"

The transport took off, and headed towards the coordinates that Grun had given them. In a short time, they reached the area. The transport landed, and Hartz and the rest of his men disembarked.

"Damn!" McKinnon cursed. "More of the buggers. We canna ge' oot now."

I looked out at the transport. How many more of them were there? They could keep us pinned down in here until our ammunition ran out.

As his troopers joined Grun and his men, Hartz contacted his master.

"Master, we have them."

"You have done well. Capture the fugitives and bring them to me."

"Yes, master."

The Wraith terminated the call.

Suddenly, Louise and her fliers swooped down out of the sky, firing upon the troopers. Several of them fell to their surprise attack, but the rest activated their rocket packs, and rose to repel the French aviatrixes. In moments, the air was filled with whirling flyers and flying troopers, each attempting to shoot the other down. Two troopers got on the tail of one of the flyers, and sent it down in flames. Another French craft suffered the same fate, riddled by the trooper's fire. But Louise and her remaining companion were too good for them, and in moments, it was troopers falling from the sky, shredded by the flyer's guns. Louise came in low, and strafed the Germanian transport as it attempted to take off, and it exploded in a ball of flame.

Hartz, seeing that he was now outnumbered, called off his surviving troopers with a curse.

"Retreat! Retreat!"

He, Grun, and the surviving troopers took to the air and fled. Louise's comrade made to chase them, but the captain's order came over her communicator.

"Leave them! Cover the transport!"

"Oui, Mon Capitaine."

"Transport! Come in. The area is secure. Make the pickup."

"Roger. Nice shooting, ladies."

The Britannic transport appeared, and began to land.

"Right, laddies!" McKinnon cried. "Let's go!"

They hustled the Molyneaux and their luggage towards the transport as I went back and helped Zorn. I helped him up, and we staggered out of the barn and towards our rescuers. Everyone got on board, and Mckinnon and Halliwell raced back inside. As the captain and I sat watching, the major and his man reappeared, carrying their two dead comrades. They lifted them onto the transport, and then boarded.

"They were guid lads, Mister Fussell. I could'na leave 'em there."

I nodded, understanding the bond between fighting men. McKinnon pointed at the machine pistol that was hanging around my neck.

"Ye're a fine shot with tha'. Ha' ye seen action before?"

"A few skirmishes. It helps to be familiar with firearms if you're a reporter in a war zone."

"Aye. It would tha'."

The transport leaped into the air, and we sped towards the Britannic lines, flanked by Louise and her comrade.

X

The Pursuit

Oberleutnant Hartz called his master to inform him of our escape. He and his surviving troopers had fled the scene, and had landed not far away. He, Feldwebel Grun, and four of his men were the only ones left alive after their failed capture attempt. He knew that his master would be displeased with his failure, but he also knew that if he didn't report our escape, The Wraith's anger would be so much the greater. He activated his communicator.

The holo of his master appeared. The giant armoured figure sat in his command chair on the bridge of the Viktor.

"Yes, Oberleutnant?"

Hartz took a deep breath.

"Master, I regret to inform you that the fugitives have escaped."

The Wraith's bloodshot eyes flashed.

"Escaped?" he echoed. *"How is this possible?"*

"A Britannic transport escorted by flyers attacked us, and evacuated them."

"And you allowed them to depart," The Wraith said. To Hartz and the listening troopers, their master's voice seemed to take on a cutting edge. It was hard to tell, because of the mask's metallic tones, but they all felt the subtle change in it.

"We were outnumbered, master," Hartz said. "I lost most - "

The Wraith slammed his fist down on the arm of the command

chair. He rose to his feet, and even through the holographic projection, his rage could be sensed. Grun and his troopers took an involuntary step away from Hartz, unconsciously separating themselves from him, the object of that rage.

"*I am not interested in your excuses, Hartz,*" The Wraith said icily. "*I do not care if a thousand men were lost. The French doctors and their cure must not be allowed to fall into the enemy's hands.*"

Hartz licked his lips nervously. How could he mollify his master's anger?

"We know which direction they took, master," he offered hopefully. "We will go after them, and - "

"*No,*" The Wraith said with finality. "*Send me the coordinates of their last position. You have done enough. Return to the* Viktor, *and report to me.*"

"Yes, master." Hartz did as he was ordered.

The information flashed up on the screen in front of The Wraith. He pressed the record button on the chair arm, and then ended the transmission.

"*Fool. I am surrounded by imbeciles.*" He dropped into his chair. It groaned under his weight. He thought for a moment, and then he punched a button. After a few moments, his call was answered.

"*Yes, master?*"

"*Hauptmann Eckhart, Hartz and his troopers failed to secure the fugitives. Take a flight and go and destroy them. They are aboard a Britannic transport, escorted by French flyers, and they are heading for Britan. Here are their last known coordinates.*" He pressed a button, and sent the information. "*You should catch them with ease; they only have conventional machines.*"

"*You don't want us to capture the transport, and bring them to you?*"

"No. There are to be no survivors. Do I make myself clear?"

"Yes, master. We will go at once."

. The Wraith terminated the call. Ten minutes later, the *Viktor's* main hanger door opened, and six gravflyers launched, and sped away in pursuit of the fugitives. The Wraith watched them until they were out of sight.

Twenty minutes later, the gravflyers spotted our transport and its French escorts. Louise called us.

"Transport, we have company. Six of The Wraith's gravflyers, and they are coming in fast."

The Britan at the controls checked a scanner that was focused aft.

"Bloody hell! They're too fast. There's no way we can outrun them."

He threw the throttle lever wide open. The transport leapt forward. Zorn and I left our seats, and went up to the cockpit hatch.

"You are correct, captain," Zorn said, looking at the display. "They will be upon us in moments."

The black shapes closed in rapidly.

"Pauke!" Eckhart cried, and they sped towards us.

"Transport, go to emergency speed. We will keep them off you." Louise and her comrade turned to engaged the oncoming enemy.

"Louise!" I cried. *"No!"*

Zorn gripped my arm.

"They are our only hope."

I watched the scanner helplessly as the icons that displayed attacker and defender closed on each other.

The two French craft closed with Eckhart and his fliers head on. Each side opened fire, and tracers flew. None were hit, and they hurtled past each other at breakneck speed, and turned to attempt to get on each other's tail.

Eckhart called to his flight.

"Destroy them. Schultz, break off and follow me."

"Jawohl, Herr Hauptmann."

"Understood. Flight attacking now."

As Louise and her comrade engaged the remaining four Germanians, Eckhart and his wingman hurried after us.

Louise got on the tail of one of the enemy. She pressed the firing button, and a hail of bullets ripped into the gravflyer, shredding it. It spiralled towards the ground, trailing black smoke.

Her comrade snapped off a short burst as one of The Wraith's craft crossed her sights. It exploded, and the wreckage spun earthward.

"Isabeau!" Louise called, "they are after the transport!"

"Go and get them, Mon Capitaine. I will look after these pigs."

Louise broke away from the fight, and rushed after Eckhart and his companion, who were closing on us rapidly. One of the enemy gravflyers came in pursuit of her, but she ignored it and pushed her flyer to maximum speed with the throttle to the wall. She knew our unarmed transport was no match for the Germanians.

As Louise closed on Eckhart and the other gravflyer, an explosion flared brightly behind her. She glanced at her rear scanner, and the icon that had represented Isabeau's autogyro faded and disappeared. She realised that now she must defeat all four of the Germanian gravflyers. Louise gritted her teeth, and bore down on the craft in front of her. In dismay, she saw Eckhart open fire, his tracers sweeping towards the transport.

The bullets tore through the hull, and there were screams from the cargo compartment. Zorn and I fell to the floor as the transport shuddered, and appeared to slow.

The transport began to trail white smoke as Louise finally got

Eckhart's wingman in her sights, and with a short burst, she shot him down. Eckhart fired again, and the smoke pouring from our damaged craft turned black.

"Merde!" Louise cried. She opened up, too far away from Eckhart to do any real damage, but she hoped that her fire would put the Germanian off his aim.

As she fired, she came within range of her pursuers, and the rattle of bullets along her starboard side made her throw her ship into desperate manoeuvres to escape them. Louise risked a quick glance at Eckhart's craft, and saw that a miracle had occurred. She had managed to hit him. His gravflyer had broken off the attack, and was limping away, trailing smoke. The transport was still flying, but was badly damaged.

Now she had to deal with her pursuers. Louise turned to attack them. They scattered as she fired, and plunged between them. But the damage to her autogyro was extensive, and in a few moments Louise realised that she could not hope to win. A glance at her instruments showed her the condition of her machine. Indicator lights were in the red, and the little craft began to behave erratically. It was this that ironically saved her life numerous times, as the enemy missed her due to its unpredictable movements. Their tracers came perilously close, but none hit her careering machine.

Louise threw her flyer into a wide circle, and the Germanians followed. Around and around they went, taking pot shots at each other. She accepted her fate, glad in the knowledge that the French doctors had escaped. She hoped that their cure was real, and worth the sacrifice she and her aviatrixes had made.

Not one to give up, however, she continued to turn, snapping off short bursts whenever an enemy craft crossed her sights. Louise fought the sluggish controls as the deadly circling continued. Once a gravflyer got on her tail, she knew she would be finished. But at least she had enabled the transport and its precious cargo to escape. Louise knew it was hopeless, but continued to fight. She was tiring; the erratic controls, and the constant turning were wearing her down. She saw some movement in her mirror, and looked to see a black gravflyer on her tail. She was in his sights.

"This is it," she thought. *"Make it quick, you bastard."* She closed her eyes.

"Tally Ho!" a Britannic voice cried in her headphones, and her pursuer exploded as a hail of bullets tore into it. Her eyes snapped open, and Louise hurled her craft out of the fight. The other three enemy craft scattered as a flight of Britannic gravflyers dove into the combat area. The Germanians, completely surprised and demoralised by the sudden arrival of the Britans, fell swiftly to their hammering guns. The hunters, now become the hunted, plunged blazing toward the ground far below.

As Louise turned to head towards the Britannic lines, the rescuing gravflyers formed up around her. She looked at the closest one, and saw Commander Symes waving at her.

Symes's voice echoed in her headphones: *"Sorry we're late, captain. That was some impressive flying. Fancy a cup of tea?"*

She laughed, and said: "Thank you, commander, but I would prefer wine if you have it."

Symes laughed too.

"I'm sure I'll be able to find a bottle."

"Or two?" Louise asked.

"Or two." Symes replied. *"Can you make it to the coast? Your ship looks pretty banged up."*

"If I do not have to perform any aerobatics, she will." Suddenly, she was crying; tears ran poured from her eyes and began to pool in her goggles. With a wrench, Louise pulled them off, and pushed them up onto her helmet. She sobbed. Her hands trembled.

"*Easy,*" Symes said. "*It's the shock. You're all right. We're here. You're safe.*"

Louise angrily wiped the tears from her face with the back of a gloved hand. She hated her reaction. She had been in hundreds of dogfights and never before had she cried or shown any emotion. Not even when she had lost close companions.

"*Captain. Louise.*"

"Oui?"

"*It's all right. What you're feeling is normal. You just escaped death. It's not embarrassing. It's just the release of tension.*" Symes's voice was calm, soothing.

"Please do not tell Zorn or Alistair."

"*Not one word. Look ahead, there they are.*"

She looked, and saw the transport, escorted by four Britannic gravflyers. She was no longer smoking. But as they closed up with us, the bullet holes that covered her hull made her shake her head in amazement. How could she still fly?

"*Captain Deville. Good to see you. We thought you were done for.*"

"Commander Symes and his men arrived just in time," she replied. "How did you put the fire out?"

"*I was lucky. The extinguisher in the starboard engine did a good job. I transferred the rest of the fuel to the port tank. It makes handling this old bus a bit tricky, but at least we didn't go off with a bang.*" He laughed.

Louise smiled.

"Was anyone killed in the fight?"

"*No. Two of Major McKinnon's men received wounds, but they are minor. Hang on, someone wants to talk to you.*"

"*Louise,*" I said. "*Are you all right?*"

"Yes, Alistair. I'm not wounded, but I'm afraid this old gyro is finished.

"*I think we might have a shiny new gravflyer to replace her with,*" Symes said.

"I look forward to that," she said.

We headed towards the base.

Meanwhile, Oberleutnant Hartz and his troopers returned to the *Viktor*. Grun and the others went to the sickbay. They took leave of Hartz gratefully, knowing that he had to go straight to the bridge to report to The Wraith. He sweated with fear, because he knew of his master's hatred of failure, and the fate of those who failed was well known to all of the Germanian forces who were under The Wraith's command. Hartz walked slowly, not looking forward to the meeting. But eventually, he reached the bridge. He paused at the hatchway, his thoughts roiling in his head. There was no excuse for his failure. He swallowed, and entered.

The Oberleutnant crossed the deck, his gaze fixed upon the giant figure that sat in the command chair. He walked up and presented himself to his master, clicking his heels.

"Oberleutnant Hartz reporting, sir." He stared into the mask, attempting to read the emotion behind it. All he could sense was anger. He licked his lips nervously. He could feel the sweat trickling down his spine.

The Wraith considered him for a few moments without speaking. Those bloodshot eyes pinned the Oberleutnant like an insect on a board.

"*Well,*" The Wraith said finally, "*what do you have to say?*"

"I apologise, sir. There is no excuse for my failure. The doctors and their cure have escaped. I will accept any punishment that seems fit to you." Hartz clenched his fists to stop his hands from trembling. His heart crashed in his chest. He resigned himself to his fate. If it was death, he hoped it would be swift and painless.

"I see," his master said. *"Very noble of you."*

The Oberleutnant stood waiting for a reprimand. The Wraith was silent for what seemed like a long time.

Get it over with, Hartz thought.

"Leave me," the giant eventually said, with a negligent wave of his hand.

Hartz stared at him in amazement, not believing that he had been given a reprieve. He clicked his heels together, and hurriedly left the bridge, thanking whatever providence that had inexplicably saved him from his master's wrath.

A bridge officer turned from his console and reported: "Sir, Hauptmann Eckhart is approaching the *Viktor*. His flyer is badly damaged."

The Wraith looked out of the massive window and saw the trail of smoke that marked Eckhart's position. He rose to his feet.

" Obermann, take over the bridge."

"Jawohl."

The Wraith strode out of the bridge, and headed towards the main hanger.

Eckhart's gravflyer came in to land, and was instantly swarmed by the fire party. The hanger door closed as they sprayed the damaged craft with foam. The Hauptmann leaped out, and got clear. His fliers surrounded him, and he was telling them of his mission when The Wraith arrived.

"Stillgestanden!"

The fliers crashed to attention. The Wraith walked slowly across the deck, his footfalls echoing loudly. He stood before Eckhart, and gazed down upon the flier.

"I am sorry to report that the fugitives have escaped, sir. They were assisted by French and Britannic fliers, who bested us."

"The French fliers had only outdated machines, did they not?"

"Yes, sir."

"And the Britans were equipped with gravflyers?"

"That is correct, sir."

"I can understand the Britans defeating you, they had craft that were as fast as your own. But the French should have proved easy meat."

"Victory does not just rely on the better machine alone, sir. They were just better in the air."

"You are saying that these French aviators were superior to your elite squadron?" The Wraith asked coldly.

"Yes, sir," Eckhart replied. "They were not just any French fliers, they were Le Rouge Chats. They are the best fliers in Europa."

"The best fliers in Europa," The Wraith echoed. *"How do you know this?"*

"I saw their squadron insignia myself."

"And you are convinced that they are better fliers than you?"

Eckhart lowered his head in shame. He raised it, and looked straight into The Wraith's bloodshot eyes.

"They are, sir. It is a fact. I apologise for my failure."

"They are women, are they not, led by a Captain Louise Deville?" "Yes, sir," Eckhart replied.

"You allowed yourself to be defeated by women," The Wraith said harshly.

Silence fell. Eckhart's fliers looked on, feeling the tension between the two.

"I am sorry, sir," Eckhart finally said.

The Wraith regarded him for a long moment.

"Give me your parachute," he said flatly.

The Hauptmann stared at him.

"Sir?"

"Your parachute, Hauptmann. Give it to me."

He held out his hand.

Eckhart looked at his comrades. They all stared at him, and he knew that they understood the meaning of The Wraith's words. Eckhart took off his parachute, and handed it to the giant figure.

But surely he wouldn't - Eckhart thought.

"Now go to the hanger door."

Eckhart, his blood running cold, turned and marched towards the hanger door. The Wraith followed, his footsteps booming loudly in the Hauptmann's ears. To Eckhart, they sounded like the footsteps of Death. His men watched, but did or said nothing. They reached the door, and The Wraith activated his wristcom. The image of a bridge officer appeared above his wrist.

"Sir!" the officer came to attention.

"Open the main hanger door," The Wraith ordered.

"At once, sir." The officer pressed a button on the console before him. The massive door opened. The sound of the rushing winds that flowed around the gravship as she sailed through the air invaded the hanger.

"Go to the threshold, " The Wraith commanded.

The Hauptmann walked over to the opening and stared down at the fields far below. They were cruising at ten thousand feet. The wind tore at him. He swayed upon unsteady feet.

"I thought Schenk's fate would have impressed upon you the price for failure," The Wraith said, suddenly beside him. His cloak whipped about in the wind.

Eckhart met his icy gaze.

"Will you jump, or force me to throw you out?"

The Hauptmann turned his gaze upon his watching men. He came to attention, and saluted them in the old fashioned manner, bringing his hand to his temple.

"For the Fatherland!" he cried. He did an about turn and then stepped into space.

The Wraith advanced to the edge, and looked down. He stood there for what seemed a long time. Finally he tossed the parachute after the unfortunate Eckhart.

"Close the door," he commanded the bridge officer, who had seen all.

"Y - *yes, sir,"* the man said, his voice shaking.

The door closed with a clang, and The Wraith terminated the connection. He walked back to the gathering of fliers, who stared at him, appalled at Eckhart's fate.

"Who is the senior officer here?"

One of the fliers stepped forwards, and clicked his heels together.

"That would be me, sir. Oberleutnant Becker."

"Hauptmann Becker now. Congratulations on your promotion."

"Thank you, sir," Becker replied.

"I want you to hunt down those French aviatrixes and destroy them."

"I will find them and deal with them, sir," Becker said.

"I hope you do, Hauptmann," The Wraith said. *"You have my*

leave to launch your flyers. Don't rest until Deville and her bitches are dead."

"Yes, sir!" Becker said. "You heard the captain! Make ready your machines. We go to hunt! For the Fatherland!"

"For the Fatherland!" his men shouted.

As they ran to prepare their flyers, The Wraith stalked back to the bridge.

XI

Welcome to Britannia

We landed in the field from which the rescue mission had set out from. As we stepped down onto the field, we met two medics with a stretcher, who put Zorn onto it and took him to the field's first aid station. McKinnon's wounded men could walk, so they followed. The Major went with them. Louise and Symes walked up to us. They had obviously put their differences aside. The two were chatting merrily away, like old friends. It warmed my heart to see it.

"Alistair!" She ran up and hugged me, and then kissed me on both cheeks in the French manner. Symes watched, his face blank.

"It's good to see you, Louise. I thought you were done for."

"Ah! Oui, so did I." She grabbed Symes's arm, and pulled him close. "But this Britan, he will not leave me alone."

We all laughed. Symes smiled.

"And a good thing too."

The pilot of the transport stepped up, and held out his hand.

Louise took it, and they shook hands firmly.

"You're a damned good flier, Ma'amselle. Thanks for saving our bacon. I'm Captain Franklin."

"Captain Louise Deville. Merci. You are also to be congratulated, sir. It would not be easy to fly a machine that was so damaged."

"Thank you."

"And now, on to more important matters. Commander, where is

that wine you promised me?" She grinned.

"I'll see what I can scrounge up."

Louise kissed him. Symes's face went red. He cleared his throat, and went off to find the promised wine, grinning like a teenager.

"He is a good man, that one," Louise said.

"Yes, he is, " I agreed.

Franklin clapped his hands together.

"Follow me to the mess, everyone. I don't know about you, but I could eat a horse."

We trooped off after him, towards one of the larger huts. We entered, and found ourselves in the mess. Familiar sights and sounds from other war zones I had been in met me. A lieutenant ran up to us.

"Sorry I didn't meet you on the field," he said breathlessly. "I'm Lieutenant Adams. I'm liaison officer here. The base commander ordered me to look after you. This way, please."

He led us to a table, where food and drink had been set out. We sat down, and fell to gratefully. Adams stood there watching us for a moment, and then nodded to himself.

"Good, good. Well, I have to be off. Bloody paperwork." He grimaced. "Sorry, ladies." He threw us a salute, and hurried off.

"This is quite good," Doctor Molyneaux said, finishing his steak.

"Only the best for the fliers, doctor," Franklin said.

"But only water or tea to drink with it," Louise said sadly.

"Perhaps not," I said. "Look there."

Commander Symes had come in, and he was carrying a satchel. He came up and took out two bottles of bordeaux and a dozen glasses. He placed them on the table with a grin.

"Ta dah!" He said, spreading his arms.

"Ah!" Louise said. "Our saviour!"

She got up and kissed him.

Symes opened the bottles, and filled the glasses. He passed them around the table, and when everyone had a glass, he said: "To our good health."

"Good health!" We cried.

The fiery liquid burned down my throat. I coughed.

"Poor Alistair," Louise said.

"It will do you good, Mister Fussell," Symes said, smiling.

I managed to smile. I picked up a water jug that was on the table, filled my glass, and drank it down. It soothed my throat. I sighed with relief.

"That's no way to treat a good wine, Mister Fussell," Franklin said, grinning.

Zorn came up to the table. His arm was in a sling.

"Captain!" Symes cried. "Here, come have a seat." He pulled out his chair.

Zorn came and sat down. Symes filled a glass and gave it to him. The captain drank it down. The commander set a plate in front of him.

"Ah. Bordeaux. Lovely. Thank you, commander."

"How do you feel, captain?" I asked.

He met my gaze. He appeared to be his old self again.

"Much better, thank you, Mister Fussell. Commander Symes, Captain Deville, I want to thank you for saving us."

"We would like to offer our thanks to you too," Doctor Molyneaux said. "If not for you, my wife and I would be lying dead, or captives." He put his arm around her.

"You are very welcome," Louise said.

"Think nothing of it," Franklin said. "All part of the service."

Major McKinnon and his comrades entered the mess, and came

over to us.

"Another transport has been arranged, and will leave in ten minutes."

"Enough time for some food, Major," Zorn said, gesturing at his meal, which he was eating with gusto.

"And a drink, perhaps?" Loiuse added, holding up a bottle.

McKinnon grinned.

"Aye, lass. Tha' would be guid."

He and his men sat down. Symes and Franklin went up to the serving line, obtained some meals, and brought them back on a trolley. McKinnon and his men set to with a will. After their hasty repast, they were given wine, which they drank off quickly.

"A pity to be in such a hurry," Madame Molyneaux said.

"A guid soldier always eats fast, Ma'am. He doesna know if it will be his last meal." McKinnon wiped his mouth with a napkin.

"Once this terrible business is over, you are all invited to our home," Molyneaux said. "We will show you the pleasure of a leisurely meal."

"Tha' will be nice," the major said. "Thank you, doctors."

"It is our thanks to you for saving our lives, major," Madame Molyneaux said.

"Time, sir," one of McKinnon's men said as he checked his chronometer.

We all stood. Each of us gazed at the other. Would we all survive this conflict? There was no way to tell.

We left the mess, and headed towards a transport that was parked on the field. Four of Symes's fliers stood by it, and their gravflyers were waiting nearby. Franklin shook hands with all of us.

"Best of luck to all of you."

"And to you, captain," I said.

"We're to be your escort," Symes said, indicating his men.

"What about you, Louise?" I asked.

"My squadron is to stay here, and be equipped with those lovely gravflyers. We will show the huns that they are not invincible." She went up and kissed Symes. "Thank you for the wine, cheri. Perhaps we will meet again."

He looked deep into her eyes.

"Count on it. Good luck."

"And to you. Au revoir."

Symes hugged her, and then he and his men went over to their gravflyers to prepare them for takeoff.

"Good luck, Louise," I said.

She hugged me.

"Good luck, Alistair."

We boarded the transport. The engines were started, and then a few minutes later the transport and our escort took to the air. We formed up, and headed towards the channel and Britannia.

At the same time, the Germanian forces were destroying all opposition. The French and Britannic ground troops were far outmatched, and their ancient hovertanks were no use against the enemy's faster, and better armed gravtanks. The French and Britannic hovertank's burning hulks were scattered all over Europa's fields. Soldiers lay dead beside them; hundreds of valiant men who were simply swamped by the vast number of troops and armour that the Germanians had put in the field. Their weary comrades were in full retreat, save for a few small rearguard groups who were soon overrun and slaughtered by the Germanians. The retreat became a rout, and soon all of the remaining French and Britannic forces awaited evacuation on the coast of France. As those exhausted troops were being taken on board every available hovership, hoverboat, and airship, the Luftangriffkraft and The Wraith's gravflyers harassed and sank and shot down many of the craft with impunity. The Royal Air Service valiantly attempted to protect the vulnerable rescue vessels, but the numerical superiority of the enemy meant that they lost many craft, as well as suffering crippling losses themselves. The French Air Force had ceased to exist.

We flew over this scene of devastation, looking down upon the wreckage of two proud armies. Black columns of smoke rose into the air over the beach that was packed with retreating soldiers. Here and there were wrecked vehicles. Some of them still burned, as the enemy gravflyers strafed the unfortunates who were attempting to take cover.

"Such destruction," Andre remarked. "France has fallen. The Huns are victorious."

"Not forever, Andre," his wife said, patting his arm.

"*Hang on!*" The pilot cried, and threw the ship forward. I looked out of the window, and saw Germanian flyers swooping down upon us.

"*Get out of it!*" Symes cried in the transport flier's headphones, and he and his flight turned to meet the attackers.

As we fled, I saw them close, and fire. One of the Britans was hit, and his gravflyer turned over, and plunged towards the sea, trailing black smoke. A Germanian craft was also hit, and exploded in midair. I clenched my fist in satisfaction. But we were hurtling away from the fight, and I desperately tried to watch as they receded in my sight.

The last sight of them that I saw was a wildly spiralling mass of flyers; friend or foe indistinguishable as the distance between us increased. As we sped away from the fight, a brilliant orange fireball marked the end of one of the combatants. Who was shot down? Was it

Symes? The transport hurtled over the channel, racing towards safety as two little black dots broke off, and came in pursuit of us. Was it Symes and one of his wingmen?

I watched as the tiny craft grew in my sight. Were they Britans or Germanians? I couldn't tell. They were too far away. But they were coming up fast. If they were Symes and one of his fliers, we were safe. But if they were the enemy...

They drew closer, and with a shock, I finally made them out. They were the gray ships of the Luftangriffkraft. We were doomed.

"Pilot!" I cried. " They're Germanians! Faster!"

"She can't go any faster!" He yelled.

We hurtled towards the cliffs of Dover. So close, but yet so far! The Germanians closed upon us. They came into range, and the closest gravflyer opened fire. The transport jinked and weaved, her pilot desperately trying to avoid the deadly tracers. We were hit, and the transport began to trail smoke. As the enemy flier lined us up in his crosshairs for a fatal burst, a group of six Britannic gravflyers appeared, and the two Germanians broke off, themselves chased by four of the Britans. The other two gravflyers formed up with us. We heaved a collective sigh of relief.

A cheery voice came over the speakers. *"Welcome to Britannia."*

We flew on to safety, and landed at an airfield. As we disembarked, four royal steamcoaches accompanied by two armoured cars with an honour guard met us. The officer in charge came up and saluted.

"I am to take the doctors Molyneaux to Her Britannic Majesty immediately. The other passengers can go with us to the hospital, and have their wounds seen to."

"Thank you, lieutenant," Zorn said. "Shall we?"

We all got onto the steamcoaches, and headed towards Londinium.

I sat back in the luxurious seat, and watched the countryside go by. Andre and Yvette were in the steamcoach with us, and they also availed themselves of the opportunity to see the sights.

"Have you ever been to Britan before, doctor?" I asked.

"Non, M'sieur Fussell," he replied.

"The countryside is lovely," Yvette said.

"Yes," I said. "But Londinium is…" I searched for the words.

"Crowded?" Andre offered. "Dirty?"

"Well, it is crowded," I admitted. "But dirty? I don't think so."

Yvette laughed. "We lived in Paris, M'sieur Fussell. We know what big cities are like."

"Of course," I said, smiling.

"They are all the same," Zorn added. "I have been to many of the world's great cities, and they are all alike."

"What do you mean, captain?" Andre said.

"There are the rich in their quarter, and the poor in their slums. It is no different whether you are in Londinium, Paris, or Sydney. All cities have these areas, and those who occupy them."

"It is the human condition," Yvette said. "There are always the rich, and the poor. Would that it could be different."

"You are right, madam," Zorn said. "There is enough food and shelter for everyone in the world to share. But greed is the thing that makes that impossible. It is greed that drives The Wraith. His lust for power over all others is the cause behind this conflict. He and Falkenberg are not satisfied with what they have; they have to take everything."

"Let us hope that they can be stopped," Andre said.

"They will be, Ma Cher," Yvette said. "Evil only conquers for a time, but good eventually triumphs."

"You are so certain, madam?" Zorn said.

"I am, captain."

"At least we have you and your cure to save our queen and her suffering people," I said.

"We will do all in our power," Andre said.

And then we had arrived at the hospital. The cavalcade halted, and we all alighted. We were met by a group of orderlies, who came forward and took the Molyneaux luggage. Zorn and McKinnon and his men were taken to a ward, as Andre, Yvette and I were escorted down the antiseptic corridors to Queen Aurelia's room.

As before, Prince Henry was sitting at her side. As we entered the room and bowed, he came forward, and offered his hand to Andre.

"Thank you for coming, doctors."

"Your Highness, it is an honour," Andre said.

The orderlies brought the luggage in, and Andre opened one of the crates and started to bring out the tools of his trade.

Yvette came over to the bed.

"How are you feeling, Your Majesty?" She took up the queen's wrist, and felt her pulse.

"I am tired." Her face was pale, and her eyes were dull.

"You are sore? Pains anywhere?"

"No. I am just exhausted."

Yvette nodded.

Andre came over with a large hypodermic. It was filled with an orange liquid. He saw the queen's inquiring look.

"It is only vitamin C, Your Majesty. "A very high dosage."

She beckoned him to come forward, and he administered the vitamin.

Yvette explained: "When we were in France, Andre, like most of the population, was struck down by drinking the contaminated water. Luckily, his symptoms were only mild; a form of depression, and not The Blight. I had escaped infection because I never drink water. I always drink freshly squeezed orange juice. Perhaps there was a connection? I experimented, giving Andre daily doses of differing strength. I found that if I increased the dosage to four times the average daily requirement I could control the symptoms. Eventually, he was cured. Heartened by our discovery, we began the same treatment on the poor souls in the hospital in which we worked. Results had been very promising. All of the affected patients had responded well; no more had died, and had in fact been improving when unfortunately the Germanian invasion had forced us to leave France and escape."

"Vitamin C," I said, shaking my head. "Who would have thought it?"

The door opened. Doctor Mansfield came in.

"I'm sorry I'm late," she said. "I'm doctor Mansfield."

"Doctors Yvette and Andre Molyneaux at your service, doctor," Yvette said.

"Madam Molyneaux was just explaining the cure to us," Prince Henry said.

"It is mainly vitamin C," Andre said.

"We can show you the formula," Yvette added.

"Vitamin C?" Mansfield said. "I would never have thought of something so simple. We tried everything else."

She came up to the bed.

"How do you feel, Your Majesty?"

Queen Aurelia sat up. Her gaze was clear. Colour had returned to her cheeks.

"I feel much better. Amazing. Not ten minutes ago, I was exhausted.

Thank you, doctors."

"We will continue to give you more injections, and monitor your progress, Your Majesty," Andre said.

"Thank you, doctor."

"Can you show Doctor Mansfield how to duplicate your work?" The Prince asked.

"But of course, Your Highness," Yvette replied.

"We have many patients," Mansfield said.

"Then let us go and see to them," Yvette said.

"We thank you for help, doctors," Queen Aurelia said.

"We will do our utmost to save you and your subjects, Your Majesty," Andre said.

"You will be provided with anything you need," Prince Henry said.

They bowed to the royal couple. Mansfield bowed also.

"Then we will go about our work," Andre said.

Mansfield led them out of the room. At last there was hope.

"Well, Mister Fussell," Prince Henry said. "We would like to hear all about your adventure."

"Certainly, Your Highness."

XII

Attacking the Lucifer

The Wraith sat in his command chair aboard the *Viktor*. He had received a communication from his servant Finke. The scientist's image hung before him on his private viewscreen.

"Master, the repairs to the Lucifer have been completed."

"Good. I am pleased with this news."

"I was also able to increase the power of the ray projector by four hundred percent. This means that the weapon will destroy biological tissue on contact, instead of just causing random effects."

"Excellent!" The Wraith said. *"Have you tested it yet?"*

"Only on sheep, master."

"Then we must have some human test subjects," The Wraith said.*"Order Commander Priller to bring the* Lucifer *to me, and you will accompany him. We will test the ray on some prisoners."*

"Yes, master." Finke said.

The giant closed the connection. His viewscreen retracted, and folded itself back into the chair arm.

The Wraith's eyes glittered. He steepled his hands, his mind swirling with thoughts of destruction.

The *Viktor* flew on.

The Emergency Council was meeting again. Reading and the other councillors were joined by Airlord Gray, General Crompton, Zorn and I. We were watching and listening to Professor Graves, who was speaking on the main vidscreen. Doctor Mansfield was by his side.

"Doctor Mansfield and I have spoken to the Molyneaux, and have done much investigation of our own, and we now know what The Wraith's weapon is," Graves said. *"It is composed of supraviolet rays."*

"Supraviolet rays?" Reading echoed.

Graves nodded. *"Yes, councillor. Supraviolet rays are a highly concentrated form of ultraviolet rays, only they are much more powerful."*

"We have seen what the effect of ultraviolet rays can have on the human body," Mansfield added. *"High exposure to UV can cause cancerous lesions to form in healthy tissue. What The Wraith's weapon does is to bring about an accelerated affect of such disease. The Blight is a form of cancer."*

The door opened, and a messenger came in, He went up to Councillor Reading, and handed him a paper that Reading perused. The councillor's face was suddenly drained of blood.

He looked up, and regarded us.

"A communication was intercepted between The Wraith and one of his underlings; Finke. He informed his master that he has increased the power of the ray by four hundred percent, and they are going to test it on prisoners."

"This modification would mean that the weapon would instantly destroy human tissue," Graves said.

"That is correct, professor," Reading said. He was still shaken.

"Such a weapon must be stopped," Airlord Gray said.

"We must send a strike mission against the *Lucifer*," Zorn said.

"But Europa is lost," General Crompton said. "The evacuation of our troops is of paramount importance. The Royal Air Service must cover the evacuation. That means that there are no fliers to be had."

"We could contact Captain Deville and ask her to stop the *Lucifer*," I suggested. "She and her squadron are still in France."

"But they are engaged in holding back the Germanian advance," Gray said.

I turned to him.

"I mean no disrespect, my lord, but I believe that that is a useless gesture. the Germanians have overwhelming numerical superiority in the air. If we leave Deville and her fliers there, they will be killed, and I think that would be a waste. Far better to have them attack The Wraith, and stop this new incarnation of his weapon."

"Are you giving the orders now, *Mister* Fussell?" Gray said. "You are a civilian, and do not have the least understanding of the situation."

"I beg to differ, sir," I replied. "I have seen many armed conflicts, and am certain that we should send Deville and her squadron against the Lucifer. The evacuation of troops can continue successfully without their involvement."

The door opened. In came Captain Smith, accompanied by Commander Symes. Symes grinned and gave me a wink.

"To take but one gravflyer away from those holding back the enemy advance would weaken us to the point that the Germanians would overrun the remainder," Airlord Gray said flatly. "To take an entire squadron is ridiculous."

"What is ridiculous, my lord?" Captain Smith asked.

Gray indicated me with an arrogant flick of his hand.

"This fool believes that we should send a strike force against The Wraith's ship. He would weaken our defences to carry out a mission that would have a very slim chance of success."

"You do not agree?" Smith said.

"Of course I do not agree. We must hold the enemy back while the evacuation is in place. The Wraith and his weapon can be dealt with after that has been accomplished."

"Forgive me, my lord," Symes said. We *are* covering the troops. Can't some of the fliers who aren't engaged in that task go up against the *Lucifer*?"

"I take it you mean Deville and her squadron?" Gray said sarcastically.

"I do, my lord."

"It cannot be done," Gray said. "They must stay and hold back the enemy."

Captain Smith walked up to the table. He took a holodisk out of his jacket and placed it on the table.

"Gentlemen. This is what Her Britannic Majesty has to say about the situation."

He activated the holodisk. The image of Queen Aurelia appeared before us. She was sitting up in her bed.

"Gentlemen. Captain Smith has apprised me of the improved weapon that the enemy possesses. We must not allow him to use it."

"But, Your Majesty, the evacuation." General Crompton said. "We must ensure that our men are safely taken off the beach and returned to Britannia."

"They will be, general. I believe that the Royal Air Service are providing cover for them?"

"They are, Your Majesty," Airlord Gray said. "But we must not weaken the forces that are allowing the evacuation to proceed. If we remove a squadron, the Germanians will surely overrun us, and slaughter our men on the beach. If the enemy achieves total superiority in the air, those men are doomed."

"I do not believe that will happen," The Queen said. *"Our fliers will*

provide ample cover for them. Commander Symes has suggested that perhaps Captain Deville and her squadron could be used to attack the Lucifer."

Gray regarded Symes with disgust.

"I believe he is wrong, Your Majesty," Gray said.

"*I do not,*" she said firmly. "*He and his squadron will take Deville and her fliers along with some bombers to destroy the* Lucifer."

Once again Gray gave Symes a withering look.

"This is your command, Your Majesty?" he asked. His face was like stone.

"*It is. You are to provide Commander Symes with a wing of bombers, and anything else that is necessary for this mission.*"

"Very well, Your Majesty. But I would like my misgivings about this mission to be set down on record. If the mission fails, I do not wish to bear the blame for such a foolhardy enterprise."

"*No blame will fall upon you. Councillor Reading, please see that Airlord Gray's wishes are carried out.*"

"Yes, Your Majesty."

"*Commander Symes?*"

"Your Majesty?"

"*Good luck. Please give Captain Deville my regards, and thank her and her fliers for all that they have done for us.*"

"I will, Your Majesty. Thank you."

She ended the communication.

"Well, gentlemen, I believe there is nothing more to say," Councillor Reading said.

"No," Airlord Gray said, "there is not. Good day, gentlemen."

He and General Crompton took their leave of us.

"I'll go and get my squadron ready," Symes said.

"Good luck, commander," Zorn said.

I walked up to Symes and held out my hand. Symes took it, and we shook hands.

"I was sure that you had been shot down," I said. "I'm glad to see I was wrong. Good luck, commander."

"Thank you, Mister Fussell. I'll see you all later."

"You take with you all our hopes, commander," Reading said. "The *Lucifer* must be destroyed. We have no way of protecting ourselves against The Wraith's new weapon."

"We won't fail, sir." He gave us all a salute, and then left.

"Well then," Zorn said, "let us return to the *Vengeance*, Mister Fussell. She is being made ready for the inevitable Germanian invasion. Good day, gentlemen."

We also took our leave.

The evacuation of French and Britannic ground troops from France had almost been completed. Heavy losses had been sustained; of hovership, airship, and supporting flyers. Only two hundred and fifty men remained, strafed and bombed by the ubiquitous Luftangriffkraft. High above the carnage, Deville and her aviatrixes were engaged with the enemy. They were outnumbered four to one; the usual numerical superiority that the Germanian fliers preferred, but were doggedly continuing to fight, knowing that if the enemy gained complete control of the air, the men on the beach would be wiped out. Suddenly, a squadron of Britannic gravflyers arrived and joined the fray. The Germanians, now outnumbered, broke off and sped inland.

"Let them go," Louise sent to her comrades. She looked down at the beach. It was clear of the enemy's flyers. For the moment. She called the Britans.

"Thank you for your help."

"You're very welcome, m'a'mselle." It was Symes.

She grinned.

"Once again you come to my rescue. Now *I* have to supply the wine."

"That sounds reasonable." He laughed. *"I thought I'd find you in the thick of it. I have new orders for you. You and your squadron are to land immediately and be briefed."*

"Very good. Red Cats, return to base."

They formed up and headed towards their field, accompanied by Symes and his squadron. They landed, and Symes walked up to Loiuse's gravflyer. She climbed out of the cockpit, and tossed her gloves and helmet onto the seat.

"How do you like her?" Symes said.

"She is a pretty little flyer." Louise came up, and kissed him.

Symes stared into her eyes.

"Not as pretty as you are. Queen Aurelia sends her regards, and thanks you for all your help."

Louise smiled.

"What are these orders?"

"They concern an attack on the Lucifer. We intercepted a transmission. The Wraith's weapon has had its power increased. The Emergency Council met, and the decision to attack the Lucifer was reached. A wing of bombers is coming, and your squadron and mine are to escort them to the target."

"The council does realise that the Germanians have achieved almost complete air superiority in France?"

He nodded.

"There was some argument about it. Several officers said that the evacuation must have air cover. They believed that the mission was foolhardy."

"When was a mission like this one not foolhardy?" She raised an eyebrow.

Symes smiled.

The other fliers came up, and Louise and Symes turned to meet them.

"Off to the briefing room," Louise said.

They all trooped off, and entered the hut where the briefings were carried out. Symes and Louise walked up to the podium. They waited for a few moments while their fliers took their seats.

Symes handed her an envelope. This contained a paper with the information on the mission that the Emergency Council had discussed. She read it once to herself, and then she explained the gist of it aloud to the gathered fliers.

"New orders. An enemy transmission was intercepted. The Wraith's weapon has been upgraded. The Britannic Emergency Council met, and the decision to attack the *Lucifer* was reached. A wing of bombers has been dispatched from Britan. We are to rendezvous with them over the coast in thirty minutes. Then we are to proceed inland, escorting the bombers with Commander Symes and his men, engage the *Lucifer*, and destroy her. Commander Symes and his squadron are to provide close escort, and we are to engage any enemy fighters we encounter. I am in overall control of the mission. We are to refuel and re-arm immediately. Questions?"

The room was silent.

"Bon. Dismissed."

There was a scraping of chairs as the fliers hurried out of the room.

High over the ravaged fields of France, the *Viktor* and the *Lucifer* sailed along in formation. The *Lucifer*, four times the size of the *Viktor*, slowly approached from her starboard side. When the two gravship's boarding hatches were lined up, a boarding tube snaked out from the *Lucifer*, and extended itself towards the *Viktor*. It connected the two vessels together with a metallic hiss. Clamps locked together, and the docking hatches on the two gravships opened. The Wraith stepped out of the *Viktor's* hatchway, and strode back towards his vessel, his footsteps echoing in the boarding tube.

Finke stood in the *Lucifer's* hatchway, waiting for him. The scientist smiled to himself, knowing that his master was well pleased with his work.

The giant figure halted in front of him. Finke bowed.

"You are to be congratulated, Finke. Is the projector ready for the test?"

"Yes, master. The test site and the subjects have been arranged."

"Excellent. Let us proceed. Come."

With his cape billowing behind him, The Wraith swept past. Finke hurried to keep up with him. The hatches on both gravships closed. The clamps were unlocked.

They both proceeded to the bridge as the boarding tube was retracted. Both ships flew on towards the test site.

Louise, Symes, and their squadrons took off, and headed towards the coordinates where they were to meet the bombers. In twenty minutes, they saw them, and went to form up with them. As they came closer, they could see that the bombers were older, conventional machines.

"Mon Dieu! Are those ancient things even going to make it to the target?" Marguerite said.

"They look like they will fall out of the sky at any moment," said another French aviatrix.

There was a confused babble of amused voices over the comm.

"Quiet!" Louise sent. "Two, six, we'll have none of that talk. These men are very brave to go into combat, knowing that the enemy has ships that are much faster than their own. It is our task to escort them, not belittle them. Understood?"

There was a chorus of *"Oui, Mon Capitaine!"* over the comm.

Louise turned her comm unit to a private channel that she and Symes had arranged before they took off.

"I am sorry for that, commander," she sent.

"Don't worry about it," Symes replied. *"We give the bomber boys some stick ourselves. Trouble is, your ladies are right. These ships shouldn't even be flying, let alone be taking on a combat mission."*

"Let us hope we can keep them safe," Louise said.

"That's all we can hope to do."

"Oui. Deville out." She changed the channel. "Red Cats, watch out for enemy fighters. Call out if you spot anything."

Once again, she received acknowledgement from her squadron.

"You heard the lady," Symes said. "Let's make sure these bombers are protected."

"Roger, Bulldog Leader." The Britannic squadron replied.

They proceeded inland, keeping a sharp eye out for enemy gravflyers. They hastened towards the target, hoping that they would not be intercepted before they could carry out their mission.

They flew over the devastated fields. Here and there a smoke column rose into the sky. They were too high to see the wreckage on the ground, but all of them knew how the Germanian advance had crushed any resistance. All of them knew the importance of their mission. The *Lucifer* must be destroyed at all costs. Perhaps none of them would return.

"Enemy fighters! Twelve o'clock high!"

Louise looked up, and saw the Germanians, forty of them, diving down to the attack.

"Bulldog Leader, we will engage them. Stay with the bombers."

"Understood. Good hunting."

She lead her aviatrixes towards the enemy, climbing hard. The Germanians had the advantage of height, and numerical superiority, but as they rushed closer, she smiled to herself. They were all old autogyros; not one gravflyer was among them. As such, they were much slower than her squadron's machines.

"Time for the dance, ladies," she said, boring in.

Tracers shrieked around them as they closed at maximum speed. Louise got one in her sights. She pressed the firing button, and the Germanian craft exploded. She quickly shifted her aim again, and with a three second burst, dispatched another. Then they were among the Germanians, and their craft formed a whirling cloud of flashing guns, whizzing tracers, and fireballs as other ships were destroyed in a wild melee.

In ten minutes, it was all over. The Germanians had been shot from the sky. Only two of her companions had been lost, and one of them had managed to bail out.

"If those old clunkers are all that the huns have to put in the air, this mission should be a short one!" Someone called.

Cheers came over the comm.

"Where are their gravflyers?" Another asked.

"Quiet!" Louise said. "We will see them soon enough. Regroup with the bombers."

The squadron formed up, and they flew back and rejoined Symes and the bombers.

A light blinked on her control panel: Symes was calling her on the private channel. She changed over to it.

"Nice work," Symes said.

"They were only old machines, completely outclassed. I do not understand why they were even here."

"It doesn't matter. They didn't get to the bombers." He paused, and then went on. *"But I'm sure you're right, the gravflyers will show themselves before this mission is over."*

"Let us stay vigilant. Deville out."

She changed the channel.

They continued on, and in thirty minutes, they sighted the *Lucifer* and the *Viktor*.

"There she is!" Louise said. "Bombers, engage the *Lucifer*. All fighters, keep an eye out for enemy fighters."

The bombers armed their rockets, and they accelerated to attack speed.

An alarm shrieked on the *Lucifer* as the oncoming attack force was spotted. The crew hastened to their battle stations. In a few moments, every station had been manned, and they were ready to defend the ship against attack. The same scene was repeated on board the *Viktor*.

The Wraith sat in his command chair, his gaze fixed upon his personal viewscreen. The mixed force of fighters and bombers were displayed there. He checked the range. Twenty kilometres. They would be in rocket range in five minutes.

He activated his wristcom. An image of Hauptmann Becker appeared.

"Hauptmann, launch your gravflyers immediately. Not one of those

bombers are to come within striking range of the Lucifer."

"*Jahwohl!*"

The Wraith ended the call, and pressed a button on his chair arm. An image of the captain of the *Viktor* appeared before him.

"*Captain Hauser. The* Lucifer *must be protected at all costs. The new weapon must not be destroyed. Do you understand?*"

"*Yes, sir. I understand completely.*"

"*Good.*"

The Wraith closed the connection.

"*Commander Priller.*"

Priller crossed the deck to stand in front of the giant figure. He clicked his heels.

"*You are to take over the ship. I will join our fighters in repulsing the enemy.*"

"Yes, sir," Priller replied.

The Wraith rose from the command chair, and strode towards the hatch. The commander took his seat, and studied the viewscreen.

"All anti-fighter guns, prepare to fire."

The Wraith stepped out of the elevator into the hanger and walked over to his personal flyer, an advanced prototype that he had been impatient to test. She was a sleek, dangerous looking machine that was constructed of crimsonite. He climbed into the cockpit, and strapped himself in. He reached out and activated the launch sequence. As the gravflyer's engines and systems came to life, the cockpit closed, and the craft rose from the deck. The Wraith aligned himself with the main hanger hatch, and pushed the throttle forward. The gravflyer rushed towards the opening, and hurtled out into the air.

He turned away from the *Lucifer*, and joined the swarms of Germanian gravflyers that were rushing to intercept the enemy.

The bombers and their escort hurtled towards their target. But it was obvious that they would not get in range in time. The enemy craft sped towards them, and Louise saw that they were all gravflyers.

"Here they come! They are all gravflyers! Red Cats, engage. Keep them away from the bombers."

"Oui, Mon Capitaine!"

The two groups of fighters plunged towards each other. Safeties were flicked off, and targets were acquired. Gunports winked as they closed at attack speed. Here, a French gravflyer disintegrated under the impact of ripping shells; there, two Germanic craft collided and spun burning towards the ground as one of them was hit and slewed into his comrade. In moments, the two groups had rushed past each other. The black gravflyers hurtled towards the bombers. Louise and her companions turned about and rushed in pursuit.

"Now for it, lads!" Symes cried. "Get stuck into them!" He got one in his sights. It was just out of range, but he hoped that it would run into his fire. He pressed the trigger, and was gratified to see that he was right as the black machine broke up and fell away burning. Then the enemy was upon them.

They opened up as they closed in. The lead bomber was hit, and vanished in a huge explosion as her rockets went off. The others plowed doggedly on towards the *Lucifer*. The Germanians ignored the Britannic fighters, and attacked the slower bombers mercilessly. In seconds, two of them had joined their unfortunate companion. Tracers burned through the air, and explosions marked where other Britannic bombers had met their fate. In just moments, half of them had been shot down.

Louise and her squadron joined the fight. Gravflyers whirled about in a deadly cloud that surrounded the bombers, and tracers flew. She got on the tail of an enemy craft, and pressed the trigger. The black ship bucked as it was hit, rolled over, and plunged earthward, trailing black smoke. Louise looked about, and saw another Britannic bomber fall prey to three of the enemy craft.

"Merde! They are being slaughtered!" She rushed towards another enemy fighter.

The Wraith targeted a bomber. He pressed the trigger, and his nose mounted cannon sent a lethal hail towards the target. The cockpit disintegrated as the heavy shells tore through it. The bomber spun out of control, and dropped away, burning. The Wraith snap rolled, and as a Britannic gravflyer crossed his sights, he fired again, and the fighter exploded into fragments.

Symes and two of his wingmen had stayed close to two of the remaining bombers. As they desperately tried to keep the enemy off them, The Wraith hurtled down from above, just as the *Lucifer* came into rocket range. The Wraith's cannon spoke again, and its shells tore the bomber apart. She broke up, and went into a flat spin. Her rockets launched in all directions as she fell. One rocket hit one of Symes's wingmen, and destroyed the gravflyer in a fiery detonation. The other craft scattered as the rockets flew wildly, but one Germanian flier was unlucky, and was hit. He joined his enemy as his gravflyer exploded.

But this had given the other bomber an opportunity. As the fighters dodged and weaved to avoid destruction, he closed in, and with a shout of exultation, launched his rockets at the *Lucifer*. They streaked towards the target. The anti-fighter guns opened up on them in a desperate attempt to destroy them before they reached their target, but they came on, unscathed.

On board the *Viktor*, Captain Hauser saw the danger to the *Lucifer*. He knew that if the rockets hit her, she would be torn apart.

"Helmsman, Put us between the *Lucifer* and those warheads!"He ordered.

"Jawohl!"

The helmsman spun the massive wheel.

The gravship began to turn towards the rockets. They were too slow! Captain Hauser clenched his fists as he stared at the racing warheads. They must have more speed! He punched a button on his command chair's arm.

"Engine room, accelerate to maximum speed!"

"Jawohl!"

The *Viktor* shuddered as her engines were pushed into maximum speed. Slowly, they began to move, and then began to accelerate. As the rockets plunged towards their target, the *Viktor* came between them and the *Lucifer*, and they impacted her hull. The warheads tore through her and exploded. The *Viktor* fell away, her back broken, and she broke apart in a succession of detonations as she dropped towards the ground, far below.

The bomber pilot uttered a curse, and was then killed as his ship was hit by a hail of tracers as The Wraith caught him in his sights. None of the Britannic bomber force now remained.

Louise quickly scanned the sky, and realised that the bombers had all been shot down. There was only one thing to do.

"All fighters attack the *Lucifer*," she transmitted.

"Oui, Mon Capitaine!"

"Roger, Red Cat Leader. Attacking now."

The Wraith looked on in amazement as the French and Britannic gravflyers proceeded to attack the *Lucifer. Fools!* He thought. *Their little guns cannot hurt her.*

"Destroy them," he sent to his squadron.

"Jawohl!

The French and Britannic gravflyers strafed the gravship, harried by the Germanian fighters and the anti-fighter guns. One by one, they were shot down as they pressed their futile attack.

Symes realised that it was useless; the *Lucifer's* armour was too strong. He changed to the private channel and called Louise.

"Louise, this is suicide. Our guns are having no affect. We must retreat."

"The Lucifer *must be destroyed. No matter the cost. You know the order, commander."*

"Yes, but to throw our lives away in an impossible attack like this is futile. Give the order to retreat."

"Non. We will complete our mission, even if we all die."

"That's bloody stupid!" he cried.

Suddenly there was silence on his comm.

"Louise? Louise!"

She had changed the channel and was no longer listening to him. Symes shook his head and changed his comm channel.

"This is Bulldog Leader. All fighters break off and retreat. Break off and retreat."

"Roger, Bulldog Leader."

"Oui, Commander."

The remaining gravflyers broke off their attack, and fled towards the coast. Symes saw the indicator light on his comm blinking. Louise was trying to call on the private channel. He ignored it. Then he heard her angry voice on the main channel as she changed over to it.

"Commander! What do you think you are doing!" She was furious.

Saving our lives, he thought. He made no reply.

The Wraith watched the fleeing gravflyers. Their attack had failed.

And there is only one reward for failure, he thought.

"*Hauptmann Becker, pursue and destroy them,*" he sent.

"*Jawohl!*"

Becker and his comrades raced in pursuit of the decimated attacking force. The Wraith turned his machine towards the *Lucifer*. The main hanger hatch opened and he brought his gravflyer in to land. He switched off his engine and systems, and as the engines whined down, he opened the cockpit, and climbed out. He walked across the hanger deck, and approached the elevator. He pressed the button, and in a few moments the elevator arrived, and the doors opened. He stepped inside.

The doors opened on the bridge deck, and he stepped out and made his way to the bridge. He entered and strode over to his command chair. Commander Priller was standing waiting for him. The giant sat down.

"*Report.*"

"The *Lucifer* has suffered no real damage, sir," Priller said. "But the *Viktor* was lost with all hands."

"*Yes, I saw it. Make sure that a report of this combat is sent to Chancellor Falkenberg, and tell him of Captain Hauser's bravery. He died a hero to the Fatherland.*"

"Yes, sir."

"*Now that we have dealt with our uninvited guests, we can proceed to the testing ground.*"

"Yes, sir."

The *Lucifer* flew on.

XIII

The Invasion Begins

Symes, Louise, and what was left of the attack force hurried towards the coast, followed closely by Becker and his gravflyers. Several stragglers had been shot down, and the Germanians were closing rapidly. They flashed over the coast, and raced across the channel.

Glancing behind them, Louise realised that the enemy was almost within range. She called Symes.

"Commander. They will be in range in moments. Let us turn and fight."

"You're right. We can't outrun them. Give the order."

"All fighters, turn and attack. Turn and attack."

"Oui, Mon Capitaine!"

"Roger, Red Cat Leader."

They turned and streaked towards the oncoming enemy. Gunports winked, and tracers flew as they each opened fire. In moments there was a chaotic whirl of gravflyers circling and firing at each other. Two French machines went down in flames, and then a Britannic gravflyer exploded in midair.

Symes got on the tail of an enemy craft. He pressed the firing button, and with a short burst, riddled the gravflyer. She rolled over, and plunged towards the channel.

Louise engaged one of the enemy. They twisted and turned,

snapping off shots as each crossed the other's sights. They circled each other, trying to get on their foe's tail.

This one is good, Louise thought. She threw her little craft into a tighter turn, straining it to its limits. The black gravflyer inched towards her gunsight, and then flipped out of the way.

Where did he go? A rattle of bullets along her port side told her the answer. She rolled and kicked the rudder, going into a corkscrew. Louise glanced in her rear scanner. He was still on her.

She wrenched at the stick, and evaded a killing burst. Her machine was damaged, and was handling roughly. Suddenly, it shook as more bullets tore into it. The gravflyer yawed in the air, a sitting target.

"Hang on, chaps!" a voice cried in her headphones.

A dozen Britannic gravflyers hurtled in, guns hammering. Her pursuer was caught by a hail of lead. His machine broke up, and fell away, trailing black smoke. Three of the black craft were shot from the sky in the surprise attack.

The Germanians, now outnumbered, turned and fled towards the French coast. The newcomers let them go, and formed up with the survivors.

"This is Top Hat Leader. Follow us to Manston."

"Thanks for saving our bacon," Symes replied.

"No problem. All part of the service."

Escorted by the Britannic gravflyers, the battered remnants of the failed attack headed towards safety.

The Germanian gravflyers returned to the *Lucifer*. A flier came up to the bridge to report to The Wraith. He presented himself before the command chair, and clicked his heels.

"Report," the armoured figure said.

"We pursued the enemy until we caught up with them over the channel. We had engaged them, and had shot most of them down. A surprise attack by a group of Britannic machines forced us to retreat."

"I see. How many of the attackers survived?"

"I do not know, sir."

"Was Captain Deville shot down?"

"I am sorry, sir. I do not know. Some of the French machines were still in the air when we retreated. Perhaps one was hers."

The Wraith regarded him silently for a few moments.

"Why did Hauptmann Becker not report to me? Was he wounded?"

"No, sir. Hauptmann Becker was shot down, lost over the channel."

"Who is the highest ranking officer remaining among you?"

"I am, sir. Leutnant Fischer."

"You mean Hauptman *Fischer. Go and have your gravflyers repaired, and see to your wounded."*

"Yes, sir," Fischer replied. "Thank you, sir." He clicked his heels together and departed.

The *Lucifer* arrived at the test site. Below them, in a field surrounded by barbed wire and several machinegun posts, were one thousand Britannic and French prisoners in a hastily erected compound. The *Lucifer* came to a stop, and descended, until she was only one hundred feet above the ground. The prisoners looked up at the massive gravship, unaware of the awful fate that was to befall them.

"Lower the projector," The Wraith commanded.

He stood at the observation window. Finke was by his side. The scientist nodded to a technician who was at the weapon's control console. The man pressed a button, and the hatch below them rumbled open slowly. As the prisoners watched in trepidation, the hatch opened fully, and then the mirrored disc of the projector appeared, and was slowly lowered. The men below cried out in terror, and rushed in all directions. The Wraith's weapon was well known. Prisoners threw themselves upon the wire in a frenzy to escape. The machineguns opened up, and men fell, but the prisoners, knowing of the horrific fate of those exposed to the violet ray, seemed to seek a cleaner death than that of those poor souls who it touched.

"Energize the projector," The Wraith ordered, watching the tumult below.

A whine began in the ship. The prisoners, hearing it, went into a madder riot than before; tearing at each other, and trampling their comrades in a desperate but futile attempt to escape. The machineguns rattled, and as the bodies piled up, more and more men leaped into their deadly fire.

"Fire!" The Wraith cried.

The ray flashed out, and the technician swept the projector from side to side. As the ray touched each prisoner, he immediately mutated, his body breaking out in disgusting pustules. Their tongues swelled up and filled their mouths, and their skin soughed and darkened to an awful purple hue. The screams were choked off as each man was affected by the ray. In moments, they collapsed, and their bodies lost their shape as The Blight devoured them alive. Soon, nothing but rotting flesh filled the compound. Several of the machine gunners were violently sick, while their comrades turned away in horror. None could bear to look upon the horrific scene.

"A successful test, wouldn't you say, Erich?" The Wraith said. *"Very successful."* There was pleasure in his voice. *"You have done great work for the Fatherland today."*

Finke nodded dumbly. "Yes," he said softly, "Very successful." He was appalled at the results, but knew well enough not to say anything. The tests with the sheep had been awful enough, but to see men mutated and killed in such a way made bile rise in his throat.

"*Retract the projector,*" The Wraith ordered.

The technician retracted the projector and closed the hatch as The Wraith returned to his command chair and activated his personal vidscreen. Chancellor Falkenberg's image appeared before him.

"*Master, the test has been successful. The weapon has exceeded our expectations. The mutation is instant, and complete. The test subjects were all reduced to masses of flesh within moments.*"

Falkenberg was ecstatic. "*Now we will give the Britans an ultimatum. Either they surrender to us, or every man, woman and child on their island will suffer the fate of the prisoners.*"

"*I had the test filmed, and will send the footage to you for your enjoyment.*"

"*I look forward to seeing it. Where is Professor Finke?*"

The Wraith beckoned, and Finke came and stood before the vidscreen.

"*Ah, professor,*" Falkenberg said, "*you are to be congratulated. Fine work, very fine indeed. We will arrange a ceremony and an award in honour of what you have accomplished.*"

"Thank you, chancellor." He still felt sick to his stomach.

The chancellor addressed The Wraith: "*And for you, my friend, your reward for your service will be as I have promised. You will rule the Britannic Empire, and the island will fall under your dominion.*"

"*Thank you, master. I am your servant.*"

The chancellor broke the connection.

"May I be excused?" Finke said. "I wish to lie down. The stress, you see." His face was white.

"But of course, professor," The Wraith said. *"You have earned your rest."*

"Thank you, master." Finke almost ran from the bridge. He hoped he would reach his cabin before he was sick. What had he done?

The Emergency Council had met at the Queen's request. Her treatment at the hands of the Molyneaux had allowed her to leave the hospital. She now sat in a throne in the meeting room, and Prince Henry sat beside her. We were watching the horrific footage of The Wraith's test. As the awful images ceased, they were replaced by The Wraith himself. He stood on the bridge of the *Lucifer*, and as the image zoomed in, we could see the gloating look in his eyes.

"Slaves of Britannia. You have seen what my weapon can now do. It has been upgraded, and now is deadly to anyone who is exposed to it. Now it means instant and horrible death to those I use it upon. Surrender to me, or your island will be laid waste. Every man, woman, and child will suffer and die if you resist. I give you three days to respond."

The image wavered, and then blanked out.

"My god," Airlord Gray said. "those poor men. This madman has no mercy in him."

"He must be stopped, and his weapon destroyed," Captain Smith added. "Your Majesty, we must mount a raid immediately, and destroy the *Lucifer* before he can attack. I will take the *Victorious* and the *Glorious*, and we will blast him from the air."

Queen Aurelia held up her hand.

"One moment, Captain. Captain Zorn, are you fit to take command of your ship?"

Zorn nodded. "I am, Your Majesty."

"Tell us, captain," the Prince asked, "are our airships a match for his gravship?"

"I am afraid not, Sire," Zorn replied. "They are not fast enough. The *Lucifer*, like the *Vengeance,* can far outstrip any of the conventional airships."

"Then we must take the *Vengeance* to meet him head on," I said.

There was a murmur of agreement.

"There is something else, "Airlord Gray added. "We have intercepted a communication that gives us details of an invasion. There is a massive build up of troops and armour, and several of Falkenburg's airships have joined the *Lucifer* on the coast. The report also says that the Luftangriffkraft are gathering a huge force of gravflyers, both bombers and fighters."

"So they intend to attack no matter what our reply to his ultimatum is," Zorn said.

"Then we must stop the armada in the channel," Captain Smith said.

"That was my thought," Gray replied.

"Captain Zorn," the Queen said, "will you lead our Britannic forces against the enemy?"

Zorn bowed. "I will, Your Majesty. Our purposes meet as one. Your island and its people will be saved, and I will finally have revenge upon the one who destroyed my family."

"May I make a request, Your Majesty?" Professor Graves asked.

"Yes, professor?" She replied.

"If we could obtain more information about The Wraith's weapon, we might be able to devise a defence against it. Perhaps this Finke could be captured?"

"During a battle?" Gray scoffed. "Impossible."

Major McKinnon stepped forward.

"Sounds like a job for me and ma laddies."

"Major McKinnon," Queen Aurelia said, "do you think you could do such a thing?"

"It would be ma pleasure to try, Yer Majesty. Plus," he said, grinning, "we could plant some bombs on board the *Lucifer* while their attention is on the fight. They willna be expectin' tha,' and it would gi'e them a nasty surprise."

The Queen smiled. "Go then, gentlemen," she said, "and make our forces ready to meet the enemy. I wish you good luck."

We bowed to her and the Prince and departed.

The Germanic invasion force departed from France. Four thousand gravflyers, half of them bombers, formed a dark cloud high above the gravships that sailed below. The *Lucifer*, accompanied by six smaller gravships, flew majestically over the fleet as it headed across the channel. Fifty thousand troops were packed into the transports that flew in the air and sailed upon the water. In twenty minutes they would reach Dover.

The Wraith sat in his command chair on the *Lucifer's* bridge. He watched the progress of the armada as it was displayed on the main viewscreen. *This is the end of the Britannic Empire,* he thought. *They cannot stop us. I will rule Britan with an iron fist.* He raised his gauntlet, made a fist, and chuckled at his own joke. Several of the bridge crew heard, but said nothing.

The Britannic air forces, hastily assembled, took off from fields all over the island. They formed up in a giant wing, and headed towards the enemy. Commander Symes led a squadron of fighters, and on his port side was Louise, herself commanding The Red Cats. Their numbers had been supplemented by fliers from Britan. They were all women, in keeping with the squadron's makeup. Louise had insisted that they were women. All around them were the total number of fighters that the Empire possessed. There were no reserves. Every machine was in the air. Every flier had manned a craft in this desperate hour. Most were outdated autogyros, but apart from Symes and Louise, two other squadrons had been equipped with gravflyers. There was also Captain Miller, who was leading Zorn's gravflyers. But there were only four hundred and fifty of them against the massive Germanic force heading their way. Behind them came the *Vengeance*, Flanked by the *Victorius* and the *Glorius*. Also with them were four smaller gravships. They flew onward, going to their destiny.

On board the *Lucifer*, a bridge officer turned and addressed his master:

"Sir, enemy craft sighted."

"Put them on the main screen."

"Jawohl!"

The image of the Britannic force appeared on the viewscreen. They were only an indistinct cloud on the horizon.

"Magnify image."

The image zoomed in, and showed the makeup of the enemy force. The giant began to count the craft displayed. Then the metallic sound that the bridge crew knew was laughter erupted from his mask.

"Pitiful!" He exclaimed. *"Most of them are autogyros! Our gravflyers will slaughter them."*

Commander Priller stood at The Wraith's side.

"Sir, What of the *Vengeance* and those gravships with her?"

"*We will deal with them. Send to the wolfpack that we are attacking the* Vengeance. *They are to escort us.*"

"Yes, sir." Priller nodded to the comms officer, and the man activated his comm panel.

"Wolfpack, this is *Lucifer.* We are going to engage the *Vengeance.* You are ordered to escort us."

"*This is wolfpack. Understood.*"

"*This will be a day to be long remembered,*" The Wraith said. "*The Britannic Empire will fall, and I will finally destroy the* Vengeance *and her master. Communications.*"

"Sir?"

"*Order half of our fighters to engage the enemy, and the others to protect the transports.*"

"Jawohl!"

As the communications officer relayed the order, The Wraith turned to Priller.

"*Now we shall see that the* Lucifer *is stronger than the* Vengeance. *Bring Finke to me.*"

"Jawohl!"

Priller clicked his heels together, and went over to the communications officer.

"Call Professor Finke, and order him to the bridge."

"Yes, sir."

The armoured figure looked once again at the pathetic Britannic force. *Soon they will lie at the bottom of the channel,* he thought. *And Zorn and his ship will plague me no more.*

"*Battle stations!*" he cried.

The klaxon howled as the two groups headed towards each other.

Zorn and I were aboard the *Vengeance*. He sat in his command chair, and I stood at his side. We looked at the image of the invaders that was displayed on the main viewscreen.

"The *Lucifer* and those gravships are coming for us," he said, pointing out the advancing craft. "Communications."

"Yes, sir?"

"Inform Captain Smith that the *Lucifer* is headed our way."

"Yes, sir. "*Victorius*, this is the *Vengeance*. Be aware that the *Lucifer* and her escort are coming to engage us."

"*Victorius here. Understood.*"

"Battle stations!" Zorn cried.

As the alarm rang through the ship, I sought a chair and strapped myself in.

"Here we go," I said to myself.

Symes looked at the oncoming invasion force. *So many of them!* He thought. He checked his instruments. Everything was in the green.

"*All fighters, this is the Victorius. Attack now, repeat, attack now.*"

"Roger, *Victorius*," he sent. *Now for it!* He called Louise.

"Good luck."

"*And to you too*," she replied.

Then there was no more time for words. They accelerated, and bored in towards the enemy. Safeties were snapped off, and gunsights activated.

The autogyros had been ordered to attack the bombers, while the gravflyers were to engage the opposing fighters. The two groups of fighters hurtled towards each other at maximum speed. They opened up, and both sides suffered casualties. They passed each other, turned, and raced back in. In moments, the air was filled with whirling craft, zipping tracers, and trails of black smoke as machines were shot down. Here and there a fireball proclaimed another kill.

The *Vengeance* and her escort headed straight towards the *Lucifer*. Down in the hanger bay were Major McKinnon and his men. They were making themselves ready to board the *Lucifer*, capture Finke, and bring him to the *Vengeance*. Equipment was checked, and checked again. All of them were clad in light battle armour, and each wore the rocket pack that gave them their name. They were armed with machine pistols and electroswords. In all the Empire, they were counted as the most elite troops that Britannia had to put in the air. They also had the charges that they would place in the *Lucifer's* engine room. These were being checked when Major McKinnon received a call from the bridge on his wristcomm. Zorn's image appeared before him.

"Major, are you ready to go?"

"Aye, captain. Tha' we are. Just gi' the wud."

"We are closing on the Lucifer *now. Get your men assembled at the hatch. I want to get you closer to the target."*

"Understood."

"Good luck."

"And to you as well, sir."

Zorn ended the communication.

"This is it, laddies. Move to the main hatch. Stand by to go."

At his side, a grizzled veteran barked orders.

"Right! You heard the major. *Get ready!*" He was Sergeant Knight, one of McKinnon's most trusted men.

The major smiled as Knight's stentorian bellow filled the hanger.

The group took up their equipment, and walked over to the hatchway.

The escort ships opened fire as they closed in, adding to the destruction. One of the Germanic gravships exploded, and debris rained down. Moments later, one of the Britannic gravships suffered the same fate. She fell burning towards the channel far below.

Aboard the *Lucifer*, Finke entered the bridge and reported to his master.

"Ah, Finke. Good. I want you to use the ray on the Vengeance."

"Yes, master."

The scientist went over to the panel that controlled the weapon. Four technicians were standing by.

"Lower the projector," Finke said.

One of the men pressed a button, and the hatch opened. Another button was pressed, and the projector began to descend.

Captain Smith was sitting in his command chair on the *Victorius*. He watched the battle on the main vidscreen. Each side were taking casualties. He knew they must keep the invaders at bay, and ensure that the *Lucifer* and her escorts were kept busy, so that McKinnon and his men could carry out their mission successfully.

"Captain." A bridge officer spun around in his chair. "There is something being deployed from the *Lucifer*."

"On main vidscreen."

"Yes, sir."

The image of the projector appeared before them. Smith's blood ran cold. The weapon! If that were to be fired....

He stabbed a button on his chair arm.

"Fire Control."

"Yes, captain?"

"Lieutenant Ogilvie, the *Lucifer* is going to use the ray. We must not allow it to fire. Target information is coming to you now. Destroy it."

"Yes, captain."

Smith nodded to the tactical officer. He sent the information to Fire Control. The forward guns began to track.

"Energize," Finke said. "Target the *Vengeance.*"

A whine began in the *Lucifer* as the projector was energised.

"We have the target, captain," Ogilvie reported.

"Fire," Smith said.

The forward turret guns bellowed, and their shells hurtled towards the *Lucifer.*

The shells ripped into the *Lucifer's* hull. The gravship shuddered and rang with the impact.

Smith brought his fist down on the chair arm exultantly.

"Good shooting, Mister Ogilvie!"

There was chaos aboard the *Lucifer.* Alarms screeched, and Finke's men desperately punched buttons on their consoles.

"Shut it down! Shut it down!" Finke cried hysterically.

The technicians powered the weapon down. The alarm was shut off.

"Report!" The Wraith cried.

"Master, the projector is disabled. We must withdraw!"

"No! Go and repair it! We must have the weapon!"

Finke came over to him, his face white.

"But - but, that is *impossible*! The damage . . . we cannot *control* - "

The giant leapt out of his chair, and took Finke by the throat.

"I do not care," The Wraith hissed. *"Repair it, or I will crush your throat."*

Finke clawed at his master's armoured gauntlets. To break free was impossible. He was held in an iron grip. His eyes bugged out as the giant applied more pressure. The bridge crew watched silently.

Suddenly, his master released him, and Finke dropped to the deck. He gasped for air, and felt his tortured throat. The Wraith loomed over him.

"I gave you an order," he grated. *"Will you carry it out, or die on the deck where you crawl?"*

The professor looked up at his master. He knew that the threat was not an idle one. He slowly got to his feet.

"I will obey, master." His throat was raw.

"Good. Be quick about it."

Finke beckoned to his men. Two of the technicians came to him. He bowed to The Wraith, and then they left the bridge. The giant resumed his seat, and gazed at the viewscreen. Around them the carnage went on.

The main hatch on the *Vengeance* opened. The Air Commandos activated their rocket packs, and one by one, they flew out of the hanger bay. They raced through the combat zone, dodging falling wreckage and streaking tracers. Several of them were unlucky, and dropped away, either hit by debris, or shredded by bullets. The rest rushed towards the *Lucifer*, evading the gravflyers that fought around them.

A bridge officer on the *Lucifer* addressed his master.

"Sir! The *Vengeance* has launched flying troops. They are coming towards us."

The Wraith activated his wristcomm.

"Sir?"

"Hartz, there are flying troops coming to attack us. Intercept and destroy them."

"Jawohl!"

The Fliegen Sturmtruppen were assembled in the Lucifer's hanger bay. They marched over to the main hatch, and as it opened, they launched, and headed towards McKinnon's group.

"*Major.*" Sergeant Knight called McKinnon. "*Flyin' pigs inbound.*"

McKinnon snapped the safety off his machine pistol.

"Righto, laddies. Let's show them how to do it!"

Both groups opened fire as they converged. Men from either side were hit, and plunged towards the channel. But the Major's men smashed through the Germanians, and raced towards their objective. Hartz and his troopers regrouped and give chase, firing as they pursued.

The Air Commandos rushed towards the Lucifer. Anti-fighter guns on board the gravship swung towards them, and opened fire. A heavy concentration of bullets tore through the group, decimating them.

"Break formation and evade!" McKinnon sent. He dodged a fusillade of streaking tracers, and several of his comrades followed. Three were unlucky; they were hit, and their riddled bodies fell like stones towards the channel.

Hartz and his troopers began to close. With short bursts from their machine pistols, they cut down several stragglers. But then they had to dodge and weave to avoid the anti-fighter guns deadly hail. Four of their number fell, shot down by their own guns.

"*Lucifer!*" Hartz called. "Cease fire! This is Oberleutnant Hartz!"

The stream of tracers continued to fly without pause. Hartz and his companions flew erratically in a desperate attempt to avoid destruction. The gap between them and their quarry widened.

"*Lucifer!*" Hartz called again. "This is Oberleutnant Hartz! Cease fire!"

"*Hartz!*" The Wraith's cold tones sounded in his helmet. "*Stop those commandos.*"

"But, master, we are being hit by our own guns. I - "

"I am not concerned with your situation, Hartz," The Wraith said coldly. *"If you are under fire from the Lucifer, then remove your troops from her firing solution."*

"Master, we are in pursuit of the commandos. We cannot avoid the *Lucifer's* gunfire, as we are in the same line of fire. The *Lucifer's* guns are hampering us. If they could cease fire for a moment - "

"No. You are to stop them. The guns will continue to protect the Lucifer. *If even one of those commandos get to us, I will hold you personally responsible."*

The channel was suddenly silent. Hartz gritted his teeth, and dodged another burst.

"Forward!" he sent to his troopers.

The Fliegen SturmTruppen plunged after the Air Commandos.

XIV

Battle Over The Channel

Symes blasted an enemy flyer, and turned to look for another target. He got on the tail of a black gravflyer, and followed it in a twisting, turning fight. They were evenly matched. Each of them was an excellent flier, and each took snapshots at the enemy as they briefly entered their sights.

"Bloody hell," Symes muttered. "This fellow's good."

They chased each other through the combat zone, firing whenever the opportunity presented itself.

Louise spotted one of her squadmates in trouble, and went to her aid. With a short burst from her guns, she shot down the Germanian, who had obviously not even been aware she had been there. She gave her comrade's gravflyer a quick lookover. When she saw that the ship was badly damaged, she called her on the comm.

"Lucienne. Your machine is done. Return to base."

"But I want to fight, Mon Capitaine."

"I know you do. But you would not last a minute with your battle damage. Return to base."

"Oui, Mon Capitaine. Bon chance."

The gravflyer peeled away, and dove towards Britannia. Louise watched for a moment, hoping that no enemy gravflyer pounced. Louise watched until her comrade disappeared. Then she threw her gravflyer towards a swirling group of fighters.

Captain Smith sat in his command chair on the bridge of the *Victorius*. He was looking at the main vidscreen, which was displaying the battle's progress in tactical icons. Suddenly a salvo of shells hit the *Glorius*, flying on their port side. The airship exploded, rocking the *Victorius*, and began to fall away, burning and spinning. The icon representing the *Glorius* vanished from the vidscreen. Smith watched in dismay, and then grimly returned his attention to the fight as the *Glorius* disappeared from view.

The Britannic autogyros, although slower than the invader's gravflyers, had been fitted with the electromagnetic guns. This armament made up for their slower speed as they took a heavy toll of the Germanic bombers. But they themselves were suffering crippling losses, as one after another was shot down by the swift Luftangriffkraft gravflyers.

The Air Commandos had managed to make their way through the withering fire that the *Lucifer* had laid down. But half of them had fallen. The major glanced to either side, and noted their casualties. He gritted his teeth in determination as they headed towards their objective, the gravship's starboard hanger hatch.

He called Sergeant Knight: "Sergeant, is that rocket launcher ready?"

"*Yes sir. Coming into range now. Corporal Pierce.*"

"*Almost there, sarge.*"

McKinnon looked at the looming gravship. *Bloody hell,* he thought. *Tha's a damn big ship.* They plunged towards her. When was Pierce going to fire? *Now! Now!* he thought.

"*Rocket away!*" Pierce cried.

The warhead streaked past McKinnon on a white tail of smoke. It hurtled towards the Lucifer, and impacted the hatch dead centre.

Seconds later, it exploded. The hatch was torn off, and fell away. The hanger bay lay open.

"Guid shootin', Pierce!" McKinnnon sent.

"Thank you, sir!" the corporal replied. He dropped the rocket launcher, its work was done.

"Let's go, laddies!"

McKinnon and his men poured into the hanger bay, and immediately encountered resistance. Machine pistols sent a hail of lead in both directions. Hartz and his remaining troopers landed behind them, and caught the commandos in a crossfire. They were pinned down.

McKinnon ducked for cover, and called out on the general channel.

"Any fighter, this is Major McKinnon. We have boarded the *Lucifer*, but are pinned down. Need assistance!"

"This is Red Cat Two. Acknowledged, major. Sit tight. I am on my way."

Sit tight! McKinnon fumed. Bullets ricocheted around him. Where was she?

Oberleutnant Hartz waved his men forward. They slowly advanced, guns blazing. To McKinnon's men, it seemed that every gun in Germania was sending a hail of steel at them.

Where the hell is this flier? McKinnon thought.

As if his thought had summoned her, one of the French gravflyers came to a jarring halt outside of the hanger bay. It was Marguerite. As she hovered there, she opened up on Hartz's troopers. She moved her ship from side to side, and mowed them down. She saw McKinnon, and threw him a salute. Then she hurled her craft away as a black gravflyer fired a burst at her. They dropped out of sight, engaged in their own battle.

The gunfire from inside the ship slackened, and the major knew it was now or never. He rose to his feet.

"Into 'em. laddies!"

His men charged the defenders, and after a few moments of savage fighting, cut them down. As his men checked the bodies and wounded, the major called Zorn.

"Captain, this is McKinnon. We've taken the hanger. Moving on to objectives."

"Good work, major. Call us when you're heading back, we will give you covering fire."

"Aye, will do. Guid luck, captain."

"And to you, major. Zorn out."

On the *Lucifer's* bridge, an officer turned and reported: "Sir. We have been boarded."

The Wraith cursed. His bloodshot eyes blazed with anger.

"Where?"

"Starboard hanger bay, sir."

With an inarticulate roar of rage, the giant surged to his feet.

"Commander Priller, take charge of the ship!"

As Priller came and sat in the command chair, The Wraith stormed out of the bridge, and strode down the corridor.

He raised his left arm, and with the push of a button on the utility unit that he wore there, he activated his undead troopers. They were held in alcoves in the bowels of the ship in a dormant state. As one, they stepped out of the alcoves and turned towards the hatch. The Wraith pressed another button, and the hatch opened. The troopers poured out of the compartment and headed towards McKinnon and his men.

The undead troopers rushed towards the main hanger. They burst in, and began firing immediately. They charged the commandos, ignoring the heavy toll the Britannic guns inflicted upon them. Behind them came The Wraith. He drew his pistol and joined the fight. His troopers advanced, attempting to force McKinnon's men out of the hanger. But the courage of the Scotsmen held, and as the undead troopers pushed forward, the commandos held their ground, drew their electroswords, and met them in a savage hand to hand battle.

Symes was under attack by two gravflyers; one of them piloted by Hauptmann Fischer. No matter what Symes did, the enemy stuck to his tail like glue.

He called out for assistance: "This is Bulldog Leader. I'd appreciate some help here." There was no reply.

He glanced in his rear scanner as tracers whipped past his cockpit. One of the Germanians was in the perfect firing position. It was Fischer.

This is it, Symes thought. He waited for the impact of hot lead.

Just as Fischer lined him up in his sights, Louise and Marguerite streaked in, guns flickering. Fischer dropped away, shot through the head, and his wingman exploded in a brilliant burst of flame.

The two French gravflyers formed up on either side of Symes's craft. He glanced over, and saw Marguerite waving. He waved back, looked the other way, and saw Louise. He gave her a thumbs up.

"That's another bottle you owe me, cherie."

"I'll buy you two. Thanks very much, ladies."

"You are welcome, commander," Marguerite said.

"Shall we rejoin the dance?" Louise said.

"After you," Symes said.

They turned and headed back into the fight.

On board the *Lucifer*, McKinnon and his men had prevailed. Only The Wraith faced them. The undead troopers lay sprawled upon the deck, along with many of McKinnon's men. But the commandos had held their ground, and proved that The Wraith's troopers were not invincible. Now the commandos covered him. If he made the slightest move, they would shoot him down.

The giant figure and McKinnon regarded each other.

"You men with the charges get to the engine room," McKinnon ordered.

"Yes, sir," one of them replied. They hurried away.

"Sergeant Knight."

"Yes, sir?"

"Go and find the scientist."

"Right away, sir."

Knight and the others headed off to find and capture Finke.

McKinnon slung his machine pistol over his shoulder and drew his electrosword. He activated it, and the blade hummed with power.

"It looks to me like ye've lost," McKinnon said.

"Is that what you think?" The Wraith replied.

He regarded the major with disdain, threw his pistol away, and drew his electrosword. They charged at each other, and their blades met in a shower of sparks and a clang of metal.

Despite having overwhelming superiority in numbers, the Luftangriffkraft flyers were being shot from the sky. The Britannic fliers, knowing how desperate the situation was, fought bravely, and pressed their attacks home even if they were wounded or their flyer was damaged. This dogged determination began to demoralise the enemy, who had expected to achieve an easy victory.

Below them, the invasion fleet had suffered appalling losses, strafed by the Britannic flyers, and also fired upon by two of the Britannic gravships. One of the transports turned to flee. The others joined it, and it soon became a rout; each ship rushed to escape the hellfire of the channel. Many of them were destroyed as they ran.

The bomber leader saw the hasty retreat and broke formation. He turned to run for home. The rest of the bombers scattered and fled, and the Germanic fighters broke away, and left them to their fate.

With shouts of exultation filling their headphones, the Britannic fliers gave chase, sending many of the unprotected bombers down in flames. Trailing smoke, their comrades ran for their lives with the RAS craft in hot pursuit. The tide of the battle was turned.

McKinnon and The Wraith were locked in combat. Electrical arcs snapped from their blades as the pair fought. They were evenly matched; The Wraith obviously had the skill of a fencer, and the major had great strength, and had also been tutored in the sword fighting arts. The Wraith's power armour gave him immense strength too. But Mckinnon was a large man, and held his own. They dealt each other huge blows that would have killed lesser men. Their armour was dented and rent, but each of them fought on.

The Britannic flyers chased the enemy craft right up to the French coast. As the Luftangriffkraft fled inland, anti-fighter guns opened up on the pursuers.

"That's enough," Symes called. "Let's go back home."

"*Agreed, Bulldog Leader,*" Louise sent. "*All fighters, head for home.*"

The formation wheeled, and went back across the channel. They looked down upon the devastation. Falkenburg's invasion fleet had been decimated. The landing craft had all been destroyed; their burning, sinking hulks covered the channel as far as the eye could see. Columns of black smoke ascended into the air. The bodies of thousands of troopers floated amongst the wreckage in the water.

On board the *Vengeance*, a deck officer reported to Zorn: "Sir, The *Lucifer's* escorts have all been destroyed."

"Very good. Communications."

"Yes, captain?"

"Any word from Major Mckinnon?"

"No, sir."

A shell from the *Lucifer* struck us. Even though she was now alone, the gravship continued to fight. Zorn regarded the viewscreen. We were approaching the coast of Britan.

"Communications, get me Captain Smith." Zorn's face was troubled.

"Yes, sir."

The main vidscreen showed the captain's image.

"Smith here."

"Ah, captain. Are we to fire upon the *Lucifer*?" Zorn asked. "In five minutes we will be over Britan."

Smith looked grave.

"I am afraid so, captain," he said. *"The* Lucifer *must not be allowed to make land. She could cause havoc with her new weapon. We are to engage and destroy her."*

I unbuckled my safety harness and rose to my feet.

"But captain, what about McKinnon and his men?"

"I am sorry, Mister Fussell, but we have had no contact with them. They must be dead. It is imperative we stop the Lucifer.*"*

"But you don't know that they're dead. You must give them more time," I said.

"Time is something that we have run out of, Mister Fussell. The Emergency Council has ordered that the enemy gravship is to be stopped at all costs. Captain Zorn, engage the Lucifer. Victorius *out."*

The communication was terminated.

The Britannic flagship's main guns opened fire. The salvo struck the enemy gravship, and she shuddered with the impacts. But her guns continued to fire. We were hit again.

Zorn brought his fist down on the arm of his chair.

"Fire control."

"Yes, sir?"

"Engage the enemy with main guns."

"Yes, sir."

I crossed the deck to stand in front of Zorn's chair. He looked up at me, and I could see the pain on his face.

"McKinnon - " I began.

"Their lives are nothing to the survival of Britan, Mister Fussell."

"You could be killing them yourself," I said bitterly.

"That is possible. They are soldiers, and know the risks of battle. They would understand."

"Would they?" I said heatedly.

Zorn turned his icy gaze upon me.

"It is an *order*, Mister Fussell. To be carried out without question. Resume your seat."

I stood there fuming. How could Zorn give an order that would send McKinnon and his men to their deaths?

"Captain, I must protest - "

"Mister Clarke," Zorn said icily, "escort this gentleman to his cabin, and ensure that he stays there until the battle is over." He turned his attention back to the main vidscreen.

Clarke came up to me and took my arm in an iron grip.

"Come on, sir," he said.

As he led me away, I heard the electromagnetic guns fire. I looked back at the viewscreen, and saw the projectiles tear through the *Lucifer.* How long could she withstand such bombardment? The hatch closed behind us, cutting off the view. Clarke marched me down the corridor.

The men McKinnon sent to the engine room burst into the control room, and killed the crewmembers there with a withering blast of machine pistol fire. The deck outside was littered with the bodies of the rest of the engineering staff. The commandos hurriedly planted their charges as they felt the impact of shells on the hull. One of them ran to the throttle levers, and pulled them to zero. The mighty engines ran down and stopped. They set the timers, and beat a hasty retreat.

The Britannic gravflyers arrived over the combat zone. The *Victorius* and *Vengeance* were hammering the *Lucifer* mercilessly. Shell after shell streaked through the air, and ripped through the enemy gravship.

"That's a fine sight," Symes said.

"*There are no enemy gravflyers about,*" Louise sent.

"*She's on her own,*" one of the Britans exclaimed.

"*And dead in the air,*" an aviatrix added.

"Let's watch the show," Symes sent.

"*The badly damaged craft should return to base,*" Louise said.

"Good idea," Symes agreed. "You heard the lady. All damaged craft, return to base."

"*Roger, Bulldog Leader,*" someone replied. "*Enjoy the show.*"

Trailing smoke, or flying sluggishly, the damaged ships limped towards home.

"Let's get a bit closer," Symes said.

"*What about their defences?*" Louise said.

Symes looked the gravship over. He nodded to himself in satisfaction.

"Their anti-fighter guns are down. Only two of their forward guns are firing. We should be in no danger if we approach from behind."

"I do not like it. It could be a trap," Louise said.

Symes laughed.

"A trap? I don't think so. I imagine that they have too much on their minds for that. I'll go and see."

"Be careful," Louise replied.

"Always," Symes said.

He descended towards the gravship, his attention fixed on the anti-fighter guns. *No use in being reckless,* he thought. *If they open up, I'm off.* But the guns remained silent. He approached and hovered only a kilometre away. *Their fire control must have been hit,* he thought. *Or the hydraulics, or even the crews for those guns could be dead. Poor devils.*

"Commander?"

He shook himself from his reverie.

"It's okay. No hostile action. The guns are down. Come and enjoy the show."

"Acknowledged. Coming down now," Louise replied.

The remaining Britannic and French fighters came and joined him. He looked to starboard, and saw Louise. He gave her a thumbs up, and then returned his attention to the *Lucifer.* They sat there and watched the battle as though they were at a show.

On the *Lucifer's* bridge, Commander Priller called the engine room. There was no response. *Why have we stopped?* he thought.

"Engine room! Respond!" He turned to a deck officer. "Karl, get down to engineering. Communications must be out. We must retreat."

Another shell hit the ship, and she rang like a bell with the impact.

'Jawohl!" The deck officer ran out of the bridge.

"Main guns, continue firing!" Priller cried.

In the ship's belly, Finke and his technicians had almost finished repairing the projector. As they winced from every impact of shell, they worked desperately to make the weapon ready. They were dangerously close to the tanks that contained the fluid the projector used to power the ray. They eyed it uneasily as they hurried to finish the repairs.

With a shattering roar, the charges in the engine room went off. The control room was obliterated, and the *Lucifer* slowly rolled to starboard.

In the hanger bay, The Wraith and McKinnon were thrown off their feet, and they slid across the deck. Bodies and wreckage tumbled around them as the *Lucifer* tilted.

On the bridge, Captain Priller and his surviving officers were hurled to the deck. Klaxons howled as the gravship rolled further. Priller grabbed onto the command chair, and struggled to his feet. He realised that the *Lucifer* was doomed, and activated his wristcom.

"Abandon ship! Abandon ship!" he cried.

The gravship heeled over, and bodies and debris rained down from open hatches and holes ripped in the hull. The giant and the major tumbled towards the open hanger hatch. McKinnon activated his rocket pack, and rose from the tilting deck. He dodged the falling wreckage, weaving in and out desperately as dead bodies and equipment flew past him. He reached a clear space, hovered in the air, and turned to see his opponent sliding towards the open hatch. The Wraith was scrabbling for a hold, but his armoured gauntlets only struck sparks from the metal deck plates as they vainly sought for purchase. In seconds, he reached the hatch, and was gone, plummeting towards the channel far below. McKinnon flew out of the ship, hovered, and peered downward. The Wraith had disappeared from view. He turned and headed towards the *Vengeance* as the *Lucifer* rolled over onto her back.

He activated his comm.

"All commandos, return to the *Vengeance*. I repeat, return to the

Vengeance." He glanced behind, and saw his men exiting the doomed gravship. he called the *Vengeance.* "Captain Zorn, this is McKinnon."

"Zorn here."

"We're on the way back, sir. The *Lucifer* is finished."

"Good work, major. And Finke?"

"I don't know, sir."

"Knight here, major. I'm sorry, sir, but we couldn't find the bugger."

"There's yer answer, captain," McKinnon said. "But I have some guid news for ye."

"What is that, major?"

"The Wraith is dead. We fought wi' electroswords, and when the *Lucifer* rolled, he fell oot the hanger hatch. I went to look, but I couldna see him."

There was silence on the channel.

"Captain?"

"I am here. That is good news, major. But we must be sure he is dead. We will send a party to look for his body."

"I dinna think that would do any guid, sir. He would sink like a stone in tha' armour."

"You are right, but I would like to be certain. Return to the ship. Once again, well done."

"Thank ye, sir."

"Zorn out."

"Righto, laddies. Home we go. Sergeant, get those men moving!"

"You heard the major! Get a bloody move on! This isn't a picnic!"

McKinnon grinned as Knight's stentorian voice hammered in his ears. The surviving commandos formed up, and flew towards the *Vengeance.*

Finke and his companions screamed in terror as the gravship

turned over. They were thrown about the compartment like rag dolls. The tank ruptured, and the deadly energy of the supraviolet ray was unleashed. It swept over the screaming men, mutating them. The awful fate that was suffered by the prisoners in The Wraith's test was now meted out to them. In seconds, they were only masses of unidentifiable flesh. The energy formed a ball that radiated outwards in a deadly sphere of destruction. It expanded quickly, catching Priller and the escaping crew. They suffered the same fate as Finke and his technicians.

Louise and Symes and their companions were watching the doomed gravship. The *Lucifer* was sinking fast, falling towards the channel. She burned, trailing thick black smoke, and small explosions went off all along her hull. Suddenly, the orb of supraviolet energy appeared, spreading rapidly outwards.

"Scatter! All craft scatter!" Symes cried.

The flyers turned away from the *Lucifer*, and rushed in all directions, desperate to escape the effects of the sphere of destructive energy.

"*Major!*" Knight's cry of alarm rang in McKinnon's ears.

He looked behind, and saw the rapidly expanding orb.

"Run, laddies!" He flicked the switch that activated the emergency power in his rocket pack. It would accelerate at maximum speed, but only for a few seconds. His men followed suit, and they hurtled towards the *Vengeance* as the energy rushed towards them.

On board the *Vengeance*, Zorn saw the expanding cloud, and cried out an order: "Helm, turn us away from that energy! Engine room, emergency speed!" The gravship began to turn away.

On the *Victorious*, Captain Smith stared at the orb aghast, and then shouted an order: "Helm, escape course! Engine room, emergency speed!"

Both ships turned to flee.

The energy rushed outwards, claiming some of the old autogyros who were not fast enough to escape. The fliers in them died horribly as the supraviolet energy swept over them. Their flyers, now unpiloted, spun and whirled out of control, and plunged towards the water.

The Air Commandos ran, mere insects in the path of the giant sphere of energy. McKinnon looked behind, and saw some stragglers overtaken. They suddenly flew in all directions, reduced to insensate masses of flesh. He gritted his teeth, and looked at his power indicator. The burn would return to normal thrust in five seconds. Did they have enough speed to escape?

The *Vengeance* sped away, easily outdistancing the wave of death. But the *Victorious*, damaged, and much slower, frantically scurried to reach a safe distance. She vibrated under the engine's emergency power. Fittings rattled, and charts and small objects rolled across desk tops, and fell to the deck. Captain Smith and his crew watched their approaching doom. They realised that they could not get clear. The rate at which the sphere was expanding meant that they would be engulfed. Their ship was too slow to escape, even though she ran at top speed. The damage that they had sustained was too great.

Smith turned to his officers and men and saluted them. They rose to their feet and returned the salute.

"It has been a privilege serving with you, gentlemen," Smith said.

The energy sphere closed in. Every man on the bridge stood waiting for the cloud to take them in its deadly grasp. It loomed larger in the main vidscreen.

Suddenly, With a thunderous roar, the *Lucifer* exploded. The expanding sphere of death dissipated as the gravship disintegrated in a huge fireball. The wreckage of the gravship drifted downward amidst a violet cloud that slowly faded.

"She's blown up!" Knight cried.

McKinnon's emergency thrust ceased. He slowed and turned. He heaved a sigh of relief as he watched the debris of the *Lucifer* fall. Sergeant Knight and the others caught up to him. They hovered there and looked on.

"All right, laddies," McKinnon said. "Show's over. Let's go home."

"You heard the major! Form up!"

The small group got into formation, and headed towards the *Vengeance.*

Symes and Louise and the other surviving flyers, all gravflyers, watched the cloud until it vanished. They saw that the *Victorious* had escaped, and cheers crackled over their headphones as they rejoiced for the flagship's getaway.

"This is Bulldog Leader. All fighters head for home," Symes said.

"Roger, Bulldog Leader."

"Acknowledged. Heading home."

"What about that victory wine, Commander?" Louise said.

"Absolutely, captain. We deserve it."

"Call me Louise," she said.

"I'm Ian," Symes replied.

"I look forward to a victory celebration, Ian."

They headed towards their base.

Aboard the *Victorius,* the bridge crew cheered themselves hoarse. Relief at their escape from an awful fate showed on every man's face. Smith allowed them a few moments to celebrate their good luck, and then he sat down in his chair.

"Helm, set a course for home," he said. "Engine room, make half speed."

His men resumed their stations, and they felt the engines reducing thrust. The shuddering of the gravship eased off, until it became the throb that was felt when she was in normal flight. In a moment, it was as though they were just on a pleasant cruise.

On the *Vengeance's* bridge, the crew cheered to see the *Victorius's* escape. Zorn watched the wreckage of the *Lucifer* fall towards the channel. He closed his eyes. *My family is avenged,* he thought. *Now their spirits can rest.*

He opened his eyes and gave an order: "Communications, get me the *Victorius.*"

"Yes, captain."

On board the *Victorious*, the main vidscreen was activated as the incoming call was received. Zorn's image was displayed.

"*I congratulate you on your lucky escape, captain,*" he said.

"Thank you, captain," Smith replied. "I must add my own congratulations, sir. The Wraith has been killed, and the *Lucifer* destroyed. Your family has been avenged. Surely this is a great day for you?"

Zorn smiled.

"*It is indeed. Thank you, captain.*"

"We will see you back at base," Smith said.

"*Just as soon as we pick up Major McKinnon and his men.*" He closed the connection.

"Helm, take us home," Smith said.

"Yes, sir."

Aboard the Vengeance, Zorn called McKinnon: "Major? Are you there?"

"*We're still here, sir. We'd appreciate a lift.*"

"Engine room, slow to one third," Zorn said.

"*One third, sir.*"

"Open main hanger doors."

"Hanger opening," a bridge officer reported.

"We're on our way. McKinnon oot."

Zorn turned to Lieutenant Clarke, who had returned to the bridge.

"Mister Clarke. Go and bring Mister Fussell to me. He has a story to write."

Clarke grinned.

"Yes, sir."

He left the bridge, to come and release me from my prison.

A deck officer reported: "Sir, Major McKinnon and his men are safely aboard."

"Very good. Close the hanger bay hatch. Helm, course for home. Engine room, best speed."

"Course for home, sir."

"Engine room, roger. Best speed."

The *Vengeance* headed for Britan. Zorn took one last look at the scene of the *Lucifer's* end, and felt a huge weight lift from his shoulders. He sat back and closed his eyes, and relaxed for the first time in many years.

The fliers landed at their respective fields. The ground crews greeted them as heroes, cheering and hailing them. Symes and Louise and their remaining comrades landed at Manston. Louise and her surviving Red Cats went and met Symes and his RAS companions. Hugs and handshakes were shared all around. And from the French girls, kisses that the Britannic fliers didn't object to.

"What about that wine, Ian?" she asked.

Symes gestured at the hut that held the bar. He crooked his arm, and Louise put hers through it.

"Right this way, ma'am."

They led the laughing, smiling fliers down the path to a well deserved victory drink.

The *Vengeance* landed at the Londinium airship docks. Zorn and I descended in the landing platform, to be met by a cheering crowd of people. I had arranged for several vidcrews to be aboard the *Victorious* and the *Vengeance*, and we had broadcasted the battle over the Imperial Vidscreen Network. The entire population had watched, with bated breath, to see the outcome. Now that The Wraith and his deadly weapon had been destroyed, they exulted in victory. As we were surrounded by a grateful and congratulatory crowd, the *Victorious* appeared overhead, and another cheer was raised for Captain Smith and his gallant crew.

The flagship docked, the gangway was lowered, and Captain Smith descended, to a tumult of applause. We went to meet him, and exchanged handshakes as the rapturous cheering continued deafeningly. Hats were flung into the air as all Londinium revelled in our triumph over The Wraith and Falkenberg's forces.

XV

The Aerocorp

Chancellor Falkenberg listened to his spy's report of the destruction of the invasion fleet. His lip curled, and his eyes blazed in anger as his agent confirmed the scattered reports that had come his way earlier that day. How had this devastating defeat happened? The invasion fleet had been well equipped, and covered by bombers and fighters. The loss of the *Lucifer* and her escort gravships had been a heavy blow. Only gravflyers had returned, routed by the combined force of the French aviatrixes and the RAS fliers. Thousands of troops now lay at the bottom of the channel, or floated lifelessly amid the wreckage of the once proud Germanian force.

Falkenberg held up his hand to stop the flow of words. His spy, his identity masked by the distortion that was displayed on the viewscreen, ceased speaking. The chancellor sat in moody silence for several minutes. His agent held his peace, knowing that to interrupt his master's thoughts was a dangerous thing to do. Even though he was in Britan, he knew that if Falkenberg wished it, he could have him killed if he displeased him.

The chancellor's fist crashed onto the tabletop. He rose to his feet, and paced angrily. His spy watched this display wordlessly. His master paced back and forth, back and forth.

"This is impossible!" Falkenberg finally cried. He turned his furious gaze back to the viewscreen. "How could those pitiful fools defeat my

fleet? We outnumbered them by four to one!" He raised his fists and shook them in fury.

"*If I may make a suggestion, master -* " the spy began.

"Well?" Falkenberg said impatiently. "What is it?"

"*The addition of Zorn's gravship turned the tide. She launched flying troopers who boarded the* Lucifer *while the battle was underway. They destroyed her by planting explosives, thereby nullifying the advantage we would have enjoyed if she had managed to bring her weapon to bear on the Britannic fleet.*"

Falkenberg listened, his face like stone. He could sense that his spy had something else to add.

"Go on," he said.

"*There was also the simple fact that although we had many more flyers than the enemy, their best fliers were equipped with gravflyers that were equal to our own. These had been provided by Zorn. They had a devastating effect upon our bombers and fighters.*"

"Zorn, Zorn! I am sick of hearing his name! Are you saying that it was his interference alone that won the day for the Britans?" He glared at the viewscreen, his face red with anger.

"*No, master. Of course not. But it went a long way to assisting them. If he had not interfered, I believe the day's outcome would have been far different. Our troops would have landed successfully, and our bombers and fighters would have smashed any opposition.*"

Falkenberg resumed his seat. He steepled his fingers in front of his chest.

"And you also believe that that French witch, Deville, was an important factor in our defeat?"

"*I do, master. She is a brilliant flier and leader, and her squadron is without peer. That is why Zorn sought her out, and brought her in on the*

Britan's side. Her fliers took a great toll of our craft."

Falkenberg silenced him with an abrupt wave of his hand. Once again there was silence as the chancellor sat in stony contemplation. Finally, he addressed his spy again.

"Has there been any word on The Wraith?"

"No, master. He was seen to fall from the Lucifer *just before she was destroyed. It is doubtful that he would have survived such a fall. Even if he had, he would sink like lead; the armour he wore would see to that. He must be dead."*

Falkenberg lowered his hands to lay them flat upon the tabletop.

"A great pity," he said. "He was a valued servant both to me and to the Fatherland. What of Finke and his technicians? They were also lost?"

"I am afraid so, master. There were no survivors from the Lucifer. *Now his knowledge is lost. We will not be able to duplicate his work, and increase the power of the weapon."*

"No, you are wrong." Falkenberg smiled. "We have other technicians who are conversant with Finke's work. Muller, Finke's protégé, is in possession of Finke's research, including the modifications that he carried out on the *Lucifer*." He leaned closer to the vidscreen. "Another gravship, larger than the *Lucifer*, is being constructed even as we speak. She will be equipped with the ray, and Muller will see to it that it will exceed the original weapon in destructive capability."

"I see. This is good news. When will she be completed and deployed?"

"Muller informs me that the gravship will be completed in three weeks. After that, she can start her trials."

"Will you put another invasion fleet together then, master?"

The chancellor shook his head.

"No. We must recover from our losses. Our forces will remain in Europa."

"What if the Britans should send their own invasion fleet? Can we stop them with our own depleted forces?"

"I do not believe that will happen. They may have stopped us, but they are too weak themselves to put together a force of that size. We are safe from invasion at the moment. I will have the gravship completed, and build up our forces. I will also send raids into Britannia, and harass their supply craft." He thought for a moment. "What of their Queen? What is her condition?"

"She lives, master, thanks to the ministrations of the fugitive French doctors. They have treated and saved many from death. Their cure is real."

"No matter," Falkenberg said. "When our new gravship is complete, none will stand before her. I will not send an invasion fleet next time. The gravship will sail over Britan, and lay waste to the country with the ray. We need not send troops to die, not when we can devastate Britan from the air. Every fighter we have will escort her, and ensure she is successful."

"A good plan, master. There is no defence against the ray."

"Go back to your position. Contact me when you have anything of interest."

"Yes, master."

The connection was terminated.

Zorn and I walked up the hospital steps, and into the foyer. We continued down the corridor, until we reached the Queen's room. Zorn knocked on the door.

"Enter."

Zorn opened the door, and we stepped into the room. Her Britannic Majesty was out of bed, and sitting in a gravchair. It was made of gold, and had a high back that displayed the Britannic coat of arms. This was a sun rising on a field of blue. Below it was a roaring lion, flanked by two pillars. Prince Henry stood on one side of the gravchair, and Doctor Mansfield was on the other. She had just examined Queen Aurelia. We bowed.

"Good morning, gentlemen," The Queen said. She looked much better. "To what do we owe the pleasure of your company?"

"Your Majesty," Zorn said, "we have just intercepted a communication that should be of great interest to you."

"A communication?" The Queen echoed.

"Yes, Your Majesty." He took a datacard out of his jacket. "May I?"

"Please."

The captain walked over to the vidscreen that had been installed in the room to keep The Queen up to date on events in the outside world. He inserted the datacard, and pressed play. The disguised image and voice of Falkenberg's spy was displayed. We watched and listened as they conferred. When the communication ended, Zorn ejected the datacard, and crossed the room to stand before The Queen.

"You have a spy in your midst, Your Majesty."

The Prince and The Queen exchanged a look.

"A spy?" Prince Henry said. "Is this genuine, captain?"

Zorn nodded. "Yes, Your Highness. I can assure you of its veracity. It is no hoax."

"When did you intercept it?" Queen Aurelia asked.

"Only ten minutes ago, Your Majesty. Mister Fussell was with me. My communications officer had been receiving a message from some French resistance fighters in Europa, when this communication caught his eye. It was not on any of our channels, so he called us over and drew our attention to it. When we heard what was being said, I made him record it, and then brought it to you."

"A spy," she said. "Working for Falkenberg."

"Yes, Your Majesty."

"And from what they were talking about, he is a spy who is very close to you, Your Majesty," I said. "Someone on the Emergency Council."

"But the men of the Emergency Council are beyond reproach," Prince Henry said. "It couldn't be one of them."

"I am afraid it must be, Your Highness," Zorn said. "The information that they discussed is known only to those men."

"This is disastrous!" Prince Henry exclaimed. "The enemy will know every move we will make, before we make it."

"You are certain that this is real, Captain Zorn? Not a trick of Falkenberg's?" The Queen said.

"I am afraid so, Your Majesty."

"What will we do?" Mansfield said.

"I have a suggestion, doctor," Zorn said. "Your Majesty?"

"Go on, captain."

"I think we should put out some false information, and monitor the men of the Emergency Council. When the spy attempts to pass it on to Falkenberg, we will have him."

"Set a trap?" I said.

"Exactly."

"Cunning," Queen Aurelia said. "I like it."

Zorn bowed. "Thank you, Your Majesty."

The Queen's face became sad. "To think that one of my closest advisors is a spy. I am not sure that I want to know who it is."

Prince Henry put his hand on her shoulder.

"Such is a ruler's lot, my dear. There is always someone who will betray you."

"But when it is someone who has been close to you, it makes that betrayal even more terrible," Zorn added.

"You are right, captain," said The Queen. "There is no bitterness to equal the feeling one has when one has been betrayed by a close companion. Thank you for bringing this to our attention, gentlemen. You have our leave to set your trap."

"It goes without saying that this cannot be spoken of outside this room," Prince Henry said.

"Of course, Your Highness," Zorn said.

"Your communications officer who received the transmission, is he trustworthy?" asked Mansfield.

"I would trust him with my life, doctor," Zorn said.

"Very good," Queen Aurelia said. "Please leave us, gentlemen. I am tired."

We bowed to them both.

"Rest well, Your Majesty," Zorn said. "We will deal with this spy."

We turned and exited the room.

Symes, Louise, and Marguerite sat drinking in The Red Lion. Each of them wore their ceremonial uniforms. The ladies were in dark blue, and Symes wore the light blue of the RAS. Their caps lay on the table. They were surrounded by a noisy crowd who had been celebrating ever since the Germanian fleet had been destroyed. Shouts and laughter rang in the air, and people hugged and kissed and sang as they celebrated. The two French aviatrixes looked on, bemused.

"Is there something funny, ladies?" Symes asked.

Louise turned to him.

"This is more like Paris than Londinium," she said with a grin.

"Why do you say that?"Symes said.

"Well, this kind of open display. I did not expect to find it here."

Symes returned her grin.

"Did you think we were cold fish?"

She gave him a mock serious look.

"Non. But many Britans that I have met are too, well..." She searched for the word.

"Serious?" I said, standing in front of the table.

Louise laughed, and with a squeal of delight, Marguerite leapt up from her chair and gave me a bone crushing hug, followed by a deep kiss. Symes coughed, and looked down at his beer.

"I'm sorry I'm late," I said, as Marguerite dragged me over to her chair. She pushed me into it, and sat on my lap. She draped her arm around my neck, and snuggled close.

"Where have you been?" Symes asked.

Knowing that I couldn't tell them about the spy, I thought quickly.

"Zorn and I were summoned by The Queen," I said. "We talked about the ceremony."

Symes snorted.

"I should think everyone would know what's going on with that." He took a pull at his beer.

"Yes," I smiled. "But you know how exacting Her Majesty is. She wants everything to be perfect."

"And so it shall be," Louise said. "We will all be decorated as heroes, and my squadron will join the RAS."

"Are you all right with that?" Symes asked. "I mean, to serve in another country's air service. How do you feel about that?"

"Oui. But of course I am." She saw the look on his face. "I was a bit hesitant at first, but The Queen explained that I can keep my rank and designation of my squadron. Anyway, we are all to join this new force that is being formed."

"And it is not only us, Mother," Marguerite said. "The Air Commandos and Captain Zorn are to be part of it too."

"Did Her Majesty say what it was to be called, Fussell?" Symes asked.

I paused for dramatic effect, and looked at each of them.

"It's called The Aerocorp."

"The Aerocorp," Symes echoed. "I like that." He took another drink.

"A toast!" Louise cried. "To The Aerocorp!"

"Alistair has no drink," Marguerite said, a mischievous grin on her pretty face.

"I'll soon fix that!" Symes cried. He rose to his feet, and began to fight his way to the bar.

"No!" I shouted. *"Ian!"*

But he either didn't hear me, or just ignored me.

"Just a little drink, Alistair," Marguerite said. She kissed me on the cheek.

Symes returned, a glass in his hand. His uniform had ensured him quick service. He placed the glass in front of me. It was filled with a deep red liquid.

"It's only port," Symes said, as he sat down. "It's good for you." He raised his glass. "To the Aerocorp!"

"The Aerocorp!" Louise and Marguerite cried.

They looked at me expectantly. I stared at the glass. *Oh well,* I thought. *It's only a little glass.* I picked it up and held it aloft.

"The Aerocorp!" I cried.

We all drank. I expected the port to burn my throat, and give me a coughing fit. Imagine my surprise when it did nothing of the sort. It was smooth, and delicious, with an almost fruity taste. I drank it all down and looked at the glass in revelation. A warm sensation began in my stomach. I felt amazing.

"Where has this been all my life?" I said.

They all laughed.

"It looks like you actually like an alcoholic drink, old man!" Symes chortled. "My Mum always has one before bed, and she's ninety eight. Swears by it." He grinned. "You'll live forever."

"It's very nice," I said. "Can I have another?"

"Oho! Off he goes," Symes said. 'I'll get you another." He went to stand up.

"No, Ian," I said, "I'll get it."

"You'll be waiting a while with that crowd," Louise said.

"No, ma'amselle, he will not."

We turned, and Zorn was there, holding two glasses. He passed one to me. It was port.

"Ah, captain!" Symes cried. "Come and join us! We were making a toast."

"Yes," he said, smiling. "I heard you."

Room was made at the table, and he sat down. He raised his glass.

"*To The Aerocorp!*" he cried.

"*The Aerocorp!*" we replied.

Once again, that wonderful nectar slid down my throat. Marguerite giggled and kissed me. Life was fabulous. We were fabulous.

What seemed like years later, Marguerite and I staggered out of a steamcab. Or I should say, *I* staggered; she was helping me to walk. I turned to the driver, and took out my wallet. I started to fumblingly look through it for money to pay him.

He held up his hand.

"Nah, That's all right, gov'nor. No charge for 'eroes tonight." He ran his eye over Marguerite, gave me a wink, and went clattering away.

"Goo' night!" I cried. I waved, and nearly fell. Marguerite and I took a few stumbling steps, and then equilibrium was restored. She took my wallet, and then put it in her jacket.

"Come on, cherie," Marguerite said. "Time for bed."

I grinned like an idiot.

"Awright," I slurred.

The steamcab had dropped us off at my flat. Symes and Louise had gone their own way. Mother and daughter had exchanged a look. Louise had nodded, and then hugged us both. Zorn had excused himself, and returned to the *Vengeance*. The evening in the pub was a blur; drinking, laughing, talking. What wonderful friends I had.

"Alistair."

"Mmmmm?"

"Where is your keycard?"

"Keycard?"

"Oui. Or do we have to kick the door in?"

I laughed. It was very loud in the early morning stillness.

"*Shhhh.* You will wake everyone!"

"They shou' be awake. *Hey! Wake up!* The heroes're here!"

"*Shhh! Quiet!*"

Marguerite grabbed my hair, and pulled my face down to hers. Our lips met, and for a long moment, the street was quiet again.

My blood was boiling in my veins. Our hearts were hammering together, and the heat of our meshed bodies seemed like fire. We broke from the kiss.

"Will you behave yourself now?" Marguerite said. Her eyes were shining.

"Yes, ma'am," I said. "Keycard's in m' wallet."

She took it out of her jacket, and searched. Then she pulled the keycard out.

"Ta dah!" I cried.

She put her finger to her lips in a shushing gesture.

I mirrored her, finally managing to bring my finger to my lips after several fumbling attempts.

"Come on," she said, and lead me up the stairs.

She put the keycard in the slot, and the door opened. We walked up to the elevator, and she pressed the button. In a few moments, it came down, and the door opened. We went in.

"Which floor?" she asked.

I held up two fingers, grinning.

Marguerite pressed the button for the second floor. Up we went. We got out, and she looked down the corridor.

"Which room?"

"Nummer six."

We wandered down the corridor to number six. She put my keycard in the slot, and the door opened. We went inside, and the door closed behind us. Marguerite led me over to the bed, and sat me down on it. Then she pushed me, and I fell and lay prone. I looked up at her. She tossed her cap onto one of my chairs, and unpinned her hair. With a shake of her head, that glorious red mane was free. Keeping her gaze fixed on me, she took off her jacket, and kicked off her shoes. Then she slipped out of her trousers, and took off her shirt. She was wearing a black bra and matching panties. She knelt down, took off my shoes, and then pulled off my trousers. She rose and came and straddled me.

Her eyes were electric.

"Are you tryin' to seduce me?" I said, my tongue thick in my mouth.

"Oui," she said, her voice filled with lust.

She unbuttoned my waistcoat, threw it on the floor, and then unbuttoned and took off my shirt. Then she leaned down to kiss me. After that, there was no more talking.

The morning came. Luckily I had heavy drapes, and they were drawn against the light. My mouth was dry, but I had no hangover. I blessed my luck, and turned to look at the girl at my side. She was awake, and looking at me.

"Were you watching me?" I asked.

"Oui. Your face is so peaceful when you sleep." She leaned towards me, and kissed me on the cheek. Then she nestled into me with a sigh, and put her arm across my chest. I suddenly felt uncomfortable.

"Marguerite, I don't think we - " I began.

She put her hand over my mouth.

"Don't say anything, cherie. I know."

"Your mother - "

"She knows where we are. She also knows that I love you."

"But she was against this for so long," I said.

"She has given us her approval. She is happy for us." She grinned.

Suddenly, she leapt out of bed. I gazed at her naked beauty, and remembered all that we had done.

"I will make us breakfast," she said, smiling, and turned to walk across the room. I watched her move like a cat. She glanced at me over her shoulder, knowing that I was watching. She gave me a wink, and then disappeared into the kitchen. *Well, that was the end of that conversation,* I thought. I lay back, and recalled the pleasures of the night. *Be careful what you wish for, Alistair,* I thought. *You may get it.*

Marguerite's voice came from the kitchen. She sang like a bird as she prepared breakfast. I felt like the luckiest man on earth.

Three days later, I was watching the parade as I had done all those many days before; it seemed like a lifetime ago. I remembered my comrades from the various Londinium news services who had been with me when the *Lucifer* had appeared and attacked. All of them had fallen in that assault. I recalled the lovely young girls who had screamed and cheered, and their harridan of a chaperone. Their screams had changed from voicing's of delight to shrieks of terror as The Wraith's undead soldiers had rampaged through the crowd. They too had all been slain. How had I survived? Luck? I did not know.

I shook my head to clear it of such awful memories. I looked about myself. Last time I had attended the procession, I had been down among the masses, standing at the edge of the road as the parade passed. Now I sat in a chair that was on a special platform that had been erected, an honoured guest of The Queen and Prince Henry. I was surrounded by Councillor Reading and his men of the Emergency Council. Only the civilian members of that august order were there; the military members were part of the spectacle.

Could one of these men be Falkenberg's spy? I wondered. *Or could it be one of the officers? Crompton? He was always argumentative. Gray? Smith?*

"Mister Fussell?"

I came out of my reverie. Reading had addressed me. He looked at me in concern.

"Are you all right, sir?"

"Yes. I'm sorry, I was remembering the attack. My friends..."

He nodded. "I understand. We all lost friends. But now The Wraith is defeated, and we must go on."

"You're right, of course. Thank you for your concern."

He gave me a smile and returned his attention to the parade. The mounted cavalry was just passing by, which meant the march past was coming to an end. A group of trumpeters who were standing on the platform stepped forward, and raised their instruments. A fanfare rang out, and the band below us played the National Anthem. We rose to our feet.

The Royal steamcoach appeared, and came towards us along the Mall. The people cheered, and waved madly. Queen Aurelia waved from her gravchair, and Prince Henry at her side waved also. The news that Her Britannic Majesty had been successfully treated by the Molyneaux had been broadcast all over the Empire.

The two doctors themselves sat not far from me. When they saw how the citizens of Londinium cheered their Queen, they exchanged a look. They held hands, and I saw tears shining in their eyes. They were responsible for the Queen's cure, and that of many of her subjects who had been stricken with The Blight. To see how much the citizens of Londinium loved their monarch, and to realise that they had saved her, affected them deeply. I caught their eye, and gave them a salute.

The steamcoach came to a stop below us. The Queen and Prince Henry alighted from it, and he held her hand and walked beside her as she ascended the steps in her gravchair. They halted at a throne that had been placed on the platform. It was for The Prince; Queen Aurelia's gravchair would serve as her throne. Prince Henry seated himself as the National Anthem ceased. We all followed suit. The Queen lifted her arm and hailed her subjects. There was a massive cheer, and then the noise of the crowd died down so that all could hear her address.

Two technicians appeared, and set a microphone before her. She waited while they set it up and retired, and then spoke.

"My beloved people. You see me here before you thanks to the ministrations of the doctors Molyneaux. They came from the beleaguered city of Paris to treat myself and those of you who were struck down by The Wraith's weapon. We honour them for their service, and welcome them into our community."

As she ceased speaking, the two doctors rose to their feet, and walked down to stand before her. A soldier from The Honour Guard came with a crimson pillow. Upon it were two medals. He handed it to The Queen, and then stood to attention beside her.

"Doctor Andre Molyneaux, I hereby award you with the Britannic Medal, for services rendered to the Britannic Empire."

The doctor stepped forward, and knelt before her, lowering his head. The Queen lifted the medal and then placed it into position about his neck. The medal hung on his chest, gleaming in the sunlight. He rose and bowed to her, and then stepped back. His wife stepped forward.

"Doctor Yvette Molyneaux, I hereby award you with the Britannic Medal, for services rendered to the Britannic Empire."

The doctor stepped forward, and The Queen repeated the sequence of before. The doctor rose and bowed, and then stepped back to join her husband. At a signal from The Queen, they turned to the populace. The crowd cheered, and they both bowed, deeply moved. Then they returned to their seats. The soldier took the empty pillow from The Queen, bowed, and then left the platform.

The combatants who had taken part in the battle of the channel were gathered below us. They stood to attention, dressed in ceremonial finery. All were clad in a dark green uniform; almost black. They were made up of members of all of the different groups that had opposed the *Lucifer*. Their officers stood in front of them in a small group.

Zorn was in that group, as was Commander Symes. Louise was there too. I caught her eye, and she winked at me. Major McKinnon and Captain Miller stood beside them. *So this is the Aerocorp's uniform,* I thought. *Very nice.* I looked closer, and could see that the arms and legs of the uniforms had double lines of different coloured piping running down the sides. *Ah, I see,* I thought. *Gold for Zorn's crew, Red for The Red Cats, Orange for McKinnon's men, and Silver for Miller's fliers.*

Another fanfare rang out, and Zorn and his companions marched up the steps, and halted before The Queen. This time two soldiers of the Honour Guard came onto the platform. They carried pillows laden with medals. One of the soldiers came up to The Queen, and handed her a medal. Zorn stepped forward, and knelt before her.

"Captain Zorn, I hereby award you with the Britannic Medal, for services rendered to the Britannic Empire."

She placed the medal around his neck. He rose, bowed, about faced, and then marched back to the group. Another medal was handed to her. Captain Miller marched up to The Queen, and knelt before her.

"Captain Miller, I hereby award you with the Britannic Medal, for services rendered to the Britannic Empire."

Miller rose to his feet, and did the same as Zorn had done. Commander Symes marched forward, and knelt.

"Commander Symes, I hereby award you with the Britannic Medal, for services rendered to the Britannic Empire."

Symes stood up, bowed, about faced, and marched back to the group. Louise gave him a wink, and then she marched up and knelt before Queen Aurelia.

"Captain Deville, I hereby award you with the Britannic Medal, for services rendered to the Britannic Empire."

Louise rose, bowed, turned about, and marched back to the group. Symes grinned at her. McKinnon marched forward, and knelt as the others had done.

"Major McKinnon, I hereby award you with the Britannic Medal, for services rendered to the Britannic Empire."

McKinnon did as the others had done, and rejoined his companions. They turned and faced the people. A enormous roar of approval rose to the sky. Queen Aurelia let it go on for a few minutes, and then raised her hand. The cheering died down.

"Let us give thanks to these our saviours. The Wraith and his weapon have been destroyed, and we no longer have to live in fear. Thanks to these men and women, and all of their fallen comrades, Britannia is victorious. From this day forth, we have formed a new contingent, made up of members from different branches of our services. They are to be known as The Aerocorp. They will respond to threats to the Empire anywhere in the world.

"We have Captain Zorn, who made us a gift of the Gravitic Drive, and his wonderful gravship, the *Vengeance*. This did much to bring about the defeat of the invaders. He is in overall charge of this new detachment.

"There is Captain Miller, who is Captain Zorn's Master of Fliers. He and his men took a great toll of the enemy craft. He will train more of our men in the operations of the gravfliers. He is in charge of the fliers on board the *Vengeance*.

"Captain Deville, formerly of France, is in command of her squadron, The Red Cats. They are the finest fliers in the world, and all of them are women. No other squadron has as many kills as these ladies. They will join Captain Miller and his fliers, and we will profit from their experience.

"Commander Symes, formerly of the RAS, commands a group of RAS fliers who have been transferred to the *Vengeance*. Their actions in the battle over the channel proved that they are a formidable fighting force. Their addition will be a most welcome one.

"Lastly, is Major McKinnon. He and his Air Commandos are also to join the gravship's complement. Their courage in boarding the *Lucifer* and planting the charges that destroyed her turned the tide of the battle. Major Mckinnon fought The Wraith hand to hand, and defeated him. The major and his men are soldiers of the highest quality, and we are certain that they will continue to excel."

She paused, thought for a moment, and then continued. "But let us not forget the treachery of Chancellor Falkenburg. He attacked the nations of Europa without warning. No declaration of war was received by any of them. They have suffered awfully; millions have been affected by The Wraith's terrible weapon. Most have died a horrific death. This battle was but the first in a war that we did not want. But we will do our duty, and render assistance to our friends in Europa. From this day forth, we are at war with Germania."

The crowd erupted. Hats were tossed high into the air. The band broke into a popular tune, and the people danced with joy.